RAVE REVIEWS FOR RONDA THOMPSON!

DESERT BLOOM

"*Desert Bloom* is a marvelous book and a joy to read. I caught myself bursting into laughter from the very first chapter."

—*Romance and Friends Book Reviews*

SCANDALOUS

"Ronda Thompson is one of those authors that you should have on your author's list. . . . *Scandalous* is a wonderfully wry Regency . . . that makes you want to come back for more."

—*Romance Communications*

"Ronda Thompson is not to be missed. An innovative writer, she is not afraid to take chances. *Scandalous* is a juicy Regency which will have you smiling over the foibles and fancies of the period. Wonderful as usual."

—*Affair de Coeur*

"*Scandalous* is a fast-paced romp readers will find difficult to put down until the last page is read. Strong characters provide high quality entertainment, while the chemistry between Christine and Gavin sizzles."

—*Under the Covers Book Reviews*

MORE PRAISE FOR RONDA THOMPSON!

"Ms. Thompson has proven herself to be a writer of distinction and power."

—*Under the Covers Book Reviews*

"Ronda Thompson continues to enchant and delight us with her wonderful gift of storytelling."

—Susan Collier Akers,
award-winning author of *Time Heals*

"Ms. Thompson's newest is a sure bet. High-tension desire and quick tempers between Wade and Cam make for an exciting, delicious read. Especially fun and engaging, this one is an unexpected surprise!"

—*Romantic Times* on *Prickly Pear*

"Ronda Thompson's *Prickly Pear* holds the flavor of a true western historical romance skillfully seasoned with sexual tension."

—Jodi Thomas, award-winning author
of *To Kiss A Texan*

"Ronda Thompson has a gem here."

—*Romance Communications* on *Cougar's Woman*

"A satisfyingly traditional Western romance."

—*Romantic Times* on *In Trouble's Arms*

A COMPROMISING POSITION

"You know you've just compromised your reputation?"

Her eyes still dancing, Lilla said, "When you consider the reputations of those present, I don't believe I've done much damage."

His smile faded. "That's where you're wrong. You've done plenty of damage." He backed her up against the wall. "You've placed yourself in a dangerous situation, Miss Traften."

"Have I, Mr. Finch?"

She knew damn well she had. Dancing with him the way she did, teasing him, testing his control. If she'd looked one bit frightened of him, staring up at him with her face flushed and her lips parted, he would have released her. But she had the look of a woman who understood what was coming. One willing to meet it head on.

"Big mistake," he said, then lowered his lips to hers.

Other *Leisure* and *Love Spell* books by
Ronda Thompson:
AFTER TWILIGHT
SCANDALOUS
IN TROUBLE'S ARMS
PRICKLY PEAR
COUGAR'S WOMAN

Desert Bloom

Ronda Thompson

LEISURE BOOKS NEW YORK CITY

To my husband, Mike, and my children, Marley and Matthew.
The greatest wish I ever made that came true, is the three of you.

A LEISURE BOOK®

December 2001

Published by

Dorchester Publishing Co., Inc.
276 Fifth Avenue
New York, NY 10001

Cover art by John Ennis
www.ennisart.com

ISBN 0-8439-4943-0

Printed in the United States of America.

Visit us on the web at www.dorchesterpub.com.

Desert Bloom

MISMATED

A hawk once courted a white little dove,
With the softest of wings and a voice full of love;
And the hawk—O yes, as other hawks go—
Was a well-enough hawk, for aught that I know.
But she was a dove,
And her bright young life
Had been nurtured in love,
Away from all strife.

Well, she married the hawk. The groom was delighted;
A feast was prepared, and the friends all invited.
(Does anyone think that my story's not true?
He is certainly wrong—the facts are not new.)
Then he flew to his nest,
With the dove at his side,
And soon all the rest
Took a squint at the bride.

A hawk for his father, a hawk for his mother,
A hawk for his sister, and one for his brother,
And uncles and aunts there were by the dozens,
And oh, such a number of hawks for his cousins!
They were greedy and rough—
A turbulent crew,
Always ready enough
To be quarrelsome, too.

To the dove, all was strange, but never a word
In resentment she gave to the wrangling she heard.
If a thought of the peaceful, far-away nest
Ever haunted her dreams, or throbbed in her breast,
No bird ever knew;
Each hour of her life,
Kind, gentle and true
Was the hawk's dove-wife.

But the delicate nature too sorely was tried;
With no visible sickness, the dove drooped and died;
Then loud was the grief, and the wish all expressed
To call the learned birds, and hold an inquest

Till a wise old owl, with a knowing look,
Stated this: "The case is as clear as a book;
No disease do I find, or accident's shock;
The cause of her death was too much hawk!
Hawk for her father, and hawk for her mother,
Hawk for her sister, and hawk for her brother,
Was more than the delicate bird could bear;
She hath winged her way to a realm more fair!
She was nurtured a dove;
Too hard the hawk's life—
Void of kindness and love,
Full of hardness and strife."

And when he had told them, the other birds knew
That this was the cause, and the verdict was true!

—Luna S. Peck

Chapter One

Lilla Traften tapped her foot impatiently, raising dust around her dainty kidskin boots. "You're certain you can't fix it?" she asked again.

Mr. Dobbs, the stagecoach driver, scowled up at her. "I done told you I can't fix it, miss. The axle is broken. We'll have to wait until someone comes along to give us a hand."

She glanced around the surrounding area. The heat made hazy lines rise from the barren ground. A few short mesquite trees and dozens of cactus dotted the flat, desolate countryside. In the distance, buzzards circled the sky. She'd been banished to hell, that's all there was to it.

"I'm thirsty," she complained. "Not to mention about to melt in this heat."

Sighing, the driver lumbered to his feet. "Why don't you climb back inside the coach and loosen your clothing? You can pull the drapes down. No one is gonna see you way out here in the middle of nowhere anyhow."

Her back stiffened. A gentleman would never say as much to a lady of good breeding. And a lady would never take such vulgar advice. Lilla glanced toward the coach. She could hardly breathe in her tightly laced corset.

"Perhaps I will take a short respite from the heat. Might I have some water?"

"I gave you half a canteen this morning," he grumbled.

"I've used it to bathe my face and wrists," she snapped. "I would like the canteen refilled."

The man's gaze slid away from her. His face turned red. "Didn't figure it'd take us long to reach Langtry. I didn't refill my water barrel at Tascosa."

"What?" She clutched the lace collar at her throat. "Are you telling me we have no water? That we're stranded in this desert in scorching heat and you didn't—"

"I have a full canteen," Mr. Dobbs interrupted. "It's just that . . . well . . ."

"Just that what?" she demanded.

He opened his mouth, then closed it. A moment later he smiled at her. More than the sight of his toothless grin unnerved her. She didn't care for Mr. Dobbs, and he didn't care for her. That much had been an immediate understanding between them.

"Nothing," he answered. "Let me help you inside the coach. I'll fetch my canteen down for you."

His offer surprised her. Lilla supposed the man did possess a few manners, crude as they were. "Thank you," she said, then allowed him to help her inside the coach. She unrolled the dusty canvas flaps that served as curtains. At least they blotted out the glaring sun. A moment later a dirty hand holding a canteen thrust through one curtain.

"Here you go, ma'am. Drink sparingly, because I don't know how long we're gonna be stuck out here."

Lilla took the canteen and cringed at the thought of placing her mouth where his had been. She set the receptacle beside her on the seat. Just the thought of having to ration the water made her mouth dry. She lifted the canteen, uncorked the top, used the skirt of her dress to wipe the spout and took a sip. The water burned her throat. She coughed. Her eyes watered and her nose ran. Yanking the drape back, she stuck her head outside.

"What's wrong with this water?" she rasped, her throat on fire. "It tastes horrible!"

The man's brows shot up. "It does?" He wrinkled his forehead. "Guess you just ain't used to Texas water. It has a little kick to it is all." His mouth twitched beneath his scraggly mustache.

"Are you sure the water hasn't been poisoned?" It wouldn't surprise her if the man had decided to do away with her.

"That water's fine. Have a few more sips. You'll see it's not so bad."

Casting him a skeptical glance, she retreated back inside the coach. She took another sip. It burned just as fiercely as the time before. She choked, sniffed loudly and tried again. The third sip went down smoother, but rather than cool her, the tainted water only made her more miserably aware of the heat. Unfastening a button or two on her high-necked gown wouldn't hurt.

After her fifth sip, Lilla had to agree with the crusty old stage driver. The water didn't taste that bad. She'd unfastened her gown all the way down the front and loosened the drawstring at the top of her chemise. Her feet were burning up. The fashionable kidskin boots were tight, pinching her toes together. She glanced around the empty coach. Did she dare remove her boots?

Another sip or two of water and she did dare. She removed her shoes, and barely hesitated before taking off her stockings as well. Lilla wiggled her bare toes and giggled.

"You doing all right in there?" Mr. Dobbs called from outside.

"I'm doing juss fine."

She thought she heard the man snicker. Maybe she'd giggled too loudly. Strange, given her circumstances, but Lilla felt rather lighthearted. Her father had banished her to Texas . . . due to a slight problem concerning her attitude about his business partner, Wade Langtry—her ex-fiancé.

Just the thought of Wade chased away Lilla's gay mood. The man had made her the laughingstock of St. Louis, jilting her to marry that hellion Camile Cordell. The Prickly Pear—that's what the inhabitants of the town called her—had to be the most unfeminine woman ever to live. And Wade had chosen her!

Lilla sighed. It was bad enough that she'd been jilted; becoming a laughingstock was unbearable.

Once Wade and his buckskin-garbed wife had left town to head back to their ranch, people began to whisper behind their hands. They'd giggled whenever Lilla passed them on the street. Even Gregory Kline, a suitor whom she suspected of wanting her only for her father's money, had abandoned her.

Well, he'd been run out of town for blackmailing Wade in order to get the deed to the Circle C ranch, she amended, but still, her choices in men reflected poorly upon her judge of character. The only two who had paid her serious court might both have been handsome, and seemingly refined in manner, but one was nothing more than an ex-gunfighter, and the other, a greedy blackmailer.

At least Gregory had paid for his crimes. The man had been completely ruined after the incident. He'd been snubbed by her father and fired from further dealings with the cattle company. He'd even sent her letters begging her to ask her father for a second chance, and declaring his undying devotion to her, but Lilla had ignored them.

Snorting disdainfully, Lilla tugged at her damp clothing. Gregory loved money, much more than he could ever love a flesh-and-blood woman—and the Texas heat reminded her that that was just what she was. She slipped her arms from the long sleeves of her dress. Although it was not cool by any means inside the coach, her upper half felt considerably more comfortable than her lower half. A moment later she struggled from the dress altogether. She removed her hat, then scooted down against the seat, placing her bare feet upon the bench across from her.

The position and lack of clothing made her feel better, but not comfortable enough. Another sip of water and she pulled her petticoats up to her knees, almost exposing the lace around the edge of her bloomers. Her legs were quite nice, she admitted. Nothing about her personal appearance caused her embarrassment. She'd been called the most beautiful young woman in St. Louis. The most sought after, as well. The perfect ornament to decorate a gentleman's home.

But, obviously, something was wrong with her. Maybe he'd never really loved her, but it still hurt when Wade had cast her aside. During the past year, she'd become the pitied "other woman" in society's eyes. In self-defense, she'd said less than ladylike things about the Langtrys. Whenever an opportunity arose for Lilla to remind the decent citizens of St. Louis that Wade was nothing more than an ex-gunfighter, and that Camile Cordell couldn't pass herself off as a true lady if her life depended upon it, she had done so with relish.

She'd become much too free with her criticisms, and her father—who was, after all, in business with the Langtrys—had found out about her bad-mouthing. As punishment, he'd told her he was sending her to the Texas Panhandle to learn some real manners. Lilla snorted. As if anyone in this cursed land knew the first thing about social etiquette! Which was another reason her father had sent her. Not only had she been instructed to learn better manners herself, she was supposed to help teach them in Margaret Pendergraft's newly started charm school.

Pendergraft, who had formerly taught in St. Louis, had recently married an old ranch foreman named Hank Riley—the very foreman who had run Camile Cordell's Circle C before Wade took over. Ooh, just the thought burned Lilla's britches. Now both couples—the Langtrys and the Rileys—had moved out to found a new town not far from the Circle C: Langtry, Texas.

Lilla supposed Wade and his new wife planned to populate the new town all by themselves. The Prickly Pear—Camile herself—never did anything by half measures. She had presented her husband with not one, but two children, a boy and a girl, and all in one shot.

"Typical of her," Lilla muttered. She hiccuped and snatched up the water canteen. The liquid moved smoothly down her throat this time. Always,

Lilla had striven to be perfect—to make her father proud. Her mother had died giving her life. The least she could do was try to be perfect for her father's sake—to gain sainthood in his eyes, the way her mother had.

Taking another swig from the canteen, Lilla wondered what her sainted mother would think of her current predicament. Here she sat, broken down in the middle of nowhere, forced to drink tainted water. And that wasn't the worst of her experiences thus far. Her mother would surely turn over in her grave if she knew her sheltered daughter had earlier shared the coach with a painted lady.

Sheltered but not naïve, Lilla had guessed the woman's profession the moment she'd laid eyes on her. Thank goodness the soiled dove had departed at the last stop, saying she'd changed her mind about Texas and planned to return to civilization. Lilla wished she could do the same. Her father had refused to give her the required funds to return home at her whim. He'd told her she would have to earn her passage from her income helping Margaret at her school for young ladies.

Lilla laughed while raising the canteen again. Imagine the belle of St. Louis forced to labor for a living! It was ridiculous . . . and for some reason, humorous at the same time. She giggled, wiggled her bare toes and burst into song.

She had no idea where she'd heard the bawdy tune, and certainly understood that a lady would never repeat the vulgar words that bounded from her lips. But Lilla didn't feel much like a lady at the moment. In fact, she felt wonderfully uninhibited. Free for the first time in her life to shrug off the responsibilities of propriety, the difficult task of achieving sainthood in Miles Traften's eyes, and simply be herself.

Grady Finch removed his hat and wiped the sweat from his brow. He could use a drink at Sally's Saloon to settle the dust in his mouth. First he had to see the banker in Langtry. He had money to add to his growing nest egg. Money he planned to use to buy a nice stretch of land from the Langtrys—the Lord willing and if the creek didn't rise.

Wade had made him foreman of the new ranch last year. Grady worked hard to prove himself worthy of the position, but he'd always had bigger dreams. He wanted his own spread, to be a man of property and influence. A couple more months of scrimping and saving and he could make Wade and Camile a decent offer on the land he wanted.

"Reckon we'll have time to do more at Sally's than just get a drink, boss?" Tanner Richards asked.

Turning in the saddle, Grady scanned the faces of his hands. Tanner might have asked the question, but all were anxious to hear his answer. "Quick as you are, Tanner, I imagine you can squeeze in time with Meg."

Tanner blushed, and the rest of the men snickered. Grady supposed he owed them town time.

They'd all worked hard the past week.

Sally, an enterprising woman, had been one of the first to arrive in Langtry. There were other ranches in the area, and where there were men, there were chances for a woman to make money.

Grady wouldn't mind a go-round with a woman himself, but he'd improved upon his past behavior after Wade gave him the promotion. Being in charge of other men, he figured he needed to set a good example. So far, he'd managed to resist the charms of the women at Sally's Saloon.

"Hey, do you hear that?"

Sparks Montgomery had asked the question. The man once handled dynamite for a mining company—thus the name, and the fingers missing from his right hand. He also had huge ears that nearly flapped on the side of his head. When Sparks said he heard something, Grady knew to stop and listen.

He lifted a hand and brought his men to a halt. The foreman didn't hear anything at first; then the sound of a voice floated over the silent plains.

"I got a gal, her name is Annie. Her teeth are gone, she ain't got any. Her legs are bowed, and they are skinny. But I love that gal, that gal named Annie."

"Is that singing?" Tanner asked.

"I'd say a sorry excuse for it," Grady answered.

Tanner edged his horse up next to the foreman. "The voice might not be music to the ears, but it belongs to a female."

Grady rubbed his jaw. "What would a woman be

doing out here in the middle of nowhere?"

Sparks placed his hands over his large ears. "Might be the only place folks allow her to sing."

Although tempted to cover his ears as well, Grady kneed his horse forward. "We'd better check it out."

They came around a bend in the road and saw a coach sitting up ahead. A wheel was broken. Cautious to a fault, Grady studied the situation. The cash he intended to deposit in the bank made him leery of a possible ambush. He halted the group.

"Might be a trap," he said.

"Could be, boss," Tanner agreed. "I've heard tales of sea witches singing a siren's song to lure unsuspecting ships onto the rocks so they'd splinter and break apart."

All of the men, Grady included, cast Tanner a skeptical glance. The cowhand listened a moment longer, then shook his head. "I don't think that's the case here."

Grady pulled his gun from the holster strapped to his thigh. "Just the same, we'd better move in slow."

The singing stopped as he and his men rode closer to the coach. Grady didn't see a driver on top, but spotted a man below, stretched out beneath the coach.

"Reckon he's dead?" Sparks whispered.

"Might be resting," Grady answered. "No shade anywhere else."

"Why not climb inside?" Tanner asked. "That'd make more sense."

The foreman shrugged. "I imagine he didn't climb inside because of the singing."

Tanner frowned. "Or because of the songbird."

"Keep your guard up." Grady dismounted. He crept toward the coach. Loud snores from the man below the coach replaced the horrible singing he'd heard earlier. The man obviously wasn't dead, but he might be pretending to sleep. Grady snuck up on him, got down on his belly and nudged him with his gun.

The man came awake quickly. His eyes widened. "I ain't got no payroll on this stage. Nothing worth stealing, mister."

Lowering his gun, Grady said, "I'm not here to rob you. I thought this might be a trap to rob me."

"No, sir," the man assured him. "Got a broken axle is all. I was waiting for help."

"Guess you found it. Climb out."

Grady crawled back, allowing the man room to exit. He dusted the dirt from his chaps. The driver scrambled out. That was when Grady noticed that the snoring hadn't stopped. He glanced toward the coach.

"How many passengers do you have in there?"

The driver scowled. "Just one. A woman."

Grady lifted a brow. "One woman is making all that racket?" At the driver's nod, he said, "At least she snores better than she sings." He turned toward the coach. "Come on out, ma'am. We're here to help you."

Blessed silence for a moment. A soft snort, and then the snoring resumed. Grady's men had joined them. They began to snicker. "Sure is a sound sleeper," he commented.

"And a pain in the ass, too," the driver grumbled, then grinned a toothless grin. "At least she was until she got herself drunk."

"Drunk?" Grady's gaze snapped back to the coach. "What kind of woman gets drunk in the middle of the afternoon?"

Tugging at his mustache, the man glanced down at the ground. "Well, to be honest—"

"Hey," Grady interrupted, answering his own question in the time it took the driver to fumble for an explanation. "Is she the new girl Sally said she's bringing in all the way from Frisco?"

"New girl?"

The foreman glanced around and lowered his voice. "Is she a . . . professional woman?"

"A what?"

Grady decided the blunt approach to a question usually received a quicker answer. "Is she a whore?"

"Oh." The man smiled.

"Yes or no?" The sun beat down upon Grady's back. His morning was fast fading into afternoon. He needed to get his money to town and his ranch hands back to work.

The driver's eyes narrowed. He glanced at the

coach again and grinned. "Why don't you have a look at her and decide for yourself?"

Although the driver's suggestion seemed odd, Grady walked over and pulled back a canvas flap. It took his eyes a minute to adjust to the dimness inside the coach. When they did, he wasn't prepared for the sight that greeted him. A pair of long, bare legs were stretched from one side of the coach to the other.

He took a moment to admire them, then stuck his head inside the window. The woman's petticoats were wadded up around her knees, her breasts nearly bursting from the frilly confines of her loose chemise. Grady swallowed hard.

Her dark hair had once been piled on top of her head; now most of it spilled over her shoulders. Her skin was pale and soft looking, her cheeks flushed pink from the heat. She had a mouth made for sin. Ripe and full of sultry promises. His gaze swept her from head to toe. If she wasn't a whore, she ought to be.

She must indeed be the woman Sally had bragged would be arriving from Frisco. No lady drank herself into a snoring stupor in the middle of the afternoon, or stripped down in broad daylight where anyone could come along and see her.

"I can give her a ride," he told the driver. "My men can unhitch the team and give you a hand into town. Langtry doesn't have much yet, but we do have a blacksmith. You can send him out to fix the wheel."

"Sounds good to me," the driver said. "Don't usually stray off the path this far, but whoever paid for the woman's expenses made it worth my while."

Grady opened the coach door. "Sally is a shrewd businesswoman. I don't imagine she'd skimp with goods like these." He climbed inside the coach and gave the woman a gentle nudge. Her skin felt warm and moist beneath his fingers. She snorted and slumped against him. Her soft breath tickled his neck; her breasts were in serious danger of spilling from the confines of her chemise.

His body, long starved for female affection, reacted with an immediacy that embarrassed him. At times, Grady really hated having to set a good example for his men. He grasped her shoulders and tried to straighten her out. "Ma'am?" He shook her gently. Her head wobbled back and forth on her neck, causing the rest of her hair to cascade down around her shoulders. "Ma'am," he said louder.

Slowly her eyes opened, but not fully, only partway. "Are we in Langtry-y-y?" she slurred.

He only caught a glimpse of deep violet before her dark lashes drifted downward again. "No, not yet, but I'll see that you get there."

Her clothing lay scattered about the coach. Grady didn't see any way of getting her back into them without taking liberties. He wasn't the sort who'd touch a woman unless she invited him. This one was drunk and in no condition to ask him anything.

After pushing the coach door open with his boot,

Grady gathered the woman into his arms and stepped outside. Conversation between his cowhands came to an immediate halt. The three who were unhitching the horses stopped dead in their tracks. Their mouths fell open.

"Holy moly. Who the Sam Hill is that?" Tanner asked.

Grady frowned at him. "This is your songbird."

Tanner ran a hungry gaze over the woman. "Don't matter to me if she can't sing. With legs like those, she can—"

"Get your tongue back in your mouth and keep your dirty thoughts to yourself," Grady interrupted, moving toward his horse. "This is Sally's new girl. I'm sure after she's recuperated, you'll all get a chance to pay your respects."

One of the hands whistled softly. "Bet we have to dig deep in our pockets to pay our respects to that one. Sally sure did herself proud this time."

Although Grady had to agree, he didn't say as much. He didn't want his men ogling the woman during the short ride into Langtry. For some unknown reason, he felt protective of her. Probably because she was pass-out drunk, half naked and innocently unaware of what she was doing to him. She'd thrown her arms loosely around his neck and snuggled her face against his neck. She felt soft and womanly in his arms.

"You men help the driver into town. I'll go on ahead."

His order received a few grumbles. Grady knew

his men would follow orders. His passenger in tow, he mounted his horse.

"Don't use her all up before we get there," someone called.

Grady shook his head. As if he'd take advantage of a drunk woman. The woman in question snuggled closer to him, her lips brushing his ear. One of her hands dropped to his lap, and stayed there. He shifted uncomfortably in the saddle. The ride to Langtry promised to be a long, torturous one.

Chapter Two

Sounds of a poorly tuned piano kept rhythm with the pounding pain in Lilla's head. Her stomach ached, her eyelids felt glued together, and she had a horrible taste in her mouth. The water. It must have been poisoned, and now she lay dying somewhere. Somewhere very close to hell.

"Make it stop," she groaned, but didn't have the strength to lift her arms and cover her ears. Her tongue felt stuck to the roof of her mouth, making her words sound funny. Slurred. "Need a drink," she rasped.

"I think you've had enough to drink."

She jumped. Whoever had spoken the words couldn't have been Mr. Dobbs. The driver had a high, squeaky pitch that grated upon her nerves.

This voice was deep, masculine—the kind that flowed over a woman like thick molasses over warm flapjacks. It might be the voice of God. At least she gave herself that hope, even though the poorly tuned piano was a poor substitute for the beautiful strums of a harp.

"Just lie back and be still. You'll feel better soon."

Yes, she mentally agreed. When she went ahead and died she'd feel much better. A hand brushed a stray curl from her cheek. The light tough of fingers against her skin felt heavenly. A thought penetrated her foggy mind. Only the devil would have a voice like that, and a touch that made a woman sigh with pleasure. More than nausea suddenly made her stomach churn. Fear gripped her. She was dying. And she would do so in a strange place all alone.

"Don't leave me here alone," she whispered.

Silence for a moment; then the surface beneath her shifted.

"There's nothing I can do for you. You'll just have to bear it until it's over."

Fear and misery made her protest. "No. Gather me in your arms and take me to heaven."

"E-Excuse me?"

She willed herself to move, to reach out for him. He didn't feel like a spiritual being. He felt very solid, in fact.

"Look, lady, you're not in any shape to—"

"Please," she pleaded. "Stay with me. I'm suffering for my sins, but I'll be good for you. I promise to be good."

"Yeah, I don't doubt that," he assured her. "But I can't stay. Under the circumstances, it wouldn't be right. Besides, I have a reputation to uphold."

Would God or Satan be worried about their reputations? Trying to puzzle out his words made her head hurt all the more. She only knew she had to convince him to stay with her, to have mercy upon her soul.

"Please," she pleaded. "Don't you have a heart?"

"My heart is not what's talking to me at the moment. Tell me again exactly what it is you want me to do."

"I want you to take me to heaven."

He sighed. She thought she heard him cuss too, but that didn't make sense.

"You're sure?"

"Yes," she answered, squeezing his arm gratefully. At least she supposed she had touched his arm, if such beings had body parts.

"All right," he agreed. "But no, ah, going to heaven until morning."

With his assurances, she relaxed. She didn't want to die, but at least he'd promised to stay with her—to see that she got to heaven. She hoped it was far away from the annoying piano pounding, and the horrible ache in her head, the twisted feeling in her stomach. He pulled her close; then she felt as if she were sinking, being sucked down into a deep void of darkness.

Her journey to heaven was a strange one—a sensation of almost feeling awake and poised on the edge of dreams at the same time. Dreams where a man held her, whispered things in her ear. His breath tickled. She giggled.

Warm lips nibbled at her neck and her throat before settling against her mouth. The kiss was quite pleasant, up until he shocked her right back into the middle of hell. His tongue crept inside her mouth. His hand closed over her breast. Lilla's lashes fluttered open. God, she strongly suspected, did not resemble a cowboy. She had a stranger's lips attached to hers. A stranger's hand in a place it had no business being. She struggled, wrestling her mouth from his. The man pulled back and stared down at her.

"It took a hell of a long time for morning to get here," he said, then flashed her a crooked smile.

She screamed at the top of her lungs. The stranger jumped up. He wheeled around as if he expected someone to be standing behind him. The motion of his hand sliding down to his hip reminded her of a man reaching for a gun. But he didn't have a gun. Her gaze roamed his backside and widened. He didn't have on a stitch of clothing, either. She screamed louder.

"What?" He frantically searched the room.

Lilla struggled up, realized she rested upon a bed

and snatched the sheets up to her neck. "W-Who are you?"

His blue-gray eyes widened. "Grady Finch. Don't you remember me?"

She had no recollection of the name, or of the man. She had no idea where she was, or how she'd come to be in a strange bed in a strange room with a strange man. Panicked, she threw back the covers and jumped up. To her embarrassment, she discovered that most of her clothing was missing. Her stomach rolled, but she kept her gaze glued on the man's face. He stood before her naked, and seemed to be either unaware or unconcerned about the matter. The door burst open.

A strange apparition entered. The creature appeared to be female, judging by the large bosom bouncing beneath her nightgown. Her hair was an unnatural shade of yellow. A large dark mole rested upon one of her three chins, and her eyebrows were darkly penciled.

"What in tarnation is going on in here?"

"She—"

"This man attacked me!" Lilla interrupted, not certain whom to be more leery of, the man or the woman. "I want him arrested at once!"

"What?" the man shouted. "I only did what you invited me to do! What you begged me to do, in fact!"

"I never," Lilla began indignantly, only to have the woman step farther into the room and cut her off.

"Keep your voices down. My girls are trying to sleep." The woman turned to her. "Now, Roxy, what's going on here?"

Lilla blinked. "Roxy? Who's Roxy?"

One of the woman's darkly penciled brows lifted. "Honey, you're Roxy. Roxy Callahan from Frisco," she explained, as if talking to someone of slow caliber.

Scared out of her wits and confused or not, Lilla knew for certain who she was. "I would never claim a name like that one," she informed the woman. "I'm Lilla Traften from St. Louis, and—"

"Traften," the man suddenly said. He frowned. "That name clangs a kettle."

"You could clang one, too," the older woman said dryly. "Cover up, Grady. It's too early and I'm too old to be having the thoughts I'm having."

He glanced down. Lilla had trouble not doing the same. He reached over, snatched the sheet from the bed and wrapped it around his middle.

"I won't go as far as to say that's better," the woman grumbled. "But maybe now I can at least figure out what's going on."

"What is going on is that this man attacked me," Lilla said. "I have no idea where I am, how I came to be here, or who this . . . this defiler of women might be," she sputtered.

"Hold on a minute," the man said. "I don't care how pretty you are, a drunkard, and a whore to boot, has no right to do any name calling."

She felt her jaw drop. "How dare you call me—"

"You were drunk," the woman interrupted. "Three sheets to the wind, and the stage driver told Grady you were my new girl."

"Drunk?" Lilla whispered. "Mr. Dobbs?" Her stomach rolled again. "The water."

"Some people like a little water with their whiskey," the man said sarcastically.

Things were beginning to make sense. Lilla recalled the prostitute who'd gotten off before reaching her destination. And the fiery water tasted foul because it had been laced with whiskey. She hadn't been dying the previous night, she'd been inebriated. Bile rose in her throat. She clamped a hand over her mouth and glanced around, desperately in need of a washbasin.

Grady had heard the expression "green to the gills" before, but he'd never seen anyone turn the color until that moment. The woman rushed to the washbasin and unloaded. Sally groaned, and he glanced away.

"Now look what you've done," Sally scolded him as she hurried to the younger woman's side. "You said you'd heard her name before. Remember where?"

Now that his head had cleared and his ears had stopped ringing from her screams, the answer came to him quickly. "I've heard the name Traften. Miles Traften is a business partner with Wade and Camile Langtry."

"He's my father," the woman said, then retched again.

He suddenly felt sick too. Grady forgot his manners and said a particularly common word, at least among cowhands, and a particularly vulgar one.

"Did you?" Sally asked with a raised brow.

"Hell, no. She was passed out most of the night. Snoring to high heaven, I might add."

The woman's head jerked up. "I do not snore!"

Running his gaze down her scantily clad body, he said, "Here's another thing you don't do. You don't sing. Or at least you shouldn't."

She opened her mouth, then turned and retched again.

"Get your clothes and get out, Grady," Sally said. "Let me get her cleaned up and dressed; then we'll sort out this mess."

He grabbed his gear and took the sheet with him when he left the room. Hurrying into his clothes, he figured he had time to get his money to the bank and get back before the woman made herself presentable.

Lilla Traften. He recalled now that she had once been engaged to Wade Langtry. She was a snooty society woman from St. Louis. An educated young miss from a wealthy family. Grady cussed the stage driver for leading him astray, Lilla Traften for being so damned tempting, and himself for going back on his principles. One look at her and he'd forgotten all about setting a good example for his men. Forgotten all about being respectable.

He'd wanted her, and had thought she wanted him too. She hadn't been so stiff and proper the previous night, he recalled. But she'd been drunk. As soon as he'd climbed into bed with her, she'd snuggled up against him and promptly passed out.

Despite the way she ground her backside into him throughout the night, he'd had the manners to leave her alone until morning. And what a morning it turned out to be.

He threw his saddlebags over his shoulder, strapped on his gun belt and moved through a door separating the back rooms from the saloon. Meg, one of Sally's girls and a favorite with Tanner Richards, sat at a table in her nightclothes. She smiled at him.

"Why, Grady Finch. I've never seen you stroll through that back door this time of morning. We were all beginning to think you're made of ice instead of flesh and blood."

He felt his face flush but didn't comment, heading toward the swinging doors that led outside.

"So, how was the new girl? She treat you right?"

"She's a pain in the ass," he muttered.

Meg laughed. "Anything I can do to help?"

Glancing at her, he noted that she'd let her robe slide off one shoulder, exposing half of her left breast. "Yeah, you can make coffee. Strong."

The seductive smile slipped from Meg's lips. "Coffee? I've got something that'll warm you up better than coffee."

Grady didn't doubt that for a moment. "The coffee's not for me." He resumed his direction toward the door. "It's for the new girl. I imagine she'll have one hell of a headache this morning."

He moved outside, the morning sun causing his own head to pound after a night without much sleep. It occurred to him to wonder what the hell Lilla Traften was doing in Langtry. Wade and Camile hadn't said anything about a visit from her before they left. He hoped she was just passing through.

His horse stood tied to the hitching post outside the saloon. Grady didn't see a sign of his cowhands' horses, or of the men. They'd obviously gone back to the ranch last night. And he could just imagine the ribbing he would take when he showed up late this morning.

Being teased wouldn't be half so bad had he done anything to be ribbed about. But then, he'd done more than he should have with a proper young lady. Snatches of the night came to him. Long legs entangled with his. Soft womanly curves pressed against him. Sweet lips and smooth flesh. He shook his head, trying to get the feel of Lilla Traften out of his mind.

Chapter Three

Lilla wanted to die. And she felt as if she had. Died and then been resurrected by a cup of strong, bitter coffee. She stood outside the disgusting saloon, her bags at her feet and her head held high despite the fact that she'd disgraced herself. Once the sickness had abated and she'd been helped into her clothing, Lilla realized that the apparition named Sally, and the young woman who'd brought the coffee, were prostitutes.

Further degraded, she'd huffed from the establishment, ordering her luggage to be brought outside. After she stood on the sidewalk for several minutes, she realized the women were not inclined to follow her orders. She'd had to go back inside and fetch her luggage—had been forced to reenter the room where she'd slept with a stranger and relive the humiliating episode all over again. She felt dangerously close to tears, certainly upon the verge of hysterics. No telling what the man had done to her—what she had allowed him to do in her drunken stupor.

Liquor had never passed Lilla's lips. Her misfortune, she supposed, or she might have known why the driver's water tasted tainted. If she could get her hands on the stage driver she'd—

A ruckus down the street interrupted her thoughts. The stage sat in front of the blacksmith shop, being hitched by none other than Mr. Dobbs, the man who had delivered her into this hell. Her grip tightened around the dainty parasol she held. Temper rarely got the best of Lilla. It was an unattractive display of emotion, or so she'd been told by Margaret Pendergraft. Still, Lilla stepped off the wooden sidewalk and moved with purpose toward the stage.

She only meant to give the man a good tongue-lashing. It surprised her almost as much as it did the driver when she whacked him over the head with her parasol. He wheeled around, a cuss word bounding from his lips. His face paled and he froze upon seeing her.

"The water has kick to it is all," she ground out, thumping him soundly again.

He lifted his arms. "Now, calm down, miss."

"Calm down!" she nearly shouted. "Have you any idea what I've been through?"

"It couldn't have been all that bad," he sputtered. "The feller I sent you off with looked like a decent sort."

"Decent!" She swatted him with her parasol again. "The man took me to . . ." She promptly closed her mouth. Lilla wasn't about to give the nasty driver the satisfaction of hearing how effortlessly he'd seen to her humiliation. She backed the man up against the stage, her dainty parasol raised and ready to deliver further punishment.

"You could use some manners," she told him.

"Yes, ma'am," he wisely agreed.

A wonderful idea occurred to Lilla. "I'll accept conveyance back to St. Louis as payment for your vile treatment of me."

By the look that crossed his face, she knew the idea of taking her anywhere did not please him. "B-But I'm not going back to St. Louis. I'm headed for Fort Worth."

"Fort Worth," she mused. She'd heard it was a wild town. She wondered how it compared to this hell hole. Glancing down the street, she saw few buildings and fewer signs of civilization. There was a mercantile, the saloon, the blacksmith, what appeared to be a bank, and a couple of adobe houses at the end of the street. A man emerged from the bank. Her stomach twisted. It was the same man she'd found herself in bed with a short time earlier.

Her first instinct was to run and hide. She considered scrambling inside the coach, but noticed that the man didn't seem interested in her. He walked with his head bent, a piece of paper clutched in his hands. Considering that Lilla had been terrified when she'd awakened to find him kissing her, fondling her indecently, she hadn't really looked at him closely.

This man, this stranger whose name she couldn't recall, had witnessed her at her worst. No telling what else he'd done. She planned to turn the man over to the law for molesting her, and needed a good description in case he tried to flee prosecution. Lilla forced herself to look him over from the top of his hat to the tips of his dusty boots.

With his head bent, she couldn't see much of his face as he neared. He stood well over six feet tall, with broad shoulders and narrow hips. Caught up in her assessment, Lilla wasn't prepared when the coach sitting beside her suddenly jerked into motion. She gasped as the driver slapped the reins and yelled, "Yaw!"

She might have been trampled had strong hands not pulled her from harm's way. The coach raised a cloud of dust. Lilla coughed, choked, sneezed and nearly cried as the cowardly driver disappeared down the rutted street. She wanted to run after the coach, plead, beg the man to take her back home. That was no longer an option. In a town the size of Langtry, it didn't take the driver long to get out. She glanced away from the retreating coach and up into a pair of blue-gray eyes.

The man who'd molested her the previous evening stared back at her. His nose was slightly crooked—broken a time or two, she imagined. He had laugh lines around his eyes, probably caused by too much squinting against the sun rather than by being easily amused. He wasn't handsome in a refined manner, but he looked rugged, masculine, like he belonged to the untamed territory.

"Seems there's been a mixup."

The comment was the most understated one she'd ever heard. "That is rather obvious, and I believe you owe me an apology, Mr . . . ?"

"Finch," he supplied. "Grady Finch."

Shame flooded her at the thought that he'd have to introduce himself after spending an entire night with her. Lilla's hand crept up to her high collar, pulling the material close around her throat. "And the apology?"

He stared past her and squinted into the distance, which proved her theory about the lines at the corners of his eyes. "You're the one who asked—no, begged—me, to stay with you all night," he said. "I'll try to remember it was the whiskey talking. Now, I think it'd be best if we both just forgot last night ever happened."

Forget? She couldn't ever remember. How dare he act as if compromising her reputation meant so little to him?

"My father will hear of this. When he finds out—"

"According to this letter, your father isn't here," he rudely interrupted. "And I don't imagine he'd like finding out his daughter got herself drunk and—"

"I did not get myself drunk," she huffed. "The driver tricked me into drinking his liquor-laced water! He should be horsewhipped for his part in this degrading circumstance." She glanced around. "Where is the law? I shall report both of you to the authorities."

"There is no law in Langtry," the man informed her. "At least not yet." He walked away, made it a few feet and turned back. "Are you coming?"

Lilla bristled. "I have no desire to go anywhere with you."

He shrugged and resumed his direction toward the saloon. It suddenly occurred to Lilla to question why the man had the letter her father had sent to the Langtrys months ago. Lilla was to stay with them during her visit. Stay with her ex-fiancé and another woman, as if her circumstances weren't unbearable enough. But a lone single woman did not set herself up in a hotel in a strange place.

Her father had counted on the WC's protection for his only daughter, and the respectability of being considered a guest of the Langtrys during her stay.

As much as she hated to do so, she followed the man. "Could you direct me to someone who might assist me in reaching the WC Ranch?" she called.

He stopped, turned and retraced his steps. "That would be me."

"You?"

"I'm foreman at the WC, and in charge when the Langtrys are away. Your pa's letter must have gotten held up. Didn't arrive until this morning, and on the very stage that brought you. Wade and Camile have gone back to close down the old house at the Circle C. Hank, Margaret and Mr. Cordell went along, too. Don't expect them back for at least a couple of months. If I'd known to be expecting you . . ."

The rude man wouldn't have mistaken her for a soiled dove and, possibly, he would have shown her more respect last evening and this morning, Lilla finished his sentence silently. This was another horrible development. The Langtrys were gone, and she had no desire to be forced into this man's vile company. Now it appeared as if she would be, as long as she remained in the Texas Panhandle.

"I want to go home," she whispered, struck by a sudden longing for her father's face and a familiar world. She didn't belong here. It had taken only a short time to know that with certainty.

Grady Finch glanced at the letter again. "Your pa says you have to earn your way home. He says you've been told what's expected of you."

"My father," she stressed, "is being an insufferable bore regarding this matter. I'm sure he will miss me shortly and send a conveyance for my return home."

He pushed his hat back, allowing her a clearer look at his face. He was younger than she'd first thought. A man in his late twenties, thirty at the most.

"I hope so. But in case he doesn't, Maria could use some help, with Camile and Mrs. Riley gone."

"Maria?"

"The Langtrys' housekeeper," he explained. "She's getting on in years now. All that cooking, mending and washing has taken its toll on her with the other women gone. Not that Camile could be hog-tied into doing much of that," he said with a smile.

"D-Domestic duties?" Lilla stammered, more unnerved by his smile than by his words. It was a disarming smile, one that changed the whole appearance of his face. One that made her draw a sudden breath.

"I have other duties to earn my passage," she assured him, then marched past, opening her parasol as she went. When the man did not readily fall into step beside her, she paused. She turned in time to see him staring at her backside.

"That's going to be a problem," he said, then sauntered toward her.

Her cheeks flamed. She wheeled around and refused to comment upon his rude observation. Lilla marched to the saloon and her waiting luggage. "I believe you offered me transport to the WC."

Grady nodded, then did the most confusing thing. A horse stood tied to the hitching post outside of the saloon. He untied the animal and mounted.

"Climb on."

She felt her mouth drop open. "You must be joking. I have never sat on a horse. I demand to be delivered by buggy!"

Rubbing his forehead as if a headache suddenly plagued him, he said, "Demand away, but it won't do any good. The Langtrys have a nice buggy, but it's at the ranch. If you want to stand here for two hours or more, I'd be happy to send the buggy to fetch you once I reach the ranch."

Stand waiting in this heat? In front of a saloon full of sleeping prostitutes? "What about my luggage?"

"It'll be fine until I send one of the hands with the buggy to bring it later."

In this godforsaken place, she seriously doubted her luggage would be here when someone returned for it. And she was not properly outfitted to ride a horse. "My dress," she worried.

"Yeah," he agreed. "That thing on the back of it isn't going to make this any easier."

"Thing?" For an awful moment, she thought she'd gotten something on her expensive gown. She tried to look behind her. Suddenly she realized what the "thing" was. "That is a bustle, and all fashionable women wear them."

He shrugged, obviously unimpressed. "Seems to me most women have enough padding back there without adding to the problem."

The man oozed insensitivity and bad manners. "No gentleman would insult a lady—"

"Oh, I didn't mean you. Last night I discovered that 'too much' doesn't apply—"

"Mr. Finch," she bit out, sorely tempted to attack him with her parasol. How dare he mention having intimate knowledge regarding the shape of her posterior? It made her stomach churn with worry over whatever else he'd become familiar with the previous evening.

"Since I can't seem to say a word that doesn't somehow offend you, compliment or otherwise, I suggest we stop talking and get moving. The sooner we ride out, the sooner we can part ways. I have work to do."

Parting company sounded good to her. And thank goodness there seemed to be someone at the WC who would see to her needs. A housekeeper, at least, who could fetch her a bath and unpack her luggage.

"What do I do?" she asked, eyeing his horse nervously.

He held out his hand. "I'll help you up."

She closed her parasol and reached for his hand. The moment his fingers curled around hers, she remembered the feel of his hands moving over her. His eyes locked with hers and darkened. Lilla wondered if he remembered, too. Probably a lot more than she could recall. He lifted her with impressive ease, settling her before him, her legs dangling over one side of the horse.

His arms went around her to clasp the reins. She felt his breath stir the damp tendrils of hair framing her face. The position was far too intimate. It tugged at memories from the previous night. Hot, forbidden memories.

Thirty minutes into the ride, Grady realized he should have insisted that the city woman stay in town and wait for a buggy. At first she'd tried to keep her posture stiff and her body from touching his. The sun and the slow ride had relaxed her. Wilted her against him. His muscles were hurting from his attempts to keep his arm from brushing against her breasts. The ride was pure torture.

She'd remained silent, but he knew thoughts churned inside her head. Questions. He suspected she couldn't remember squat about the previous night. He had a mind to let her believe the worst. It would serve her right. Acting uppity to him. Staring down her perfect little nose like he wasn't good enough to lick the soles of her shoes. He'd known women like her before. Women who had snubbed his mother, called her names, made her cry.

"A-About last evening," she finally stammered. "What . . . that is . . . did." She stopped and drew a shaky breath. "What I'm trying to ask is if—"

"Spit it out," he drawled, annoyed by the heat and the ache in his arms from trying not to touch her.

The woman released her white-knuckled grip on the saddle horn and pushed a long strand of midnight-colored hair behind her ear. She had a very nice ear. He remembered nuzzling it just that morning.

"I need to know what exactly happened between us last night."

He tried not to smile. "You don't remember?" Of course he knew she didn't, but he liked making her uncomfortable.

"No," she admitted. "I don't recall much of anything after taking a few sips from the driver's nasty canteen."

"Do you remember singing?"

Her cheeks flushed. "I do not sing."

"I know," he assured her. "But you gave it a try."

"So you keep saying," she bit out. "Mr. Finch—"

"Grady," he interrupted. "After last night, seems silly to be so formal with one another."

She straightened. "Last night is what I'd like to discuss, not how horribly I sing."

"And snore," he added.

Blushing again, she said, "I had no idea I did any such thing."

"Surprised someone hasn't complained about it before now," he muttered.

Her face snapped toward his. "No one before you has been in a position to know whether or not I snore!"

A man could get lost in those violet eyes of hers. Grady had trouble speaking, thinking, breathing. His gaze lowered to her mouth. He remembered the sweet feel of it beneath his, the firm mound of her breast beneath his palm. "What do you think happened?"

The heat made her hair curl around her face. He didn't know if her cheeks were so pink because of the heat or embarrassment. "Obviously, I'm not certain. I-I thought you were God."

He smiled. "I get that reaction a lot."

When her brow knit, he knew the sarcasm was lost on her. He'd played with her long enough. Having her complete attention was hard on a man. "If anything had happened between us, you'd know."

She frowned. "How would I know?"

Grady thought about it for a moment. "I can't think of a nice way to put it."

"You've hardly minded your manners up to this point," she said. "Why not, as you suggested to me, just spit it out?"

He had no problems with that. "For one thing, you wouldn't have still been wearing those fancy underclothes come morning. And there'd be other signs. More than your head would have been aching this morning."

Her stare remained blank for a moment; then her gaze widened. She glanced away from him. "Even if you didn't take full advantage of the situation, you should apologize for kissing and groping me."

"We had our ideas of heaven mixed up," he said.

"Besides, I got the impression you didn't mind so much until—"

"Until I realized I was being molested," she snapped. "The matter has been discussed to my satisfaction. I'll thank you not to mention it again."

"You brought it up," he muttered.

"And now I'm ending it." She sat stiff-backed, her chin tilted at an arrogant angle.

The woman's mannerisms were a complete contradiction to the soft, willing female he'd held in his arms last night. The one who kept grinding her round bottom into him, rubbing her long legs against his, making little moaning sounds when he touched her. Grady shifted in the saddle. The sun suddenly felt ten degrees hotter. He had no business thinking the thoughts running through his mind. She wasn't a woman used to climbing into bed with strange men.

Judging from her reaction when he'd kissed her, she wasn't even used to having that done properly. Lilla Traften was a cut above him, and that was fine with him. He didn't cotton to her type. Never had and never would.

"Damn, it's hot," he swore.

"I would appreciate it if you would refrain from cursing in front of me," she clipped. "But you're right. I don't know how anyone tolerates this insufferable heat."

He glanced behind him, thankful they'd at least put Langtry behind them and would reach the ranch in less than an hour. By the time he turned back, Lilla had lifted her dainty parasol from the saddle horn.

"Don't," he said, but too late. She opened the contraption with a snap. His horse, easily spooked, was startled by the noise and flurry of motion within his side vision. The animal bolted, then reared. Grady made a grab for the saddle horn. The force of Lilla's slight weight smacked against him and threw him off balance. They both slid off the horse's rump.

He landed with a jar, then felt the breath knocked out of him when she fell on top. Through the pain shooting through the back of his head, he heard the thundering of a horse's hooves. His mount knew the way home, and was obviously in a hurry to get there.

Grady cussed again. The silly flowers in Lilla's dainty hat tickled his nose. She groaned and rolled off of him.

"Are you all right?" she asked breathlessly.

Staring up at her, he almost laughed. Her dainty hat now sat on the side of her head and her dress and petticoats were twisted around her knees. But this was no laughing matter. They had a long walk ahead of them.

"You spooked my horse," he said, then struggled to sit. He grabbed his hat. "Smashed my hat, too."

"I-I'm sorry," she stammered. "How was I to know the silly beast would be frightened by—"

"You already told me you didn't know about riding. A thinking man would assume you'd ask before doing something like that, since you don't know squat about horses or the danger of being stranded out here without water or protection from the sun." He lumbered to his feet and dusted off his clothes. "I hope you wore your walking shoes. Afoot, we'll be lucky to make the ranch in two hours. That's if the coyotes or rattlesnakes don't get us first."

Chapter Four

Coyotes and rattlesnakes? Lilla glanced around. All she saw were miles of flat land, sparse grass and cactus. She was sorry she'd spooked the blasted animal. She'd only meant to protect her skin and find a little shade. The sun burned the back of her neck, and her eyes burned too.

A tall shadow fell over her. "You're not going to cry, are you?"

She tried to blink back her tears. "No," she answered, but her voice shook.

"Are you hurt anywhere?"

Lilla shook her head. "I believe you broke my fall."

"Yeah." Grady rubbed his neck. He crammed the smashed hat back on. "Let's get moving."

Lilla would have preferred to sit and stew in self-pity a while longer, but the foreman's lack of manners had her quickly abandoning her tears. He walked away without offering her a hand up. She opened her mouth to mention his oversight, then noticed a huge hairy spider crawling toward her. Lilla bit back a scream and struggled to her feet. She hurried to catch up with him. His long strides forced her to keep hurrying. Only a few minutes into the walk, her shoes were pinching her toes together.

The day grew hotter. Thankfully, she still had her parasol, which offered her a small amount of comfort. A while later, she started to limp. Sweat ran in the valley between her breasts. She lagged behind.

"You coming?" the man called over his shoulder impatiently.

"Be right with you," she assured him, then caught her foot in a hole. She fell, coating her expensive dress with dust. When his shadow fell over her again, she wanted to sigh in relief over the added shade.

"Problem?"

Glancing up, she swore she would not cry. "I stepped into a hole," she informed him. "There are holes everywhere."

"Snake holes," he explained.

She scrambled up so fast her head spun. She swayed, but he steadied her. His hands lingered too long upon her shoulders. She brushed past him and kept walking, or rather, limping.

"Why are you limping?"

Without an answer, she plodded onward. Her feet were screaming inside her tight lace-up shoes, but she wouldn't complain. Her horrible circumstance was one of her own making. She wouldn't afford him an opportunity to point that out to her.

"Bet you have blisters the size of silver dollars on your feet," he said, falling into step beside her.

If Lilla were a wagering woman, which she was not, she wouldn't take that bet. "My feet are hurting," she admitted. "These shoes are too tight."

"I thought as much." He took her arm and pulled her to a halt, then went around and stood in front of her. "Climb on."

She stared at his broad back. "Beg your pardon?"

"Throw your arms around my neck and wrap your legs around my waist."

His suggestion sounded vulgar to her. "Do what?"

"Didn't your pa . . . father ever give you a piggyback ride?"

She did recall seeing other children ride on their fathers' backs. She'd thought it looked like wonderful fun, but her father had told her that hoisting children around in such a manner was undignified. In fact, her entire childhood had been rather restrained. Being the businessman he was, Miles Traften had demanded that she act like a lady from an early age. She quickly learned to do so properly, staying out of sight and keeping quiet so as not to disturb his meetings and gatherings.

"It wouldn't be proper," she said quietly.

He turned. "Neither was getting yourself drunk yesterday and stripping down to your skivvies. You're not in St. Louis anymore. Do you want to limp around here all day in the sun being proper? Or do you want to reach the ranch before nightfall?"

Responding any way besides the latter would make her look like an idiot. Not that she hadn't done a wonderful job of acting that way already. Her current situation had never arisen as a topic at Margaret Pendergraft's School of Charm and Etiquette for Young Ladies in St. Louis. Lilla glanced around. It wasn't as if anyone would see her in such an undignified position.

"I'd like to reach the ranch before nightfall," she answered.

"At least we can both agree on one thing." He turned around and waited.

If anyone had told Lilla that on her first day in the Texas Panhandle, she'd be forced to mount a man and ride him across the desert, she wouldn't have believed them. She'd have thought it was one of those tall Texas tales meant to pull her leg. Speaking of legs, she didn't care for the thought of hers wrapped around Grady Finch's waist.

* * *

Grady didn't mind her legs wrapped around him. He had to hike her skirts up to get a good grip beneath her knees. Her silk stockings felt nice beneath his hands, but he imagined his calluses had torn holes in them. He also didn't know how a woman who weighed so little could grow so heavy so quickly. She had one arm wrapped around his neck, practically choking him, and held the parasol over both their heads with the other.

He moved along, stumbling over holes and wondering if his face had turned blue from lack of air. His feet were starting to hurt, too. His eyes burned from staring straight ahead. He lowered his gaze and stared at the dirt for a while. To rile her, he started to sing.

"I got a gal, a gal named Annie. Her teeth are gone, she ain't got any."

Rather than rile her, his singing seemed to relax her. His passenger loosened her grip around his neck. Her chin was propped upon his shoulder and her hand had slid down, barely grasping her silly parasol, which now rested on the top of his hat. She snored softly in his ear.

"Great," he muttered.

After stumbling a few feet farther, he stopped to catch his breath. The distant jingle of a bridle had him quickly glancing up. Through the haze of heat rising from the ground, he saw a group of mounted men. The riders moved forward.

He jostled his traveling companion. "Wake up. We have company."

Her mouth brushed his ear. "What?"

Grady shook her again, trying to ignore the wave of pleasure the touch of her lips against his ear sent through him. "Wake up and climb down or I'll never hear the end of this."

Her arm automatically tightened around his neck. "Who's coming? Are they outlaws? Indians? What—"

"They're from the WC," he gasped since her arm choked him. "And I'm glad to see them under the circumstances, but I'd be happier if you weren't riding on my back with that damn parasol perched on top of my hat."

She breathed a sigh of relief. "Thank heavens. We've been rescued." She scrambled off of him and brushed her skirts into place.

Grady took a moment to enjoy the absence of her cloying weight and catch a decent breath. His pleasure was short-lived. His cowhands quickly closed the distance. They gaped at them like country bumpkins at their first county fair. The men did have enough sense, he noted, to bring along an extra horse.

"Your horse came back to the ranch without you," Tanner said, his eyes glued to the bit of fluff standing beside Grady.

"Yeah, that's what I figured when I saw you coming." Grady steered Lilla toward the extra mount.

"Ain't you gonna introduce us to your woman, boss?" Tanner asked.

His companion's spine suddenly went ramrod straight. She marched over to the man. "I am not his woman. I am Miss Lilla Traften from St. Louis, and you will kindly remove your hat while being introduced to a lady."

Tanner's fingers scrambled for the brim of his hat. He quickly snatched it from his head. "Sorry, miss, you do bear a striking resemblance to the whore—"

"Tanner," Grady warned. "Keep your mouth shut. The lady wields a mean parasol." He walked up behind Lilla and nudged her in the direction of the horse. "Seems we were misinformed as to Miss Traften's identity when we first came across her. She's a guest of the Langtrys and will be treated as such."

"You mean she ain't a—"

A glare from Grady cut the man off in mid-sentence. If Lilla's back got any stiffer, he thought she'd snap. She groaned when they reached the horse, and he had to agree with her. He was used to long hours in the saddle, but he wasn't used to having a desirable, if snooty, young thing sharing the saddle with him. The quicker he got her to the WC, the sooner she could become someone else's problem. He wondered what Maria would think of Miss Lilla Traften. And what Lilla would think of the ranch.

The house was ghastly on the inside. The place looked nice enough when they'd ridden up—a large, two-story structure with a fresh coat of whitewash and a lovely porch that encircled the entire house. But the inside—Lilla shuddered again. There was obviously one thing Camile Langtry did not do well. Decorate.

Crude pieces of furniture covered in cowhide graced the spacious living area. What pieces weren't covered by hides were covered by leather, which she supposed was the same thing without the hair. From what she could see, however, the house was clean and well kept, which she suspected was the handiwork of the short, round Spanish housekeeper standing before her.

"Maria, this is Lilla Traften. Lilla, Maria. Lilla's come all the way from St. Louis for a visit. I didn't get the letter from her father until this morning."

It was on the tip of her tongue to tell the man that the use of her first name was not appropriate, given their short acquaintance. Then Lilla recalled that she'd spent the night in bed with him and refrained from saying anything. The housekeeper shocked her by stepping forward and throwing her arms around her.

"This house has been too quiet. It will be nice to have another woman for company."

Although Lilla considered the servant presumptuous for thinking of her as company for her, rather than as the Langtrys' guest, she didn't say as much. By society's standards, it was rude to treat others' servants with anything but patience. However, all Lilla required of the woman was for her to take orders and go about her business quietly and efficiently. She also felt uncomfortable being hugged. Intimate bodily contact was not anything Lilla was accustomed to . . . up until yesterday, anyway.

Her father had never been one to openly show affection. Lilla had learned early in life not to form attachments to the many nannies that came and went throughout her childhood. Her little heart had been broken with each tearful good-bye, each promise to send her letters or visit her. She soon learned to keep her feelings guarded, her relationships with others cordial but unemotional.

She pulled away from the woman. "I'd adore a bath. I'm wearing an inch of dust. And where am I to stay during my visit? I wish to—"

"First things first," Grady interrupted. "Maria, would you mind fetching me a basin of water, a towel and some liniment? Please?" he stressed, his gray-blue gaze falling upon Lilla. The housekeeper nodded and hurried off. "Sit," he ordered.

Frowning at her seating options, Lilla settled stiffly into a leather chair. She assumed he intended for her to wait until his own needs had been met by the housekeeper before he turned the woman over to Lilla. It startled her when Grady knelt before her.

"Let me see those blisters."

She jerked her feet beneath her dress. "You'll see no such thing."

She sighed. "I've seen more than your feet, lady, and I don't know how folks do things in St. Louis, but here we show respect to other people. Maria has been with the Cordells since Camile lost her mama. She's part of the family. Don't come in here spouting orders for baths like she's some kind of—"

"Housekeeper?" Lilla interrupted. "Isn't that what you told me she was?"

"Yeah," he agreed. "But that's just a title. We can't call her Camile's mother, or Tom's wife, but she's more than a woman who does all the hard work around the house." Grady gently cradled her foot and began unlacing her boot. "You could use a few lessons in manners."

Lilla was about to inform him that she'd traveled to this godforsaken country to teach manners, but Maria returned with a short towel draped over her arm, a basin and a suspicious-looking tin.

"Here is what you need, Mr. Grady," she said, handing him the items. "I will see to preparing the lady a bath."

Grady lifted his gaze to Lilla expectantly. She didn't know what he wanted until she noticed the housekeeper still standing there, as if waiting for some type of acknowledgment.

"That will be fine," Lilla said, turning her attention back on the man who slipped one dainty boot from her foot. When he frowned at her, Lilla glanced back up and added, "Thank you very much, Maria."

The woman smiled and hurried off.

"That wasn't so hard, was it?"

His attention returned to unlacing the other boot.

Grady had removed his hat upon entering the house. His hair was the color of coal and in bad need of a trimming. It curled around his collar. A few strands hung rakishly across his forehead. She felt tempted to brush the stray strands away from his handsome face. Of course she refrained from doing anything so intimate.

Intimacy with a stranger obviously didn't bother him. His fingers strayed from her foot up the calf of her leg. She jerked away.

"What do you think you're doing?"

"Removing your stockings. I can't doctor your blisters with your stockings in the way."

"I'm perfectly capable of tending to my own—" She suddenly coughed. A rancid smell filled the room. He'd opened the tin. "Good Lord, that stinks," she choked out.

He nodded. "Yeah, doesn't smell too pretty but it does the trick. Usually takes two to apply the liniment. One holding his breath and smearing it on, while the one getting doctored holds his nose. I figure the sooner I spread it on, the better those blisters will start healing."

Lilla snatched her reticule and retrieved a perfumed handkerchief. She lifted it to her face. "Close the container. I will not allow you to put that foul-smelling stuff on my person."

His jaw tightened. "If you want to wear shoes for the next week or so, you will. It may smell, but if you keep it smeared on your feet for a couple of days, it'll heal those blisters right up."

The blisters stung painfully, and she couldn't walk around with bare feet for the next week or more. "All right. I'll remove my stockings. I need a moment of privacy, please."

He set the tin on the floor beside the water basin, rose and turned his back. Lilla shuffled beneath her dirty skirts to remove a stocking. She kept a sharp eye trained on Mr. Finch. His shoulders were broad, tapering down to a thinner waist and slim hips. His dusty denims hugged his backside in a becoming manner. Her eyes watered, tearing up not at the sight of such male perfection, but because she had to ease the stocking from the part of her foot where the blisters had popped and molded silk to flesh. She bit her lip to keep from crying out.

One stocking successfully removed, she went for the other one. This time she couldn't keep her pain silent. Grady wheeled around. He flinched at the sight of her stocking plastered against the big ugly spots that were once blisters.

"Let me," he said, bending. "I'll make it quick."

Lilla nodded, wadded the material of her dress between her fists and pressed her lips together tight.

He yanked.

She winced.

A second later his hands were on her feet, placing first one, then the other into the washbasin's tepid water. The water made the blisters sting worse. Lilla bit back a groan. He washed her feet thoroughly, then gently dried each one with the towel.

She gagged and pressed her handkerchief to her face when he removed the lid from the tin again. His fingers, long and looking more suited to piano playing than hard work, soothed the foul-smelling liniment over her aching feet.

Despite the horrid smell, Lilla began to tingle . . . and not just in her feet. The coolness she'd felt upon entering the house fled. It had never occurred to her that having her feet rubbed could be . . . well, she couldn't really say what it was, having never experienced the pleasant sensations his touch brought her.

"You have nice toes."

"I'll thank you not to notice," she said, annoyed that her voice sounded breathless instead of stern. No man had ever complimented her feet.

He glanced up at her. "For some, turning a blind eye is as hard as turning the other cheek. I'm finished here. If you want to thank someone for something, be sure you thank Maria for fixing that bath for you. I trust you'll treat her with respect and kindness during your visit."

The man trusted no such thing or he wouldn't be warning her. Lilla was appalled that he'd give her directions concerning the matter. Her servants at home were never treated harshly. She told them what to do, and they either did their job or she dismissed them.

"I will behave suitably," she assured him.

He replaced the lid on the liniment and rose. "Keep this on your feet for the next couple of days.

I know it smells, but it'll see those blisters healed quickly."

The liniment and the smell would be more easily tolerated if he agreed to apply them daily for her.

"I have the bath ready for you, miss," Maria said, breaking into Lilla's shocking thoughts. "And a room I think you will like."

"Lovely," she said, smiling at the woman.

"Don't get your feet wet again," Grady commented. "Let that liniment soak in good."

How was she to bathe without getting her feet wet? Not that Lilla would pose the question to him. Genteel society frowned upon discussions about intimate subjects. He didn't give her a chance anyway. The man simply turned and left. No "good day," nothing.

"Rude," she muttered.

"Would you like to see the room now?"

Lilla lumbered to her aching feet, not at all poised under the circumstances. She swept up her shoes and ruined stockings. "There is nothing I would like better," she answered, but didn't add *besides going home*.

Maria retrieved the tin. "I will bring this for you."

"Lovely," she said again, her smile beginning to feel forced. "Lead the way . . . please," she added.

Lilla didn't realize how exhausting her trip to Texas had been until she'd bathed. She got her feet wet despite Mr. Finch's instructions, then put on a fresh nightdress and found solace in a feather-down bed decorated with a lovely frilled comforter. Maria had explained that the room had been decorated with Camile's old furnishings from the Circle C home, which Camile had never appreciated. Thinking of Wade's unfeminine bride, Lilla could well see why not.

Picturing the Prickly Pear among such frills brought a smile to Lilla's lips. Even the slight expression took more strength than she had, and she closed her eyes, easily drifting off to sleep. Her slumber was plagued with dreams. Disturbing memories of gentle hands and a deep voice lulled her deeper into the black pit of oblivion. She was aware of being shaken awake a time or two, encouraged to eat. She ignored the woman, content to exist in her dream world, safe from the reality her life had become.

Someone who she assumed to be the housekeeper, Maria, kept the stinky liniment applied to her feet. She knew they weren't Grady's hands on her, but smaller and less capable ones.

"You must wake up, miss."

The frilly curtains that matched the comforter upon the bed were snatched back, flooding the room with light. Lilla groaned and flung an arm across her eyes.

"Too much sleep is not good for a young lady," the voice persisted. "It puts pounds around the waistline and makes the spirit lag."

Lilla lowered her arm and squinted toward the

window. She recalled the premature lines around Grady's eyes and forced her gaze to widen. "I don't believe it is your place to tell me what I need or don't need," she gently scolded.

The Spanish woman frowned. "We have no 'places' in this house. We are all a family."

Struggling up, Lilla said, "Not to be rude, but I am a guest. And guests are to be treated differently."

Moving forward, the woman straightened the covers. "I do not see why. To me, the greatest compliment is to treat a stranger as we would treat one of our own. Is it not the same in your household?"

Lilla had to admit it was not. The servants were ordered to fuss over the guests, probably to the point of annoyance, since no one seemed to stay long. "It's a nice tradition," she admitted.

"Then I will treat you as I would treat Camile, who is like a daughter to me."

Something akin to pleasure warmed Lilla. She'd never had a mother—not one who wasn't a saint as well as a ghost, anyway. It had been years since another woman treated her with anything but social politeness. "That would be nice," she found herself responding.

The housekeeper's sweet expression faded. "Good. Get your lazy body out of bed, get dressed and downstairs. Breakfast will be served in ten minutes."

She marched from the room, leaving Lilla stunned. No one, not even her father, had dared to say anything so rude to her. She should report the woman's disrespectful behavior . . . but report it to whom? Grady Finch was in charge during the Langtrys' absence. Lilla rose, wincing when her sore feet met the hardwood floor. She hobbled to the window.

Below, she spotted a barn, horses grazing in the distance and a structure of sorts not far from the house. The door to the structure opened and a man stepped out. He adjusted his hat and moved toward the house. Lilla struggled to lift the window.

"Mr. Finch!"

He glanced around.

"Up here!"

His head tilted back.

"I must speak with you!" she called down.

"Up there?" His brow rose.

Lilla realized she wasn't decently attired to be yelling out a window at him. Not that yelling out a window was proper, either. Her nightgown was modest, but an unmentionable all the same. "Downstairs!" she specified. Recalling Maria's time limit, she added, "Give me ten minutes." She closed the window and stepped back. A short time later, she was surprised to find the front foyer empty. She'd specifically told him ten minutes.

Maria rushed into the room. "There you are. Hurry or miss breakfast." She bustled out again.

Everyone in Texas lacked manners. Lilla glanced down at her bare feet, aware that she wasn't proper, either. She couldn't tolerate the thought of squeezing her feet into her shoes again. A fresh coat of liniment had been applied earlier by Maria. Lilla's nose twitched. The smell alone would probably ruin her appetite. Not having investigated the rest of the house, she moved toward the open archway where Maria had disappeared.

A moment later, she stepped into the dining area. The scene that greeted her caused her a moment of panic. There were at least ten men seated around the table. Grady Finch was one of them.

"Miss Traften," he drawled. "We're waiting for you."

She never imagined that the cowhands took meals inside the house. And it was obvious they were gathered for breakfast. Heaping bowls of freshly baked biscuits, scrambled eggs, cream gravy and thick slabs of bacon were piled high on the table. Her mouth watered. She suddenly felt starved. A chair next to the foreman seemed to be the only seat available. Lilla walked to the chair and waited.

"Have a seat," he instructed.

"I'm waiting for you to hold my chair. And gentlemen should rise when a lady enters a room."

All eyes turned to the man seated next to her. He nodded, and the cowhands lumbered to their feet. She'd forgotten how tall Grady stood until she glanced up at him. He grasped the back of her chair and pulled it from the table. Lilla seated herself. He shoved her chair back up to the table, so close it nearly cut her breath off. The noisy scrapes and shuffles of men resuming their seats followed. What happened next could only be called pure chaos.

The men lunged for the food. Biscuits flew, spoons clinked against glass bowls and plates. Food was shoveled into mouths before it even had time to hit the plate. Grabbing rather than passing seemed to be the rule. Lilla was stunned by the drama unfolding before her. She fully expected fisticuffs to break out at any moment.

"Better take something before it's all gone," Grady said next to her, slopping a large portion of gravy on two biscuits he'd managed to catch in the free-for-all.

"This is disgusting," she whispered.

He spooned a bite into his mouth and shook his head. "No, Maria's the best cook around. Meals don't last long at this table."

"A meal? Is that what you call this?"

A man across the table tossed a biscuit on her plate, then grinned at her as if she should be beholden for the scrap. Maria entered, her arms loaded with more food. She quickly deposited her burdens and hurried out again.

More diving for food followed the housekeeper's departure. Lilla could stand no more. She rose, her chair scraping loudly against the hardwood floor.

"Stop this instant!" Chaos came to an immediate halt. Lilla drew herself up. "This is the worst display of poor table manners I have ever witnessed."

"On a drive, the men are used to eating in a hurry, and doing without if they aren't fast enough to spoon full portions," Grady informed her.

"I don't care what they're used to. You're not on a drive now, are you, Mr. Finch?"

"No," he answered. "If we were on a drive, we wouldn't be at the ranch."

"More's the pity," she muttered. "We shall conduct breakfast like civilized people. Follow my instructions."

All eyes turned toward the foreman again. "You do eat like pigs at the slop trough," he said. "A short lesson in table manners won't hurt any of you."

A couple of men groaned, silenced by one steely look from Grady. Lilla sat. She took a cloth napkin from beside her plate. "This article goes in your lap and is to be used frequently," she said to a man who had pieces of scrambled eggs lodged in his mustache. "Dishes are to be passed. Take a small portion of each entrée."

"What's an entrée?" a cowboy asked.

"A fancy name for food," Grady answered. "Get to passing. We have work waiting for us."

When breakfast continued in a more mannerly fashion, Lilla couldn't help but smile at Grady. He smiled back, which made her heart do strange things inside her chest. He really was quite handsome, she decided.

Maria entered again. The woman drew up short. "Is the food not good?" she asked.

"The food is fine," Lilla answered for the men. "I have just instructed the men on the proper way to consume a meal." Rather proud of herself, she added, "I'm surprised Margaret Riley hasn't insisted that these men attend her classes. I suppose I will take over her position at the charm school in her absence. That is the reason for my visit. To help with the school."

Maria blinked, and Grady Finch nearly choked on his food. Lilla reached over and gave him a gentle pat on the back. The room suddenly seemed too quiet. She glanced around the table, noting that all men wore expressions of surprise.

"I'm perfectly qualified," she said. "Margaret once considered me her most prized pupil." When no one commented, she felt defensive. "I assure you I know—"

"Could I have a word with you in private?"

Although Grady was polite enough to ask, he didn't give her time to answer. Lilla found him out of his chair and pulling out hers before she could respond. He took her arm and steered her from the dining room. Once in the large living area, he faced her.

"Seems there's been another mixup."

A prickle of unease raised the fine hairs on the back of her neck. "Another mixup?"

He nodded. "Margaret doesn't have a school. She planned to open one when she first moved to Langtry with Hank, but it didn't take long for her to realize there was no point to it. See, there aren't any young ladies around these parts. I mean, not the kind who'd want to learn manners."

Lilla felt her knees weaken. For a horrible moment, she feared she might faint. Her face must have paled, because Grady steered her toward a seat. She plopped down. "But she wrote to me about her plans for the school. She said she'd have so many students needing instruction in this part of the country, she'd probably require help. If I hadn't mentioned as much to my father, he'd never have gotten the idea to send me here to aid her when I . . ."

She maintained enough sense to refrain from telling Grady she'd purposely bad-mouthed the Langtrys to anyone willing to listen in St. Louis, thus bringing about her fall from grace with her father. "No school? No students?" she repeated.

"I'm afraid that's the long and short of it."

This couldn't be happening. Lilla's only means of escape from this godforsaken place was the charm school. She had calculated, according to what Margaret charged for lessons in St. Louis, that three or four months' worth of lessons to a handful of wealthy misses would earn her passage home. She couldn't even inform her father of her predicament. He'd decided to visit various stockholders in his cattle company during her absence. She had no idea where he was, how to contact him, or when he would return.

"I believe I'm going to be ill," she whispered.

Chapter Five

Grady tried to keep his eyes from straying to the top window of the boss house. For two days he hadn't seen hide nor hair of Lilla Traften. Maria said the young woman had taken to her bed, and no amount of persuasion had been able to lure her out. She hadn't been eating well, either. All this fuss over a silly charm school. She wasn't tough enough to handle Texas. Her father had been a fool for sending her to the Panhandle.

Women like her didn't belong here—weren't suited for the harsh realities of tumbleweed life. Women like her were a burr beneath his saddle blanket. Her kind had turned up their noses at his mother, swept their skirts aside when she passed them on the street. Sarah Finch did what she had to do after his pa died. She'd tried to get decent work, but she was too pretty to hire, as far as women were concerned, and the men she worked for were always grabbing at her, trying to touch her.

She'd married again in an effort to take care of him. Grady had been only six at the time, but he still remembered his stepfather. The man had ended up nearly beating both him and his mother to death. After that, his mother had taken Grady in her arms and said that sometimes people had to make sacrifices for love. She told him she would make sure her boy never took a beating off a drunk again. She'd promised him he'd never go hungry, be cold, or have to sleep in the streets. She'd kept her promise.

A shadow appeared at the upstairs window, a ghostly image, there one minute, gone the next. Grady abandoned saddling his horse and took off for the house. He went inside and up the stairs, not bothering to knock on Lilla's door. She stood by the washbasin, her features pale, her high-necked nightgown floating around her like a cloud. In that instant, she looked like an angel to him.

"What do you think you're doing?" she snapped. "How dare you come into this room without asking my permission?"

Her angel image quickly fled. His words were short and to the point. "Get dressed and go downstairs. Do you think you're just going to hide away up here forever?"

"I-I'm not hiding," she sputtered, rushing to the

bed to hold her robe in front of her. "I'm . . . well, I'm waiting."

"Waiting for what?"

She straightened. "I'm waiting for my father to come fetch me, or to send me the passage home."

Grady frowned. "I just sent that letter for you two days ago. It'll be a while before he receives it."

"I'm aware of that. I'm biding my time."

He stepped farther into the room. "Could be time better spent. As I've said before, Maria could use some help with—"

"I am not a hired hand," she interrupted, turning to slip into the robe. "I came here to teach lessons, and since I have no students, that leaves me little else to do."

"If Wade and Camile were here, I'm sure they'd give you the money to return home, but—"

She wheeled around. "I hadn't thought of that." Color returned to her cheeks, sparkle to her eyes. "You could give me the money, Mr. Finch. I will simply have my father repay you once I return home and he returns from his business trip."

Grady could, but his money was precious at the moment. He needed all he had for the land. Besides, that sounded too simple to him. "I think your pa meant for you to earn your way home."

When she moved toward him, the nightgown billowed around her legs beneath her robe. He wished he didn't know what lay beneath all that soft cotton and lace.

"But that is not an option, now is it, Mr. Finch?"

Her violet gaze lifted. She looked very helpless, but rather than soften toward her, his body did the opposite. Her long, dark hair hung down around her shoulders. He had an urge to tumble her to the unmade bed and rumple it some more.

"I asked you to call me Grady."

"Grady." She touched his arm. "You could loan me the money, couldn't you?"

The temptation of her mouth became a stronger one when her lips parted. She fluttered her eyelashes.

"I could." At the smug smile suddenly shaping her mouth, he added, "But I won't."

Her smile faded. "You won't?"

He shook his head. "I need every cent I can scrape up right now. As soon as Wade and Camile return, I'd like to make them an offer for a prime piece of land they're willing to part with."

She looked somewhat stunned. "An offer?"

"I plan to buy my own spread," Grady explained, and just saying it made him feel ten feet tall. "I'm going to own a place just as fine as this one someday."

"Why in heaven's name would you want to? From what I've seen of it, this ranch is nothing but cactus and dirt. There isn't even a decent civilized town within riding distance. You must be insane."

Insulting him was one thing, insulting his soon-to-be pride and joy was another. "The WC is as fine a ranch as any in the territory. I plan to work hard and make sure mine is every bit as good."

"How romantic," Lilla said dryly. She quickly snatched her hand from his arm. "I consider you the lowest form of humanity if you won't come to the aid of a lady in distress."

"And I was wrong about what I thought the first time I saw you. You'd make a lousy whore."

She blinked. "What did you say?"

"You heard me." He stepped closer to her. "You're the one who should take a few lessons from the girls at Sally's. When they want money from a man, they make it clear that the exchange is flesh for coin. They don't go about it in a sneaky way. You bat your lashes and touch me without any intention of giving up a damn thing."

"I simply used my feminine wiles," she insisted. "It's a perfectly acceptable practice among ladies."

"You're not among ladies," he pointed out. "You're not even among gentlemen. That might work with your daddy, but try it again with me and this is what you'll get."

Grady knew he shouldn't, but he'd been itching to taste her lips. And he wanted to show her that he wasn't pudding in her hands—wasn't a man she could easily manipulate. She'd think twice about flirting for the purpose of getting what she wanted from him.

Lilla knew what he planned. Some small part of her wanted him to kiss her. She'd been terrified and confused that morning in Sally's back room. But she did remember thinking that what he did to her was quite pleasant before she'd regained her senses. When his face moved closer now, she didn't step back. Her lashes drifted downward as his lips brushed against hers.

The kiss started out tender; then, as before, he nudged her lips apart. She felt his tongue probing her mouth and tried to struggle. He pulled her closer.

"Even a lady should learn to kiss a man proper," he said against her mouth.

She had trouble connecting the word *proper* with what Grady Finch was doing to her. But she supposed a lesson in proper kissing wouldn't hurt. Of course, she wouldn't dare ask what she might be doing wrong. Instead, she'd follow his lead. She allowed the contact of their lips. He cupped her chin, slanting his mouth across hers. When his tongue explored her mouth this time, she admitted that it wasn't so horrible after all.

Curious, she touched his tongue shyly with her own. He made a noise in his throat, a sound that reached deep inside her and touched her where no man had before—where no man had dared.

His hands slid up her back, molding her to him when she thought they were as close as two people could get. She softly sucked his tongue deeper into her mouth. Her arms went around his neck, threading her fingers through the silky hair that curled around his collar.

"Whoa. You learn fast," he broke from her to say, his voice husky. "Too fast."

He held her one moment and stepped away from her the next. Lilla stumbled, might have fallen had she not recovered herself. Her face flamed with embarrassment. She'd been brazen with him, clinging to him like a damp shirt, and he'd been able to walk away from her.

"I should slap your face," she said to cover her humiliation. "No gentleman would kiss a woman the way you just kissed me."

"You knew I wasn't a gentleman going into it," he reminded her, moving toward the door. "But I'm more of a gentleman than either of us would have guessed." He grabbed the door handle and glanced over his shoulder. "What I really want to do is give you another lesson." His gaze shifted to the bed. He left it at that, and left her alone.

Lilla stumbled to the rumpled bed and collapsed. She fanned her face—tried to catch a normal breath. "Good Lord," she whispered. She had to get home. She had to get home soon!

Grady was right, although Lilla hated to admit it. She couldn't hide in her room forever. What had possessed her to allow him to kiss her? He wasn't a man befitting to her station. Not a gentleman of means. Not a gentleman at all, although she supposed he could have taken greater liberties with her than he had.

The thought of him doing so brought a blush to her cheeks. She patted the curls arranged atop her head, gave herself a once-over in the mirror and headed for the door. She would join the men downstairs for breakfast, if for no other reason than to break the boredom she felt. Avoiding Grady was out of the question. She'd decided she would face him, pretend as if nothing had happened between them. If he was indeed any kind of gentleman, he would go along with the pretense.

Sounds of clanging and chaos greeted her before she reached the dining room. From the sounds of it, the men had completely forgotten her instructions regarding meals. Just as she suspected, the sight that greeted her upon entering the room caused her blood to churn. A biscuit flew across the table in the shuffle. It ended up on the floor. To her disgust, one of the men picked it up and sat it on his plate. Lilla glared at the offender. He must have felt her regard, because he glanced up. His gaze widened and he elbowed the man beside him. The next man elbowed the next and so on until she had the room's attention.

Grady glanced at her, and the heat that suddenly flared in his eyes assured her that he had not forgotten what had taken place between them upstairs. He set his napkin aside and rose. The other men lumbered to their feet, making the worst racket possible in the process.

Maria entered, caught sight of Lilla and said, "It is about time you came out of that room. I need some help in the kitchen." She hurried back out without waiting for a response.

Lilla bristled. She didn't care for being treated

like family by Maria. Menial chores were not her strong suit. Grady lifted a brow. She knew he expected her to refuse. Maybe if Lilla was nice to Maria, he would soften and give her the money to return home. It was worth a try. She smiled at him and walked toward the kitchen. Her smile faded as soon as she entered the other room.

There were dirty pots and pans everywhere. Food bubbled on the wood-burning stove, and the room felt hot enough to melt a rock.

"Stir the gravy before it becomes too thick," Maria instructed. "I must get these biscuits out before they burn."

Lilla maneuvered her way around the housekeeper and stirred the bubbling gravy. It splattered all over her expensive gown. "Well, good grief," she huffed. "Now I've ruined my dress."

Maria paused while pulling a tray of biscuits from the oven. "There is an apron there by the dry sink. Put it on."

Lilla couldn't remember ever having worn an apron. The minute she finished tying the strings around her waist, Maria shoved a bowl of piping-hot biscuits into her hands.

"Take these to the table. Tell the men the gravy will be out in another minute."

Although she didn't like Maria ordering her around like a servant, Lilla felt relieved for any excuse to exit the messy, overheated kitchen. She took the bowl and hurried out. She walked to the head of the table where Grady sat, handed him the bowl and said, "Pass, don't throw."

"Uh, we're out of gravy," a man informed her.

Lilla cast him a frosty glance. "I shall bring more out in a moment. And we do not begin sentences with 'uh.' "

"We don't?" he asked weakly.

"No, we don't," she answered and walked regally, if reluctantly, back to the kitchen.

The rest of the morning passed in a blur. She couldn't see how so few men could eat so much food. And she couldn't see how Maria alone managed to cook for all of them. Of course she usually had Camile and Margaret to help, Lilla supposed. The house obviously needed more servants.

Once all the food had been carried out, Lilla decided she could do with a bite herself. She walked into the dining area to find it nearly deserted. That wasn't so bad, but the food was gone and the one remaining cowboy was Grady Finch. He stood, his hat in his hands, as if waiting for a word with her. She kept her distance, nervous to be alone with him.

"None of your men could have possibly chewed any of the food I brought out," she said. "For them to have finished this soon, it must have been rude manners as usual at the table. Shoveling and swallowing."

"We have horses to break this morning," he said. "The sooner we get them broke, the sooner we can move on to something else."

And the sooner he left, the sooner she could breathe normally again. She swore the man got better-looking every time she saw him. She'd told herself she would forget about the kiss they shared upstairs, but she hadn't forgotten, not one small detail of it.

"Uh, thank you for helping Maria out this morning," he mumbled, running his fingers over the brim of the hat he held. "It was nice of you."

"I don't intend to make it a habit," she assured him, flustered by the sight of his long, skilled fingers gently caressing the hat's crease. "And we don't start sentences with 'uh,' " she reminded, then recalled that being nice to Maria held a motive, and not being nice to Grady might undo her strategy. "Uh, I mean—" Lilla immediately cut herself off, realizing she had committed the same slip.

The smile that slid across Grady's mouth riled her a little, and made her feel strange inside. His smile was his best asset. The smile and his blue-gray eyes. Oh, and his long, dark lashes. His shoulders were also very broad. He had a strong jaw line, a nice chin . . .

"I must go home," she blurted. "I cannot stay here indefinitely. I insist that you provide me with the funds to travel to St. Louis."

His smile faded. "In case you've forgotten, I don't work for you. No one here works for you. Anyone with manners should know that he or she should earn their keep when they can't pay their way."

"I helped Maria this morning," she sputtered. "That should be worth something."

He glanced at the mess on the table. "Are you going to help her clean up the breakfast dishes? Will you help her with the laundry, the baking and—"

"Now hold on. You can't force me to work like . . . like . . ."

"Like those you consider beneath you?" he asked, his eyes turning a stormy gray. "Tell you what I'll do. I'll pay you a dollar a day to help Maria. If you want to go home, you'll have to earn your way."

"A dollar?" she squeaked. "I'll never earn my passage back home! I'll grow old in this godforsaken place!" She tried to rein in her temper, realizing that her anger was not ladylike. And maybe there was something to Grady's plan. She had come to Texas to teach, and teach she would. "I'll take your offer if you promise to find me students to expand my income."

He moved around the table toward her. "And where the hell do you think I'm going to find students?"

She met him head on. "I don't know, Mr. Finch, but if you want me gone, and I know that you do, you'll find me some. And paying ones."

His eyes narrowed. "Folks here don't have the kind of money your father has. They can't pay a lot for something they might figure is useless anyway."

"I'm willing to negotiate on the cost of lessons." He stood too close. Her heart began to beat rapidly. "I will adjust the price according to income. Say—"

"A quarter a lesson," he said.

"That's robbery!"

"Take it or leave it."

The man was totally unreasonable. Her servants back home made more money than she would. Still, Lilla didn't see that she had much choice. Maybe he'd find her a good number of students, and she could get home quicker than his offer suggested. Or if worse came to worst, Wade and Camile would return and surely loan her the money needed to return home.

"When are the Langtrys due back?"

A dark brow lifted. "Looking for an easy way out?"

Something in his tone, the way he said the words, struck a sour note. Her life had been easy. She asked for something and she usually received it. And she didn't see any fault with a person getting what they wanted, what they deserved. Grady made finding an easy way to solve her problems sound bad.

"I'm just curious as to when to expect them," she answered, trying to appear nonchalant.

He smiled, letting her know he didn't believe her for a moment. "Fact is, I'm not sure when to expect them. They figured two months to get things in order, but said it might take longer."

Well, that settled the matter. She couldn't wait

around for that length of time without making an effort on her own. "And you will find me students?"

"I'll try," he answered. "That's as good as I can give you."

Knowing that men sealed a bargain with a hearty shake, she extended her hand. "Then we agree? A dollar a day for helping Maria and twenty-five cents per student, per lesson, at the charm school?"

He took her hand in his, and the shock of pleasure that raced up her arm surprised her. He must have felt it too, because he jerked his hand away.

"Agreed," he answered.

They stood staring into each other's eyes for a few moments, until Maria bustled into the dining room. It was a good thing. Lilla had a sudden fear that more kissing might have ensued.

"Miss Traften has agreed to help you during her stay," Grady said to the housekeeper. "Isn't that right, Miss Traften?"

At the gleam of hope that entered Maria's gaze, Lilla nodded. "I must warn you that I'm not used to doing household chores, but I believe I'm a fast learner."

The minute the words left her lips, Lilla wished she could snatch them back. Grady had said she was a fast learner upstairs.

"That she is." Grady smiled slightly. "She catches on real quick."

"You must change that dress," Maria said. "Do you have old clothes?"

"Old clothes?" Lilla wrinkled her nose. "I most certainly do not."

The housekeeper eyed her from head to toe. "Maybe we can find something of Camile's. She is taller than you, but we will go upstairs and look."

Without waiting for an answer, Maria grabbed her hand and pulled her along. Lilla glanced helplessly over her shoulder at Grady. He replaced his hat, nodded a good-bye and headed outside. She shuddered. From what she recalled of Camile's wardrobe, it wasn't even fit for a man to wear, much less a woman. And Lilla Traften swore she wouldn't be caught dead wearing a pair of men's pants.

Chapter Six

Grady's teeth knocked together. He gritted them and wound his hand tighter into the rope. The filly beneath him had plenty of fire. She cut to the right, then to the left. She kicked up her heels and nearly unseated him.

He tightened the rope again, listening to the whistles and cheers of his men. He'd ridden wilder horses than this one. In fact, he had a long-standing record. Grady hadn't been thrown from a wild horse in more than four years.

The filly crow-hopped. He managed to hang on. She reared, came down hard enough to rattle his teeth again, and then bucked some more. He noticed that the hands had grown silent. That was strange. Usually they whistled and cheered each other on until either the man or the horse gave up. A quick glance up found them all staring toward the house. He followed their gazes.

His eyes landed upon a nicely rounded female bottom. A bottom swathed in tight-fitting buckskin pants. Lilla was currently bent over a tub of wet laundry. She straightened, and the sun glinted off her dark hair. Her fingers barely gripped the pair of longhandles she raised to the clothesline. She dropped them. It was his undoing. She bent to retrieve them from the dirt, and the next thing Grady knew, he was eating a face full of it himself.

"Hey, Grady got thrown!" someone shouted.

All faces lining the corral swung back toward him. Grady sat in the dirt, his pride bruised more than anything else. Damn, what was Lilla Traften doing wearing a pair of Camile's tight buckskins? And why'd she have to look that good in them? Why was her hair darker than midnight, soft and silky to the touch? Why were her eyes the same shade of violet that painted the sky come sundown? Her mouth, he wasn't even going to think about that, or the way her innocent lips made him hunger for more than kisses.

"You all right, boss?" Tanner Richards called.

Grady shook his head to clear his thoughts. He rose and dusted off his chaps. "She just jarred my senses for a minute."

A grin broke out across Tanner's mouth. "Which filly got the best of you?"

The men turned back to watch Lilla hang laundry. She glanced over her shoulder, realized everyone was staring at her and hurried toward the house.

"Yeah, you'd better run," Grady muttered. He was tempted at that moment to give her the money to return to St. Louis. The sooner she left, the sooner he wouldn't be having the kind of thoughts he did about her. But he'd worked too hard for that money, came too close to his dream, to throw it away because of one snooty girl in a pair of buckskins.

The filly, he noted, stood quivering in a corner of the corral. His men were still staring at the house, and he didn't like the direction their thoughts had probably taken.

"What do you say I break this one and we head into town early?" he called.

All faces turned back to him again. An eruption of hoots and cheers broke out. A night of drinking and whoring should take their minds off what none of them had any business slobbering after.

With his pride at stake, he made fast work of the filly. His horse had already been saddled by one of the hands before he turned the green-broke filly out to pasture. The men ate a quick meal outside, then Grady swung up into the saddle, ready to lead his men into sin.

They rode hard, conversation cast by the wayside in exchange for speed. When they reached Langtry, the town looked deserted. Good, Grady thought; the other outfits hadn't reached Sally's yet. There'd be no scrapping over women or waiting for drinks to be served. Grady didn't plan on getting drunk or sharing a back room with a woman. He was there to keep his men in line—to make certain none of them lost their temper and got into a fight, or worse, got themselves shot. He was their mentor, their protector, their shining example. And he really hated it at times.

Squeals of delight met his men when they entered the saloon. The women had obviously been twiddling their thumbs, waiting for company. Sally stood behind the bar, polishing the well-worn surface. He ambled over to her.

"You boys are early," she commented. A slight smile formed upon her plump, red lips. "How's your woman doing?"

He frowned. "Last I knew, I didn't have one. Who are you talking about?"

She chuckled softly. "That green-in-the-face, high-and-mighty miss you spent a night with in one of my back rooms."

"Oh, that woman," he said flatly. "Well, she's not green-colored anymore." Grady removed his hat and set it on the bar. "How about a drink?"

"A little early for you, isn't it?"

He ran a hand through his hair. "I'll take my time with it."

Sally grabbed a glass. "Heard that about you from a gal in Tascosa. Course, none of my girls know for sure if you take your time or hurry through it like most men. A few of them have said more than once they'd like a chance to find out."

The woman tried to use his conceit against him. Probably tired of not getting his monthly earnings like she did from most every other cowboy in the territory. Still, a man could be curious. That didn't cost anything.

"Any in particular interested in finding out?"

Her smile stretched. "Meg said she wouldn't mind riding you hard and putting you up wet. Oh, and Delores thinks you're packing a big gun. Said she wouldn't mind pulling your trigger."

His face flushed. Damn. Did women really talk like that about men behind their backs? He knew one who wouldn't. Trying to shake the thought, he slowly took in the scene around him.

Meg sat at a table with a couple of Grady's men, picking her teeth with a knife. His gaze dipped to the low bodice of her dress. She had nice assets, if a man could get past the teeth-picking. Delores stood, her leg propped up on a chair, flirting with Tanner Richards, who everyone knew had special feelings for Meg. The slit in her dress showed more leg than a man usually saw unless he wanted to pay for it. The harder Grady looked, the more he realized Delores should refrain from showing her legs. They had more hair on them than his.

He shuddered and turned back to the bar. Sally set his drink before him.

"Are you turning up your nose at my stock?" she asked, no longer smiling.

"Your girls are fine," he quickly assured her.

"But they could use a bit of polish." He glanced toward Meg, who still picked her teeth with a knife.

Sally snorted. "As if those sorry excuses for men who work for you couldn't. Take a look around."

Sipping his drink, he turned from the bar and studied his men. Smitty White still had lunch lodged in his mustache, which wasn't unusual. Sparks Montgomery belched loudly. Tanner Richards sat talking to Meg, but beneath the table, he scratched himself in a place a man shouldn't handle in public. Grady frowned.

"I guess they could use some polish, too," he admitted.

"Burns me up that Lilla Traften didn't turn out to be Roxy from Frisco. I was hoping a gal from more civilized parts might take these girls in hand and teach 'em some manners."

An idea suddenly popped into Grady's head. A god-awful idea. One that made him smile just the same.

"How about you and me discuss a little business?"

Sally's dark brows lifted. One of her chins quivered. "I haven't had an invitation as tempting as that one in some time. And it is tempting, especially since I've seen for myself how big your gun is."

Grady tugged at his collar, suddenly uncomfortable. "That wasn't the kind of proposition I had in mind."

"Figures." Sally poured herself a drink and

leaned closer to him. "So what *do* you have in mind?"

Lilla settled her aching bones on the front-porch steps. Even with the men gone for most of the day, Maria had had several chores for her to do. There had been the mess to clean up after breakfast, the laundry, a light lunch she'd helped prepare for the men before they left, although they ate outside while they busily saddled horses as if in a hurry to be on their way. It wasn't until dinnertime that Maria told her the men had all gone into town. Saturday nights, she had informed Lilla, were for drinking and whoring, as far as the men were concerned.

The news had upset Lilla. Men should be more civilized. She wished Maria hadn't enlightened her as to the men's whereabouts. And one man's location in particular. She had no idea why the thought of Grady spending time with another woman bothered her. Except maybe he shouldn't kiss one woman and then run to the arms of another. It reeked of bad manners. It also made her long for home, where men were gentlemen and treated a woman and her feelings tenderly.

A bout of homesickness overtook her. The barren landscape made her heart ache with loneliness. But then, she'd always been lonely. Her father was a busy man. She'd managed, she supposed because of her father's position and wealth, to have friends throughout her life. But Lilla had never formed deep attachments to anyone. Her childhood had taught her not to get too close to people. Not to care too deeply. Certainly not to count on them staying around for very long.

But at least in St. Louis she didn't feel as if she'd dropped off the face of the earth. She glanced at the flat country before her. It was ugly, barren and somehow cold despite the Texas heat. Then she noticed something she hadn't seen before. The sunset. Such vivid colors streaked the sky, the sight took her breath away. A big, glowing ball sat level with the ground, ready to slip away and bring the night. She was so enraptured by the sight, she almost failed to hear the men returning from town.

Sounds drifted to her. The jingle of bridles—a soft laugh—muted male voices. She hadn't expected to be awake for their return. They had gotten an early start, and she supposed that was the reason the cowhands had come back before sundown. She stretched her neck, trying to see in the direction of the barn. Men dismounted, leading their horses inside. Not long afterward, the horses were shooed out to run freely.

The men began filing out, and she started to rise and go inside. She'd changed from the buckskin pants Maria had found for her. If Lilla had thought for a moment that someone might see her in them, she would have refused to wear them in the first place. She did have to admit they'd been comfortable, however, and much less restraining than a dress.

"Evening."

She jumped and sat back down.

Grady smiled. "Didn't mean to startle you."

"I didn't see you approach the house." Her gaze roamed over him from head to toe. He didn't look any different than when he'd left. Not messed up or however she imagined a man would look after involving himself with. . . .

"Glad you changed out of those buckskins. You shouldn't wear them around the men."

Her mouth probably dropped open. "Considering where you've been all afternoon, I can't believe you have the nerve to lecture me about decency."

"I'm not lecturing you." He stepped closer. "I'm saying you should take care how you dress around the men. You don't want to give them ideas."

"I'll wear whatever I choose," she suddenly decided. "Besides, they should be used to the sight of a woman dressed in men's clothing. Camile—"

"Is Camile," he broke in. "She's different."

Lilla frowned. "She certainly is."

"You make that sound bad." Grady took another step, forcing her to lean her head back to look up at him. "Camile is all woman, don't think otherwise, but the men consider her an equal, too. They take orders from her the same as they would Wade, and they know better than to be eyeing parts of her that are spoken for. You haven't earned their respect."

She grew tired of looking up and stood, nearly bumping heads with him in the process. "And I suppose it will take roping something, or learning to swear and roll tobacco to earn their respect?"

"No." He leaned closer to her. "It'll take becoming comfortable in your own skin. It'll take finding out who you really are, and being brave enough to be that person. It'll take understanding that manners don't make the man, or the woman. Camile Langtry might be a little rough around the edges, but she has a good heart, and she's one of the finest ladies I've ever met."

His defense of Camile started a suspicion. "You're in love with her," she whispered.

He stepped back as if she'd punched him. "That's crazy. I've known her since she was just a kid. Hell, since I was just a kid, too."

"And you fell in love with her over the years," she insisted.

The tattletale lowering of his gaze gave him away. He recovered quickly. "I'm just saying, when or if I choose a woman to be my wife, it would be someone like her. A woman who understands the land and my dream of owning a ranch. A woman who can hold her own in this untamed territory."

He'd described her true opposite. That was fine with Lilla. He was the opposite of what her father would expect for her. She couldn't care less if Grady found her lacking in qualities he would demand in a wife. And she would prove to him that she didn't care.

"I wish you luck in finding such a woman," she said. "Good night."

"I'm not looking," he assured her. "And I came to tell you something."

She paused on the step, turning back to face him.

"I rounded up some students for you while I was in town."

Her heart leapt. "You did?"

He nodded; then his gaze slid away from her. "Is the day after tomorrow too soon to start your lessons?"

Lilla bounded down the steps. "Day after tomorrow is wonderful." Here she'd thought he'd spent his afternoon in town drinking, and probably doing worse, and he'd been finding her students. "I don't know how to thank you."

She wondered why he had trouble looking at her. Embarrassed, she supposed, because he'd done something nice for her.

"No need to thank me. Good night."

"Wait." She reached out and took his arm. "You haven't told me who, how many, what—"

"I'm not sure yet," he interrupted. "I just put the word out. You'll have to wait and see who shows up."

Her spirits sagged. "Then there is a possibility no students will attend."

He lifted her chin. "I promise you'll have students."

She stared into his eyes. Suddenly she became aware of her hand still resting upon his arm—of how close they stood to one another, his fingers intimately cupping her chin. For a woman who felt uncomfortable merely hugging another person, she didn't mind touching Grady Finch, or being touched by him. His gaze darkened, then lowered to her lips. She thought he would kiss her again. He released her chin and stepped away.

"Good night," he said, tipping the brim of his hat.

The slight disappointment she felt while watching him walk away worried her. He'd had no business kissing her either time he had, and no business even considering it tonight. For all she knew, she'd mistaken the look in his eyes, the way his gaze lingered over her mouth, as if he were hungry to taste her again. Considering how little she knew about the subject of desire, it had been foolish to suppose he'd been tempted. She wasn't his type of woman; he wasn't her type of man. That was the end of the matter.

When he disappeared from sight, Lilla's spirits suddenly lifted. She might have students. No, Grady promised she *would* have students. She'd be doing what she'd been sent to do, which would please her father, and the extra income would help her return home. She could hardly wait for the day after tomorrow, anxious to see what sort of students the Texas Panhandle would provide.

Chapter Seven

Grady used Wade and Camile's smart buggy to drive Lilla into town. She'd gotten all gussied up, and he had to admit she was easy on the eyes. He tried to ignore his feelings of guilt as she prattled on about bringing social graces to Langtry's young female population. He pulled the buggy to a halt in front of Sally's Saloon. She turned to him, her voice dying in mid prattle.

"What are we doing here?"

He tugged at his collar. "I figured this was the best place to have your lessons. Look around; besides the mercantile, the bank and the blacksmith, there ain't much else."

"I cannot instruct proper young ladies inside that

disgusting place. And you mustn't say ain't. It sounds horrible."

"Sounds better'n most things I say," he muttered. Grady turned to her. "Sometimes folks have to make due with what they have. You can't expect everyone to ride out to the ranch for lessons. No one would come."

Her violet gaze strayed to the saloon. "But I can't imagine these young women's parents agreeing to let them enter a saloon, for lessons or otherwise."

"I wouldn't worry about their folks." He tugged at his collar again. "Hell, we used to hold weddings and most social functions inside the saloons at Tascosa. They were usually the nicest places. Granted, Sally could do some sprucing up in there—"

"Oh, all right," she interrupted. "But I'll have no riffraff traipsing in from the streets."

"I'll speak to Sally about it." Grady jumped down, went around to her side and lifted her from the buggy. He liked the way his hands fit around her waist. Her fingers rested upon his shoulders. He felt the heat of her touch through his shirt and her dainty lace gloves. When she wasn't talking, she had the sweetest mouth.

"Grady . . . ah, Mr. Finch?"

He realized he hadn't let go of her. Grady released her and took a step back. "After you." He watched the sway of her bustle as she walked onto the planked sidewalk and paused before the swinging doors at Sally's.

"I'm a bit nervous," she admitted. "Do I look all right?"

She looked like a pretty flower growing in a patch of weeds. "You look fine," he assured her, then pressed his hand to her back and ushered her inside the saloon. Half of her students were waiting; the other half would arrive shortly.

From the corner of his eye, he watched the smile she'd plastered on her face before entering the saloon fade. Her gaze widened. She glanced at him accusingly.

"You want to bring social graces to Langtry's young women?" He nodded. "These are Langtry's young women."

He expected anger, maybe a temper tantrum, but not the tears that suddenly welled up in her eyes. Without saying a word, she turned and marched right back out of the saloon. Grady turned toward the women, some of whom, he noted, hadn't bothered to change from their nightclothes.

"Stay put. I'll have a word with her."

Sally stood behind the bar and raised an eyebrow as if in doubt that any words were going to do the trick. Grady set his jaw and marched outside. Lilla had already climbed back into the buggy. Her pretty mouth was pinched together tight, and she stared straight ahead.

"You said you needed students," he began.

She refused to respond.

"Hell, Lilla, who needs manners more than the students I've provided for you?"

Again she said nothing, staring straight ahead as if he didn't exist. Grady wasn't used to being ignored by women. It rubbed him the wrong way.

"I should have known you'd turn tail and run the moment things didn't go as you planned. To be a Texas woman, you've got to show some spunk."

Her gaze swung toward him. "Spunk? What does that word mean?"

"Backbone, courage."

"Oh, I see." She lifted the harness reins, slapped the horse's back and nearly ran over Grady.

He cussed and dove for cover. He glanced around for a horse, but there wasn't one in sight. He relaxed. If Lilla meant to leave town, she was headed the wrong way. He would catch her on her way back.

Sure enough, she seemed to realize her error. She turned the horse and buggy at a speed that lifted the wheels of one side off the ground. He ran into the street, afraid she'd overturn the contraption and get herself killed.

The wheels hit the rutted road, bounced her up in the air, but she never slowed down. She headed straight toward him, and by the look on her face, she didn't plan on stopping. Grady moved out of the way, but when she came even, ran beside her and grabbed the side of the buggy.

She slapped him lightly with the end of the reins. "Is this spunky enough for you?"

The next time she tried to slap him, he grabbed the reins and pulled himself into the seat beside her. The horse and buggy nearly ran over his men, who were just entering town. Horses reared and scattered. Cuss words flew. Grady managed to bring the excited animal hitched to the buggy under control. He slowed the horse to a halt.

"Are you crazy?" he exploded.

"No. I just have spunk," she shot back. "And you're the crazy one if you think I would lower myself to consort with a group of women who make their living by unscrupulous practices!"

"At least they're willing to earn a living," he said. "Not everyone is born to a good life the way you were. Some people have to do whatever they can to survive."

Lilla was fuming mad. She couldn't believe he had the nerve to defend the honor of women who in her opinion had none. The man was cruel for setting up her hopes, only to dash them upon the rocks.

"I will not associate myself with those women," she ground out. "Not for any price."

"Fine," he snapped. "I'll tell Sally her money isn't good enough for you. She agreed to pay more than I thought. A silver dollar for each girl, for each lesson." He shoved his hat back. "That'd be six dollars a day, one day a week that you don't have to help Maria. Then there's the men."

"The men?"

He nodded. "I nearly got myself lynched when I told them they had to take lessons in manners. They all said they'd be the laughingstock of the ranching industry. Half of them threatened another strike like the one we had a while back in Tascosa."

The thought of teaching men manners hadn't occurred to her, but the cowhands who worked for the WC Ranch were certainly in need of instruction. "How much is each man willing to pay?" she asked.

Grady pulled his hat down tight. "A quarter a lesson, like we agreed."

"Now, wait a minute." She turned to him. "I only agreed to a quarter for young ladies who were of a less fortunate background—"

"A quarter a lesson," he interrupted. "I have nine men. That comes up to two dollars and twenty-five cents a day on lesson day. If you refuse to teach these folks because of your principles, it will take you twice as long to earn your passage home."

"I could simply bide my time until the Langtrys return," she reminded him.

His eyes narrowed. "You could. But I don't think you will. You have more spirit than that." Grady handed her the reins and jumped down from the buggy. "I need a drink. The choice is yours."

She watched him walk toward the saloon. His men were waiting for him. None of them looked pleased as they dismounted and followed him inside. Lilla glanced down at the reins in her hands. The decision was hers to make. Spirit? He thought she had spirit?

Lilla refused to acknowledge the rush of pleasure

coursing through her. He'd only paid her the compliment as a challenge. If she refused to teach the students he'd provided, then she would appear spoiled and useless to him. She would still be Daddy's precious angel, a woman who couldn't think for herself. A woman without spunk. A woman who had once let a Texas hellion steal her man and had done nothing about it.

With resolve, she took the reins and turned the buggy toward Sally's Saloon. She had a moment of conscience. What would her mother think of her? Lilla smiled. She knew for certain that her mother would not approve, nor would her father, even though it was by his doing that she found herself in her present situation.

The knowledge gave her a heady sense of independence. It seemed she'd always been under someone else's thumb. Her proper father's or society's. This time she'd been given a choice, issued a challenge, and she intended to show Grady Finch that she could rise to the occasion.

Once she reentered the sinful place, Lilla's enthusiasm fled. The atmosphere inside was, she suspected, very much like it was on a Saturday night. The men laughed and flirted with the women. The women did likewise. Grady stood at the bar sipping a glass of spirits. First thing first, she thought. Lilla approached him and snatched the glass from his hand.

"There is to be no drinking during lessons."

He easily reclaimed the glass. "It's just water, and I'm not one of your students."

She placed her hands upon her hips. "You set the example for your men. They look up to you. They won't take my lessons seriously unless you take them seriously. I demand"—she hesitated when his jaw muscle clenched—"I ask that you join the men for lessons, as well."

Their conversation had quieted the room. Lilla would have preferred that it remain a private issue. Men were known to balk if a woman tried to take the lead. She strongly suspected that this particular man would too. Grady was used to issuing instructions, not following them. She thought he would refuse, but instead, he set his glass aside and shrugged.

"Sure. Hell, why not? I can't get much done without the men at the ranch anyway."

She smiled, then sobered. "First lesson, Mr. Finch. Men do not swear in front of ladies. It shows bad manners and disrespect for the lady."

A man snickered. "Not many ladies present."

Lilla wheeled around and approached the man. "In my classroom, all women present are ladies. You are to remember that, Mr. Richards."

A woman sitting at a nearby table let out a soft laugh. Lilla glanced over at her. It was the woman who'd served Lilla coffee her unfortunate first day in Langtry. Richards, who sat beside her, turned red in the face. Lilla might have made the man squirm more, but she noticed that the woman wore a nightgown, and none too modest a one at that. And she wasn't the only woman who'd forgotten to get dressed that morning. It would not do.

"I wish for all of the men to leave," Lilla said.

A chorus of whoops followed her statement. When the noise died down, she continued, "Only until the women make themselves presentable. You may all wait outside until I give you permission to join us again."

"I don't know. The old gal looks plenty presentable to me," one cowhand said, nodding toward the woman who'd given Lilla coffee.

Lilla cast him a frosty glare. "Our lessons today will begin with introductions. The 'old gal' has a proper name, and you will use it from this day forward during lessons."

"Well, I-I—" the man stuttered.

"Outside, men," a voice at the bar instructed. "You heard the lady."

The men rose from their chairs. Lilla cast Grady a thankful smile, although she really didn't want the men to believe he was in charge of her lessons. She would talk to him about the matter latter.

Once the men had all filed out, she turned to the women gathered. There were six of them. Lilla's spirit had trouble taking flight. It would take a miracle to turn this coarse-looking group into ladies.

"I expect all of you to dress for lessons," she said. "And in clothes that do not display all of your womanly wares. Have you more modest clothing? Something perhaps you would wear to church?"

The woman whose name she had just defended burst into laughter. "Oh, that's good."

"Langtry doesn't have a church yet," another dove said—a slim girl who looked beaten down and used up for her young years. "And if it did, the likes of us wouldn't be allowed inside."

"I'll drink to that," an older woman said. She rose and sashayed over to Lilla. "I'm Delores, and I don't give a tinker's damn about being a lady. Unlike some here." Her gaze strayed to the younger girl. "I'm a whore and proud of it. All I care about getting from the men is money, and that's the simple truth. You're wasting your time and ours."

"Delores," came a firm voice from behind the bar. "I run this place. I say when you're wasting your time."

The woman bristled. "She ain't got no business in here, Sally. A snotty miss like her. Looking down her prissy nose at us like we was no better than horse dung. And her spending the night in a back room with Grady Finch when she was in town no longer than a minute."

Lilla's cheeks blazed. Good Lord, she'd forgotten that the women would think . . . they would believe . . .

"I told you all that was a misunderstanding," Sally said. "Grady and the lady didn't do more than swap a little slobber."

"I wouldn't mind swapping more than slobber with him," the buxom blonde sitting at the table said, causing more than one woman to laugh and nod her head. "A waste of man, that one. Maybe she can tell us if the rumors floating around about him are true."

"Now, Meg," Sally began.

"Yeah, tell us," Delores interrupted. She grinned at Lilla. "Is he really hung like a mule?"

Lilla frowned. "Pardon me?"

"His equipment," the coffee server said, wiggling her brows as if that were a clue regarding the confusing discussion. She sighed when Lilla didn't respond. "His co—"

"Meg!" Sally barked. "The lady isn't here to trade bedtime stories with you gals. She's here to teach manners, so watch yours and try to have a thought in your empty heads besides the size of a man's . . ." Her voice trailed when her gaze landed upon Lilla. "Ah, pride. Go on in now and get dressed, all of you. Wear your cleaning dresses. They at least cover you up."

"But those dresses are ugly," a pretty Mexican girl complained. "They don't show nothing to catch a man's eye."

"They will do nicely," Lilla said, still trying to puzzle out the earlier conversation. What in the world had she committed herself to? She seriously doubted she could teach manners to women who cared nothing about having them. These women were beyond help. Beyond salvation. A dollar per girl per lesson had sounded too good to pass up. Now she found herself reconsidering her decision.

Chapter Eight

The decision was reevaluated a short time later, and without positive results. The women had dressed, and yes, they wore shapeless shifts that did little to enhance their attributes. But as one of the women had claimed, the dresses were ugly to the point of distraction. Lilla kept wanting to add a lace collar here or take in a bit of material there, or in some cases, such as with the buxom blonde, let out a good deal.

Lilla sat at a table and removed a tablet, a feathered pen and an ink well from her reticule. "To make proper introductions, I need to know your names. One at a time, step up to me so I may record your names and more easily commit them to memory."

The buxom blonde was the first to approach her. "Meg's my name. I, ah, liked the way you put that Smitty White in his place. I don't cotton to being called the 'old gal.' "

Nodding acceptance of the compliment, Lilla asked, "And what is your last name?"

The woman's face turned red. "Don't have one, far as I know."

Lilla glanced up at her. "You have no last name?"

Meg shrugged. "My folks died when I was little. No one would take me in 'cause they died of something other folks were afraid they might catch from me. The townsfolk threw scraps to me in the streets, and that's how I grew up until I was old enough to get decent meals by tending drinks, and then by entertaining men."

A shudder raced up Lilla's back. What a horrible way for a child to live. "If you don't have a last name, I think it would only be right that you give yourself one."

The woman's brow furrowed. "You mean I can just pick out any old name I like?"

"I don't see why not," Lilla answered.

Meg chewed her bottom lip, her face a mask of concentration. Suddenly she smiled. "My favorite food is fresh-baked bread."

"That's nice," Lilla responded.

"Can I be Meg Bread?"

It was a horrible name. "How about Meg Rye, or Meg—"

"Pumpernickel," Meg interrupted. "That's who I'll be. Meg Pumpernickel."

Lilla tried not to laugh. She neatly penned the woman's name. "And who is next?" she called, not glancing up.

"I'll be next. I'm Gap-tooth Kate."

Lilla glanced up and was nearly startled into falling from her chair. The woman before her smiled broadly. She had a gap between her front teeth a horse and buggy could drive through. "I-Is it Kate, or Katherine?" she stammered.

"Well, it's Katherine, but I ain't been called that in a long time. Not since my teeth grew in."

It came as no surprise to Lilla. "Katherine, what is your last name?"

"O'Conner."

Lilla should have guessed an Irish name by the red hair and freckles. "Katherine O'Conner," she said as she wrote. "That is a very lovely name."

"I guess it's a mite better than Gap-tooth Kate," the woman agreed.

"Let us move along," Lilla urged. "We don't want to leave the men standing outside in the heat."

Women stepped up and Lilla penned their names. Delores had a last name the others giggled over. Dupe. Delores Dupree. Lilla suggested a slight alteration, and she became Delores Dupree. The last girl seemed hesitant to approach her. She was the thin girl who looked as if she belonged in a schoolroom instead of a saloon.

"I don't want to tell my last name," she admitted shyly. "I'm from Kansas, and most of my kin have a reward attached to our name."

"Oh," Lilla said. "Then let's begin with a first name."

"Violet," she said quietly.

"Violet is a lovely name. Would you like to choose a new last name?"

The girl nodded enthusiastically. Lilla waited while the girl fidgeted with her ugly dress.

"It's hard to pick when there's so many that might be nice."

A good while passed while Violet twisted her fingers together and stared at the ceiling.

"Just pick something," Delores demanded. "We'll be here all day."

It didn't escape Lilla's notice that the girl flinched. "I can't choose," she blurted. Her soft blue eyes beseeched Lilla. "You pick for me."

"You should choose yourself," Lilla said gently. Something about this girl bothered her. Something besides the obvious. She didn't appear to belong with the other brazens at Sally's.

"She can't do nothing for herself," Delores said. "Always has to be told what to do and when. Addle-brained," she explained. "And scared of her own shadow. 'Mouse' should be her last name."

Violet's eyes filled with tears. "I hate mice."

Lilla certainly cared nothing for the filthy creatures, but she had a cousin in Boston who would faint dead away at the sight of one. "How do you like the name Mallory? I have a favorite cousin in Boston whose last name is the same."

"Mallory," Violet repeated, as if testing it on her tongue. "I like that just fine."

"Then it's settled." Lilla penned the name into her tablet. "Now, if you ladies will excuse me for a moment, I will call in the men and take their names, as well."

Since there were ten of them, it took a while to get through taking the names. Lilla had insisted that Sparks Montgomery give her his real name. It turned out to be Homer, much to the delight of the other ranch hands. She supposed the man was in for some teasing. Next she instructed the women to form a line behind her, and the men to form a line in front of her.

Acting as hostess, Lilla began the introductions. "Mr. Smithton White, allow me to introduce to you Miss Delores Depree. Miss Dupree, Mr. White."

"Delores and I've met." A lewd grin spread across Smitty's mouth. "Many times."

Rib-poking and crude laughter resulted. Lilla was not amused. Her parasol lay with her teaching tools. She fetched it. "We will try again. This time I will instruct you as to what to do or say, Mr. White. And be certain to tip your hat while being introduced to a lady, or to a gentleman on the street."

Introductions were made again, but before Smitty said anything rude, Lilla turned to Delores.

"It is the lady's place to acknowledge the gentleman introduced with a short bow."

"I ain't bowing to him," she said with a snort. "Not unless he's paying me to."

"And you'd charge more than it was worth to have you do it, too," Smitty shot back.

"I charge so much for you because you smell!"

Smitty's face turned red. "And I could knit a blanket from the hair on your legs!"

"Now, lady and gentleman." Lilla stepped between them. It was a mistake. Delores threw a punch and hit Lilla in the eye. She stumbled back a step, her face throbbing.

"Hey!" Grady was suddenly there, shielding her body from the two combatants. "Why'd you do that, Delores?"

Holding her smarting eye, Lilla heard Delores answer, "I meant to hit Smitty, not the lady."

"No brawling during lessons," Grady growled. He turned and drew Lilla close, studying her face. "Are you all right?"

Her hand still covered her throbbing eye. "I-I think so." She lowered her hand, and he whistled.

"You're going to have a hell of a shiner. I'd better get you back to the ranch so we can get that doctored."

He turned her toward the door. Lilla dug in her heels. Although there was nothing she'd like more than to hurry back to the ranch and never return to Sally's Saloon, Grady had taken charge again. Like it or not, these were her students, this was her classroom, and Grady was not going to ride roughshod over everyone, Lilla included.

"No," she said firmly, pulling away from him. "First we're going to finish today's lesson."

"The longer you wait to—"

"Resume your position in line, Mr. Finch," Lilla snapped, using her good eye to glare at him.

For a moment, he looked as if he would argue. He also appeared as if being ordered around by a woman didn't sit well with him. Lilla held her ground. He muttered something and rejoined the men. Lilla approached Delores.

"I believe you were going to bow to Mr. White, Miss Dupree," she reminded.

"Didn't mean to punch you," the brunette said. "But I ain't bowing to the likes of him."

Lilla begged to disagree. She stabbed Delores in the middle with the tip of her parasol. The brunette doubled over.

"And now, Mr. White. You, in turn, will bow in acknowledgment of Miss Dupree." She aimed her parasol, but found no need to prod the cowhand. He quickly bowed.

Introductions proceeded. Meg's chosen last name drew a few snickers as did Sparks Montgomery's first name. Violet could hardly look the cowhands in the eye, which made Lilla wonder how the shy girl managed to do anything more intimate with the men.

"Now I shall introduce the men to the men, and the ladies to the ladies," she decided.

Her decision met with murmurs of protest.

"Hell, we all know each other," Tanner complained. "This is wasting our time."

His foreman frowned and looked as if he might say something. Lilla wouldn't have Grady being looked upon as the authority figure in her classroom. She stepped up to Tanner, who eyed her parasol with trepidation.

"Let me say again, gentlemen do not swear in front of ladies, Mr. Richards. Nor does a gentleman even address a lady unless she speaks to him first."

"The hell you say?" He winced. "Oh, sorry."

"Are you saying they can't talk to us unless we talk to them first?" Meg asked.

"She said 'ladies,' " Tanner answered before Lilla had a chance to speak. "That don't apply here, except for Miss Traften."

Lilla wanted to thwack the man. Grady stepped from his place in line.

"What say you and I go outside and have a talk, Richards?"

Tanner's face paled. Lilla realized that Grady was not being cordial, and the prospect of a "talk" outside was not a pleasing option. Any talking going on during her lessons, however, would be her decision. "Step back in line, Mr. Finch," she clipped. "You may talk to Mr. Richards after you've both been properly introduced to one another."

"Could I have a word with you?" Grady asked, his jaw muscle tight.

"After lessons you may," she answered. "Give

me your hand, Mr. Finch, and we shall show the other gentlemen the proper way to shake."

He didn't look pleased but walked from his place in line and did as she instructed. Lilla slid her hand into his. "You are to take the man's offered hand with a good grip, but not so tight as to squeeze." She slipped her hand from his until he only held two fingers. "Never shake in this manner. Only allowing a portion of the hand is a sign of snobbery, or an indication that you intend to snub the person to whom you are being introduced."

Grady's hand felt warm, his hold firm. Lilla had trouble concentrating. "If you are being introduced by a third party, or you are conducting the introduction between two men who are not acquainted with one another, it is always proper to introduce the inferior to the superior, the younger to the older. And of course, if a lady is being introduced, the gentleman to the lady."

She glanced up into Grady's eyes, noting that they looked more blue than gray this afternoon. "If you are acquainted with both parties being introduced but the parties themselves are not acquainted, it is proper to say something about one party in order to start a conversation between them."

"Excuse me," Grady said, his brow puckered. "I don't understand."

The warmth from his hand sent a tingling sensation shooting up her arm. Lilla tried not to jerk away. "W-Well, say I am introducing you to a man you have never met. I would say, 'Mr. Finch is the foreman of the WC Ranch, and an expert on the cattle industry in this area.' "

He smiled. "You would?"

His teeth were straight and white. His lips were nicely shaped.

"Lilla? Ah, Miss Traften?" he corrected.

She realized she'd been staring and felt a blush creep into her cheeks. Along with the heat in her face, she noticed a throbbing around her injured eye. Lilla pulled her hand from his. "Yes, something of that nature. I believe we should cut the lesson short today. My eye feels as if it might be swelling shut."

Grady gently tilted her face up to his. "I told you we should see to that as quickly as possible." He leaned forward and looked closer. "It's starting to swell, all right."

She became aware of everything about him. The length of his dark lashes, the tiny lines around the corners of his eyes, his slightly crooked nose. A bandanna rested against his tan neck. He swallowed. She glanced up. He stared at her. Not at her injury, but into her eyes. His fingers traced the line of her jaw, so light she wondered if she only imagined his touch.

Lilla knew she should look away—pretend she hadn't been staring at him or remembering things better left forgotten. She couldn't seem to make herself glance away. Not even if it meant the difference between living and dying, drowning or breathing, salvation or ruin. Only one thing managed to penetrate the foggy recesses of her mind. A woman's dry words. Sally's voice, she believed.

"There's a room in the back. You two help yourselves."

Chapter Nine

Lilla's eye turned a deep shade of purple. Grady had slapped a piece of raw meat on it as soon as they returned to the ranch two days ago, and although it did seem to help the swelling, it didn't do much about the bruise. She didn't know what had gotten into her to stare at him the way she had inside the saloon. If Sally hadn't spoken when she did, if she hadn't dryly asked if they wanted a room for doctoring her eye, Lilla might have stayed like that forever.

She glanced into the mirror at her face again, sighed and went about straightening her room. When she moved the teaching manual she'd intended to study the night before, a piece of paper drifted to the floor. She stooped and retrieved it. It was a letter, one she'd received shortly before her banishment to Texas. Another declaration of love from Gregory Kline.

Lilla smiled, wondering what the proper Mr. Kline would think if he saw her at that moment—if he knew she'd been consorting with soiled doves and doing manual labor. He'd be shocked, she supposed. Even blackmailers like Gregory had certain standards where women were concerned.

Kline thought she was a spoiled, empty-headed doll who could further his career, line his pockets with her father's money, stay safely within the bounds of propriety and never stray from the path beaten for her by society. But she *had* strayed, evidently. She'd never entertained wicked thoughts about either Gregory or Wade Langtry when either man courted her. Not the kind of thoughts that she now kept conjuring about Grady Finch. The kind of thoughts that got nice girls into trouble.

The clanging of pots outside interrupted her musings. Lilla glanced down and frowned over the tight cotton shirt she wore and the buckskin pants hugging her hips. The Lilla Gregory knew wouldn't be caught dead in such unfitting apparel, but she had laundry to do, and she wouldn't soil one of her good gowns in the process. And she somewhat enjoyed this newfound freedom. Grady wouldn't tell her what she could or could not wear.

She replaced Kline's letter inside of her manual, laid the book on the dresser and went downstairs.

Maria had gathered the piles of laundry on the

front porch. A pot of lye soap and water was boiling upon a fire built over a pit in the ground. Another large pot of clean water sat next to the lye for rinsing. Lilla realized she'd have to haul all the laundry from the porch to the pots. She sighed and gathered up an armload.

"Can I give you a hand, Miss Lilla?"

From nowhere, Smitty White had materialized. Lilla smiled at him. "That is a very kind offer, Mr. White. And a very gentlemanly one, as well." She transferred her burden to his arms and turned back toward the porch. She bent and gathered another armload, only to turn and find Smitty ready for the next pile.

"You scoop 'em up and I'll tote 'em over to the pots."

"All right," she agreed. "That sounds like a plan."

"Not a very good one." Grady sauntered toward them. "I sent you to the house to tell Maria when to expect us back for supper, Smitty."

The cowhand flushed. "I saw Miss Lilla in need of some help and—"

"I know, you thought you'd be gentlemanly and give her a hand."

Smitty nodded, but Lilla couldn't figure out why the ranch hand looked ill at ease. She supposed laundry wasn't part of Smitty's duties.

"I'll go on in now and tell Maria," the cowhand said.

Grady stepped closer. "Lilla will tell her. Return

to the corral and help saddle the horses."

"Yes, boss." Smitty hurried off without even tipping his hat to Lilla in parting.

She turned to Grady. "You shouldn't discourage a man from helping a lady."

He took the clothes from her arms. "I told you not to wear those tight pants. Smitty was helping himself more than he was helping you—helping himself to a nice view every time you bent over and scooped up an armful of laundry."

Lilla's temper immediately rose. "You don't know that for a fact."

"Yes, I do." He moved to the pots and dumped his armload of laundry. "I watched him watch you. He had his tongue dangling out of his mouth like a loco mule."

She didn't like the idea of being ogled by the lanky cowhand. "Then you should say something to him. Tell him it isn't polite—"

"Hold on just a minute," he interrupted. "You can't mold a body like that one into tight-fitting clothes and not expect a man to stare."

His gaze swept over her. Lilla's heated reaction to Grady boldly staring at her was different from the irritation she'd felt about Smitty's gawking. "I must be loco, too," she muttered, moving around the laundry so she could bend without having her backside facing Grady. "And you're the one Sally's girls compare to a mule, by the way."

He stepped up on the porch and reached for another armload. "What?"

She dumped her load into his arms. "Oh, something they said. I didn't understand it. Some reference to you and a mule."

"What? Like, 'he's stubborn as a mule'?"

Chewing her lower lip, she tried to recall the reference. "No, that wasn't it. I would have understood stubborn as a mule."

He shrugged and turned toward the dump pile.

"*Hung* like a mule," Lilla blurted. "That was it." She smiled, pleased that she'd recalled the reference.

Grady missed a step and nearly fell off the porch. "What did you just say?"

She frowned. "Is that bad? I mean, the way they were giggling, I didn't really think that it was bad."

The laundry fell from his arms. "You don't know what that means?"

Lilla didn't consider herself ignorant and didn't care for anyone implying that she might be. "Farm animals are hardly a subject much discussed within my social circle, Mr. Finch."

He laughed and shook his head. "I don't imagine so."

When he started to walk away, she said, "Well, what does it mean?"

"I don't have time to explain. The men are waiting for me. Tell Maria we should be in around sundown for supper."

Her gaze roamed his broad shoulders and lower as he walked away. "All right, you can explain it to me over supper. Pleasant conversation should accompany a good meal."

He stumbled again and turned around. "Why don't you ask Maria what it means? And bear in mind that Sally's girls don't know firsthand, ah, so to speak."

"All right," she said, then went about gathering up the load of laundry he'd dropped. "I'll ask Maria."

She thought she heard him laughing as he continued on toward the corrals.

Grady's amusement died the moment he spotted Smitty White. He marched up to the cowhand and shoved him back against his mount.

"Keep your eyes in your head and your thoughts off of that one! Understand?"

"Hell, boss, you can't blame a man for looking," Smitty defended, his voice high.

Grady could feel heat flush his face. "I can and I will." His gaze included all of the men. "You'll show Miss Traften proper respect while she's here, or you'll answer to me. Everyone clear on that?"

Heads were quick to nod. Tanner Richards, always braver than the others, said, "Seems to me you do your fill of looking at Miss Traften. How come it's all right for you but not for the rest of us?"

It was a good question. One he didn't have an answer for. Or did he? Grady moved to his horse. He patted the spirited bay affectionately. "The way

I see it," he said, swinging into the saddle, "it's my job to watch Miss Traften during her stay. I'm responsible for her safety."

He didn't give the men time for comments or arguments but kneed his horse into a gallop, knowing the others would follow. They would spend the day counting cattle, looking for new calves, branding if they found any. They rode in silence. As always, when they moved to a certain section of rich grassland, Grady left the men and rode up upon a rise.

Below sat the prettiest stretch of dirt and grass he'd ever seen. There were cottonwood trees lining the valley where a thick stream wound its way through the territory. He wanted that land more than anything he'd wanted in his life. It was his chance to make something of himself, the way his mother would have wanted him to. And Wade and Camile wanted him to have the land, too. Without the couple agreeing to cut out a land section from theirs and sell it, he wouldn't have a chance of buying such a prize. And for a decent price.

He imagined the house he'd build, the children who'd come running when his woman rang the dinner bell. His woman? Grady frowned. He couldn't picture himself strapped with a woman and children. In fact, there wasn't a woman he'd think about taking as a wife. Was there? There was one, his mind argued, and even provided him with a picture of her delicate features and violet eyes.

Grady shook the image from his thoughts. Lilla

didn't belong with this land. She belonged in the city, with her fancy folks, attending to her fancy doings. She did have more spirit than he'd first given her credit for, he admitted. He smiled, recalling the way she'd nearly run him over with the buggy, and she'd taken a damn good punch from Delores without losing her legs beneath her.

He had about as much sense as a rock for staring down at his future home and trying to imagine her there—even to consider her wanting to share his dreams.

She belonged in St. Louis under the protection of her father. Miles Traften, he felt certain, had better things in mind for his only daughter than the likes of him. Grady's would be a hard life cut from a hard territory. Not a place for expensive lace or fine ladies.

"Hey, boss, we found some new calves!" Sparks Montgomery shouted up to him.

With one last glance, Grady sighed appreciatively, then turned his horse toward a long day's work. The fancy Hereford bull Wade bought in Fort Worth last year had proven his worth. The men herded a large group of cows and new calves toward him. Grady removed his branding equipment from his saddle as Tanner Richards gathered wood to start a fire.

They made a rope corral, and had a hell of a time getting the calves separated from their mamas. Once the calves were secured, and two men sat on horseback to keep the fretful mothers at bay,

Grady leaned down and held the WC brand over the fire.

"Reckon Miss Lilla will want to keep on with those silly lessons?" Tanner asked him.

"I figure she will," Grady answered. "She hasn't said different."

A couple of the men groaned. "This is damn embarrassing, Grady," Sparks said. "What are we gonna do if some of the other outfits find out we're taking charm lessons?"

Poking the fire, Grady answered, "We've had this conversation before. I don't know why any of you are bellyaching about it. You get an hour of free time once a week in town, and the money for the lessons is coming out of my pocket, not yours."

"It's the principle of the thing," Tanner argued. "We ain't fancy dudes from back East. We're cowboys and—"

"And don't any of you have a scrap of good manners between you," Grady interrupted. "Lilla needs the money so she can return home."

"Hell, why don't you just give it to her? You're paying her to help Maria and for our lessons anyway."

The foreman spit on the branding iron to see if it was hot enough. "It's the principle of the thing," he repeated. "Her pa wants her to earn her way, and I don't see where it's going to hurt her to learn a lesson or two in the bargain."

"You got something against her?" Sparks asked.

Tanner laughed. "He'd like to have something

against her. Something in the front of his pants."

Grady's gaze lifted from the fire to meet Tanner's. "Never rile a man who's holding a branding iron, Richards. I told you all to show her proper respect."

Tanner eyed the branding iron. He laughed nervously. "Hell, I was just funning you, Grady. Sides, it's the truth, ain't it?"

It was the truth, but Grady would be damned if he'd say so. He felt like he'd made a fool of himself at Sally's Saloon—staring into Lilla's eyes, thinking how he'd like to pull her into his arms, kiss those sweet lips of hers, run his hands over more than the delicate curve of her jaw. The saloon could have burned down around them, and he didn't think he'd have been aware of anything but her. If he had a lick of sense, he'd heed his own warnings concerning Lilla.

He lifted the branding iron, watching it glow red, then noticed that Sparks and Tanner were still waiting for an answer. He glanced past them and called, "Take one down, I'm ready."

Iron in hand, he rose and walked toward the unfortunate victim. The calf bawled pathetically for its mama. Grady hated branding. The calves had thick hides and he knew it didn't hurt them for more than a minute, but it always made him a little sick to press the tool to the calf's hindquarters. The stench of burnt hair assaulted his senses.

Despite the smell, he smiled, recalling when he'd first arrived at the Circle C with Tom Cordell. He hadn't been more than thirteen and had asked why they couldn't just draw a brand on the cows. To tease him, the outfit had wrestled him down and drawn a CC brand on his butt with charcoal. Full of hurt over the loss of his mother, a boy poised on the threshold of manhood, he'd given more than one cowhand a taste of his fists. No one had treated him like anything less than a man since. And of course the charcoal had easily come off, teaching him why branding was a necessary evil.

"Bring me the next one!" he shouted, releasing the calf. Grady poked the iron back into the fire and wiped the sweat from his brow. The afternoon promised to be a long, hot one. He found himself anxious to return to the ranch, ready for the cooler temperature of the house and the pleasant scent of lilac that hovered sweetly around Lilla Traften.

She represented all in life he'd been denied. Everything beyond his reach. Spoiled, sheltered Lilla, who didn't understand crude references to men's private parts. He wondered if she'd asked Maria the question yet.

The moment Lilla's gaze met Grady's over the dinner table, she felt her face heat up. She set the last dish of mashed potatoes on the table and walked to her seat. When he rose to hold her chair, her gaze automatically lowered to the front of his pants. She quickly glanced away.

Grady leaned close to her ear when he scooted

her chair up to the table. "I told you none of them know firsthand."

She stiffened. Flustered, she said, "I have no idea what you're talking about."

He didn't pursue the issue, thank goodness, but he did have a slight smile hovering over his mouth when he reseated himself. Lilla focused on Maria, and was pleased when one of the men rose and drew her chair back from the table. The housekeeper sat down, cast Grady a dark look, then bowed her head and folded her hands for grace.

Lilla could hardly concentrate on the prayer with Grady sitting next to her. She kept thinking about Maria's blunt answer to her question concerning mules and men. Judging by the conversation between the women at Sally's, such an asset in a man was not considered a fault. Lilla clasped her hands together tighter. Her gaze slid sideways. The foreman had respectfully bowed his head, but he still wore that amused smile.

"I wouldn't think it was anything to be smug over," she muttered.

"What are we discussing?" he asked under his breath.

"Nothing," she whispered. "Only talking to myself."

"You wish to add to the prayer, Miss Lilla?" Maria asked from the other end of the table.

Lilla glanced up. She had the room's attention. She smiled. "Amen."

A chorus of amens followed. Dinner progressed

in a somewhat organized manner, but she could tell that the men wanted to resort to their usual tactics of shoveling and throwing. Perhaps they needed a distraction to help their impatience while waiting for dishes to be passed.

"It is customary during a formal dinner to converse with the person seated next to you," she said. "This weakens the temptation to eat quickly, thus allowing your food to set properly, which causes fewer health problems."

"I do get an awful case of the trots after every meal," one man admitted.

"*Pleasant* conversation," Lilla stressed. "And only with the person seated next to you."

She turned to the man seated on her right, only to discover Smitty White grinning at her. Considering the incident with the laundry, she quickly turned in the opposite direction. Of course that left her staring into Grady's blue-gray eyes.

Intelligent thought did not visit her, and Lilla couldn't think of anything to say. Several moments ticked past. She felt grateful when Grady had to pause from staring at her in order to pass her the platter of fried chicken. Maria had wrung the bird's neck and plucked it earlier that day while Lilla finished the laundry. She was relieved she hadn't had to witness that awful event.

She and Grady were back to staring at one another.

"Did you have a nice day?" he finally asked.

Unfortunately, Lilla took a moment to consider

the question rather than respond automatically. "No," she answered. "Did you?"

He dished a heaping helping of buttered greens onto his plate. "Can't say as I did. We branded calves today. The smell of burnt hair . . . well, it's not anything I should discuss at the dinner table."

Lilla nodded in agreement. She made a pretense of eating, moving food around on her plate.

"How are your feet?" When she glanced up, he frowned. "Oh, sorry. Don't guess I should talk about blisters, either."

"No. But my feet are fine."

Their eyes held for a moment. She glanced away. They ate in silence until the meal became awkward. "Surely you did something today you found pleasant," Lilla commented.

Grady lifted his napkin and wiped his mouth. "I did sneak away and look over that land I plan to buy from Wade and Camile."

"Ah," she said. "Cactus and dirt. That does sound pleasant."

His gaze cut toward her. "Not much cactus there. Good grassland, and there's the prettiest river that snakes through the valley, and trees that line the bank."

"Trees?" She lifted a brow. "I was beginning to think that Texas had no trees."

He laughed. "Sure, we have trees. And not all the land is flat. That's what is so unique about the Panhandle. We have canyons, and bluffs, even a hill or two."

"You actually like it here, don't you?"

"Sure I do. I wouldn't stay if I didn't." He laid his fork aside, turning toward her. "There's nothing in the world like sleeping outside. Lying beneath a blanket of stars and listening to the fire crackle and the coyotes howl in the distance. The soft lowing of cattle as they bed down for the night. Sometimes the smell of rain on the air even though the storm is miles away."

His eyes danced. He felt a passion for his way of life, for the land. Lilla envied him in that moment. Other than fancy clothes and the things her father's money could provide for her, she couldn't recall feeling passionate about anything in her life. She'd been the good daughter, the proper little lady—done what she was told, become what was expected of her. She'd never had a dream of her own.

"But you wouldn't understand," he said, the light fading from his eyes as he turned back to the meal.

"No," she agreed quietly. Lilla resumed her meal, noticing that the table around them had fallen silent. She glanced over the men while they ate, catching Sparks Montgomery's eye.

"We ain't got much pleasant to talk about," he explained. "I mean, besides what we do here on the ranch and what we do in town on Saturday night, not much else happens. Langtry ain't exactly St. Louis. No fancy parties and such."

Lilla suddenly had an idea. "What would you all think about having a dance?"

"A dance?" Tanner Richards repeated. "You mean, a shindig?"

"I'm speaking of a formal dance," she corrected. "One where we all dress up and waltz—"

"I ain't gonna strut around like a peacock," Smitty White interrupted. "Won't make a fool of myself with the only gals we have around these parts."

"You do that every time you go into a back room with one of them," Tanner said, causing the table to laugh.

"Gentlemen," Lilla said, her voice stern. "You are not to refer to the ladies at Sally's as gals. We've gone over that issue before." Seeing the lack of enthusiasm on the men's faces, she turned to her left. "Mr. Finch, you'd enjoy attending a nice social event, wouldn't you?"

Grady tugged at his collar. "I don't dance," he said softly.

"You don't dance?" Lilla repeated loud enough for everyone to hear. "Why not?"

He shrugged. "Never learned how."

"I'll teach you," Lilla decided. "I will teach all of you, and the ladies as well if they don't know the steps."

"I don't care to learn," Grady said, returning his attention to the meal as if that were the end of the matter.

Lilla had finally gotten her passion up for something, and she wouldn't allow him to snub her plans. "Why don't you care to learn?"

His face flushed. Lilla thought he might be blushing.

"It's . . ."

"Sissified," Tanner Richards provided. "We don't dance."

"Sissified?" Lilla didn't understand the term. "What—"

"It isn't manly," Grady said, then again turned to his meal as if he'd dismissed the conversation.

Lilla begged to disagree. "Many a woman has lost her heart to a man who moves gracefully across a dance floor. I, for one, am very attracted to men who dance well."

A set of blue-gray eyes lifted to her, a spark of interest ignited within them. "Are you saying women think more of a man who can dance than one who can't?"

"Oh, *sí*," Maria, usually silent during meals, said. "In my mother country, a man who can dance the flamenco can steal more than a woman's heart. It is a dance of seduction, a dance—"

"It is improper." Lilla frowned at the woman. "I once saw the dance performed by Spanish royalty visiting my father, and I must say we were all shocked by the display. I mean to teach all of you the waltz, or a nice—"

"This flamenco," Tanner Richards rudely interrupted. "You say it makes the gals hanker after a man, Maria? Gets 'em fired up and easy to—"

"Mr. Richards, kindly do not interrupt. It's not polite."

Tanner glanced at Lilla. "You just did."

To her embarrassment, she realized he was right. "Never mind," she said. "It is clear to me that none of you care the least bit about learning social graces."

"I might agree to learn that flamenco," Tanner said.

"Hoping to catch Meg's eye," Sparks explained to Lilla. "He's got a soft spot for that whore, and don't like sharing her with no one else."

"Sparks," Grady warned. "Watch your mouth."

"It's true," the big-eared man defended. "He moons after her like a titty-starved calf. I don't know why he don't just ask her to marry him and be done with it."

"I ain't marrying no whore," Tanner said between clenched teeth. "And you just shut your pie hole about her, too, Montgomery."

"I can say whatever I want, Richards," Sparks countered.

Lilla thought a fight might ensue. Grady quickly brought the men under control.

"You two want to bump heads, you wait until dinner is over and take it outside behind the bunkhouse."

The look that passed between the men said they intended to do just that.

"Sparks likes Meg, too," Smitty whispered beside her. "She won't give neither one of them more than an hour in the back room."

Her cheeks burning over the discussion, Lilla refused to comment. She also had trouble letting go of her idea to plan a dance. It was the only thing she really knew how to do well. Host a gala. As Tanner and Sparks finished the meal and threw threatening looks at each other, another idea occurred to her.

"Perhaps Meg could be wooed by a man with more social etiquette. One who didn't always greet her with cow manure on his boots. A man who could dance."

Grady cast her a sideways glance, smiled slightly and returned to his meal.

"You reckon?" Tanner asked.

She shrugged. "It would certainly be a change from what she's used to."

"Suppose I could learn that flamenco Maria talked about?" Sparks said.

"I said 'social etiquette,' " Lilla reminded stiffly. "A nice waltz will turn her head more than a vulgar display said to have originated with the Gypsies. Besides, I don't know the flamenco and have no desire to learn it in order to teach you."

"But you expect the men to learn something they don't want to learn," Grady pointed out.

"Now, hold on, boss," Tanner said. "If Miss Lilla thinks Meg . . . ah, the whores . . . I mean, the ladies at Sally's would cotton to such a shindig, maybe we shouldn't be so fast to say no."

"If a two-left-footed billy goat like you can learn to dance, then so can I," Sparks muttered.

"You two would look like chickens scratching for

feed," Smitty said with a laugh. "Now, I have the grace that Miss Lilla says is needed to dance."

One man spewed a mouthful of food across the table. "You can't even rope without getting tangled up, White."

Arguments broke out around the table. Lilla clanked her spoon against her glass. "Then it's settled," she said smugly. "I will teach all of you to dance."

"But that will have to count as part of their lessons," Grady said beside her. "I can't spare them for more than the time we've already agreed upon."

Lilla nodded. "All right."

"Hey, wait a minute, Grady," Tanner said. "You're talking like it's just us that has to learn to dance. You're gonna learn, too, ain't you?"

Grady didn't give the question much thought. "No. I don't dance."

"Then we don't dance." Sparks threw his napkin down. "It was you who said we had to do this foolishness in the first place. You're the one who's always saying you wouldn't ask any more of us than you'd ask of yourself."

"You have said that several times, boss," Smitty joined in. "Seems to me if we're willing to learn, you should be willing, too."

Lilla had trouble keeping a straight face. Grady suddenly looked very uncomfortable.

"All right," he surprised her by agreeing. His gaze swung to her. "But only the flamenco, and

Miss Traften has to agree to dance it with me at the social."

Displaying poor table manners, Lilla allowed her mouth to drop open. "I will not," she assured him.

"Then it's settled. No dancing at all."

"B-But I don't know the dance," she defended.

He smiled, nearly as smug as she'd been earlier.

"I know the flamenco," Maria said quietly. "I will teach you, and I will teach Mr. Grady. The dance is not usually performed by a couple, but by a lone man or woman, but we can improvise."

Lilla had the pleasure of seeing Grady's smile slip from his mouth. She might have been amused by his shortsighted strategy in the matter, had she not been appalled at the thought of being a party to such a lurid display of dancing.

"I refuse," she said.

"Then so do we," Tanner countered.

Grady was back to smiling.

Proper upbringing battled with Lilla's will to be the victor in this situation. She'd always had a stubborn streak. One her father had tried to tame, one Margaret had convinced her was better left hidden beneath a polite mask of submission. Her gaze roamed the men lining the table. It came to rest upon their foreman.

"You have a deal, Mr. Finch."

Chapter Ten

"A dance?" Delores grumbled. "What do you mean we're having a dance?" The brunette glanced over her shoulder. "And where are the men?"

"I thought it best if I instructed you and the men separately. Much less disruption than when all of you are in the same room."

"Don't sound like much fun," Delores grumbled.

"I think it sounds nice," Violet said in her soft voice.

Delores snorted. "And what would you know about dancing? What do you know about anything? You can't even bring yourself to do what you're supposed to do around here and pleasure the men."

Violet's face turned red. Sally, working behind the bar, poked her head up.

"Leave her alone, Delores. Young Violet keeps this place clean, and if she wasn't such a good cook, you wouldn't be getting such a fat ass."

The saucy brunette glanced behind her. "My ass isn't fat."

"Smitty White says it is," Meg said. "Course, he likes his women plump back there."

Lilla's ears were burning. "Ladies. Let us return to the subject at hand. I thought you would all enjoy a social. Dressing up and learning to dance, being treated like ladies by the men."

"That ragtag group wouldn't know a lady if they stepped on one," Meg said. " 'Sides. What's the point? They all know what we are anyway."

A murmur of agreement followed. Even shy Violet seemed sadly resigned to her fate in life. Lilla's frustration level rose.

"People who don't demand respect rarely receive it." Thinking Violet might be her best ally, she turned to the young woman. "Where is your pride, Violet?"

The young woman drew herself up, but Delores's words quickly deflated her.

"Hers was beat out of her a long time ago," the brunette said. "Ain't that right, Mouse? Your daddy firmly believed that sparing the rod spoils the child. And he thought so much of you, he went and sold you for a case of whiskey."

Horrified, Lilla glanced at Violet. The girl's big blue eyes filled with tears and she ran from the room.

"You're gonna run that gal off, Delores," Sally grumbled. "Why do you always pick on her?"

"I bet it's because she's pretty," Meg said. "And she don't have hair on her legs a grizzly would envy."

Delores wheeled toward the buxom blonde, her eyes narrowed. Lilla wasn't in the mood to witness a scrap between the two, and she was concerned about Violet. It took a great deal of willpower, but she walked to the door leading to the back rooms and pushed it open. She stepped into the hallway. Wicked thoughts immediately assaulted her.

Cool sheets and hot skin. A man's mouth greedily exploring hers. The feel of a large hand molded firmly against her breast. Shaking her head, she proceeded down the hallway. She found Violet inside a modest room, weeping.

"Delores shouldn't have said such cruel things."

The girl's head jerked up. Tears ran down her pale cheeks. "It's the truth. My pa did sell me for a case of whiskey. And he beat me something fierce while I was growing up."

Lilla was outraged. Although her father hadn't been one to openly show affection, he'd always been kind to her, loved her in his restrained way. She couldn't imagine a man taking his fists to his children, or selling one for any amount of money or goods.

"How could he?" she whispered. "And you can't be more than . . . what? Sixteen?"

"As far as I remember, I'll be seventeen come

next month," Violet said. "But my pa sold me to a man who ran a whorehouse in Independence when I wasn't more than fourteen. Pa was broke, like he usually was, and he wanted a drink, like he usually did. This man stopped by our place to water his horses and saw me sweeping the porch. He had a wagon filled with liquor. Said he'd give my pa a bottle for me. I heard them and I was scared, but my pa said no, and I almost loved him in that moment. Then he said I was worth at least a case."

Tears stung Lilla's eyes. "Where was your mother? How could she let—"

"My ma was dead," Violet said. "Oh, she was still breathing, but she'd been dead for a long time. There were five of us kids, me being the oldest. My ma just did her work and sat her bruised self in the corner at night, quiet like the rest of us, hoping our pa wouldn't take notice of us until he'd drank enough to pass out."

Lilla couldn't contain the shudder that raced down her spine. "How horrible."

"I thought it was," Violet admitted. "But after a night on the road with Victor Vega, I changed my mind. He wasn't any better than my pa, but along with drinking and slapping me around . . . he . . . he did worse. Said he had to break me in for my new position in his whorehouse."

Lilla felt sick. "The man took advantage of you?"

Violet nodded, her dirty hair falling in her face. "That night, and many other nights over the next two years. The only good thing about it was that he'd decided he didn't want to share me. I was a whore. But at least I was just his whore."

"Why didn't you run away?" Lilla moved further into the room. She sat down on the bed Violet kneeled before.

"Because I had no money, no place to go. Then one day I just couldn't take any more. I thought about stealing money from Victor the night I ran away, but too many people with my family name are thieves, and I wasn't going to add that to my sins. I crept out while he was snoring drunk. Didn't take nothing but the clothes on my back, which weren't much good."

"So you escaped. What a relief that must have been."

The eyes Violet turned upon Lilla were the eyes of a woman too wise for her young face.

"I found out there are worse things than being a whore. Starving so much you have to walk bent over because your belly hurts. Shaking so badly from the cold you can't fall asleep at night. I was about to turn back when Sally and her girls came along in a wagon headed for Texas. She took me in, fed me, gave me clothes, and I told her I'd work for her."

"Is what Delores said true? I mean, about you not entertaining the men?"

"I thought I could." Violet's face flushed. "But the first time I came back here with a man, I started shaking and crying. He went up front and got Sally. She came back and I told her what had happened to me. I told her I couldn't ever let a man touch me again. I figured she'd throw me out."

"But she didn't," Lilla said softly.

Violet shook her head. "She said I could stay if I'd help her keep the place clean and cook for the girls. So that's what I do."

Lilla sighed. "Haven't you thought about going somewhere else? Cooking for an eating establishment or working for—"

"Won't no decent folks want to have dealings with me," Violet said. "This is my home, and I can't say it's not the best one I've ever had. Delores gets on me, I don't know why, but for the most part, the rest of them are decent. The men don't bother me, knowing I don't go to the back rooms. I make sure when they look at me they don't want me the way they might want Meg or Delores or any of the others."

Understanding dawned upon Lilla. That was why Violet let her hair go dirty and hang down in her face. Violet probably wasn't reed thin but wore clothes much too large for her body. The young woman had wisely decided to disguise her frail beauty as a safety measure.

"You're not addle-brained," Lilla said with a smile.

Violet smiled back through her tears. "No, ma'am. But I have learned how to make myself unappealing."

Lilla gently touched her cheek. "It's a shame to hide that lovely smile beneath stringy hair. I believe your hair would be lovely if you wore it clean and brushed back from your face."

"Why would I want to?" Violet asked. "No sense in being pretty if all it will get you is on your back."

"A woman should take pride in what she's been given," Lilla argued.

With those soulful blue eyes staring up at Lilla, Violet said, "That's easy for a woman to say who ain't never had nothing taken away from her."

"I suppose you're right, Violet." Lilla rose and walked toward the door, deeply disturbed by Violet's past. She was shaken, too, by her own naïveté. Things like this took place in the world outside her protected boundaries, and she had allowed high society to shape her judgment of the people who experienced them.

"Miss Lilla," Violet stopped her. "I think a dance would be nice. I could cook, and it would be a chance for something besides drinking and whoring to go on here."

With resolve, Lilla said, "You will have your dance, Violet. That, I promise you."

Although Lilla wanted nothing more than to slink into a dark place and weep over Violet's sad life, she wiped her tears away and straightened her spine. Delores and Meg were still bickering when she walked into the saloon. Neither, she noted, had any bruises . . . yet.

"Choose partners, ladies. We are going to dance."

* * *

Grady thought Lilla acted subdued during dinner that evening. Her thoughts seemed to be somewhere else. He swore her eyes watered a time or two, as if she might be on the verge of tears. Later, as he made his rounds to check the place, he heard soft weeping. He followed the sound, finding Lilla on the front steps of the house, her face buried in her hands.

"Lilla?"

When she glanced up, he saw the sparkle of tears streaming down her cheeks in the moonlight. She quickly wiped them away. "I-I didn't think anyone would be up at this time of night."

He stepped closer. "Are you all right?"

She sniffed, then glanced around as if looking for something to wipe her face with. Grady pulled a bandanna from his back pocket and handed it to her. She snatched it and blew her nose.

"I'm fine," she answered, handing the bandanna back.

"Why don't you just hang on to that," he said. "You're going to end up washing it anyway." He moved up the steps and sat beside her. "You didn't sound fine a minute ago. I heard you crying."

She waved a hand. "Women cry sometimes, Mr. Finch. And there doesn't always have to be a reason."

He shook his head. "That doesn't make much sense."

"That's one of the few advantages of being a woman. We don't have to always make sense."

Grady didn't think she'd cry for no reason. "Did something happen today? Something in town?" He tensed, turning to study her face in the moonlight. "Did any of the men get out of line while you were teaching them dance lessons?"

"No," she answered quickly. "I-I'm homesick."

"Oh." He breathed a sigh of relief that he wouldn't be rousting out any of the men to beat them senseless. "I guess you're missing your father and all your fancy friends." Grady felt guilty for exposing her to elements she'd been sheltered from all of her life. "I don't expect you have much in common with Sally's girls, or any of the rest of us, for that matter."

"No," she agreed, and he swore her eyes filled with tears again.

"Life here isn't that bad, is it?"

A tear rolled down her cheek, and he took the bandanna from her fingers and wiped it away.

"No, it isn't that bad," she answered, but her voice quavered. "Things could be much worse for me. I've never seen the world from anywhere but the safety of my father's domain. I knew that some people didn't live the way we did. I just never realized how ugly a place the world might be for some."

"You're sure something didn't happen in town today?"

She shook her head. "No, nothing. Just something I learned that upset me."

If she'd learned something from Sally's girls, he

suspected it wasn't anything a sheltered miss like Lilla should know. "Those women say things to shock you," he pointed out. "Things better left unsaid around an innocent."

She lifted a brow. "What kind of things?"

He stuffed the bandanna back into her hand. "Things concerning men and women."

"Oh, you mean information such as Smitty White prefers women with large, ah, posteriors?"

"To set things straight, he likes that part of a woman in particular, large or otherwise," Grady answered. "Yours isn't large, and he didn't mind slobbering over it that day he helped you with the laundry."

Even in the darkness, he saw her blush. "We shouldn't be having this conversation. It isn't decent."

"I'm sure you've heard worse in the time you've been here."

"Yes, I'm receiving quite an education," she said dryly.

Once, hearing her say as much would have amused Grady, but now he didn't like the thought that her view of life was being so thoroughly tarnished. "Male and female matters," he said, then cleared his throat. "You know much about them?"

Her face turned a shade darker. "I assume you're not asking because you believe that I can enlighten you about the subject. That leaves the unpleasant possibility that you hope to enlighten me. I've been told the basics, thank you very much."

She looked stiff and proper, but her hair hung around her shoulders, and her lips were far too tempting to belong to a prudish woman. Lady or not, she oozed sensuality.

"I didn't want you to get the wrong idea," he explained. "That it's just about bumping and grinding against one another and—"

"Mr. Finch!" she interrupted, her eyes flashing in the night. "You have crossed the boundaries of decency. Not that this is the first time you've done so," she added irritably. "I don't care to hear your—"

"Call me Grady," he said. "I like the way you say my name."

He didn't realize that his face moved closer to hers until he saw her lips part. "Mr. Finch," she warned, but in a breathless voice. "Grady," she whispered, then seemed to shake herself. "I should go inside now. It's late."

"Yeah," he agreed, pulling back.

But she didn't rise and go in.

"Since you were rude enough to begin the conversation regarding men and women, I suppose it would be ruder to leave it unfinished." She turned to him. "To set your mind at ease, I am aware that how a gentleman treats a lady is a far cry from . . . from what takes place in Sally's back rooms."

Grady thought about it for a minute. "I wasn't

talking about gentlemen and ladies. I'm talking about men and women."

"Within my circles, men and women *are* ladies and gentlemen."

"Maybe on the outside," he agreed. "But most of us are the same on the inside. Just because you're a lady doesn't mean that I don't feel . . ." He shut up.

"Don't feel what?"

He tugged at his collar. "Manly urges when I'm around you."

"Oh." Her eyes widened.

"And just because you're a lady doesn't mean you can't feel . . . "

"Womanly urges?" she suggested.

"Right."

"I'm not positive what a womanly urge feels like," she admitted.

"I was afraid you'd say something like that." He stood, telling himself that now was a good time to say good night.

She rose as well. "Aren't you going to explain?"

Moonlight danced in her hair. He saw the streaks on her cheeks left by her earlier tears. Her pouty mouth drove him crazy.

"I can't think of a way to explain it so you'd understand. Well, I can, but—"

"Then please do," she insisted. "As I've pointed out, it's rude to start something and not finish it."

Grady figured that if Lilla understood what womanly urges were, she could better fight them off when confronted with them. Besides, it was just a harmless lesson.

"Sometimes showing is easier than telling."

Lilla suddenly found herself in his arms. His mouth captured hers. His boldness enraged her, but somehow it also excited her. Grady was a physical person. She'd learned that about him. He didn't mind touching her. In fact, it seemed in his nature to openly express his feelings. He said what he thought, did as he chose. He wasn't like anyone she had ever met. He reminded her of something half tame, half wild, and part of his appeal was that she never knew when he'd abandon logic and react out of pure instinct.

The way he did tonight. She met his kiss with more awareness this time. When his tongue slipped into her mouth, she greeted him with her own. He deepened the kiss. The feel of his mouth moving against hers made her heart beat faster, her face feel hotter. She might be inexperienced, but she knew enough to realize he had impressive skills when it came to kissing.

He nibbled and teased her lips until she placed her hand against the back of his head to keep him still. It was perhaps a mistake, she decided a moment later, because all of his attention became focused upon the complete fusion of their mouths.

She never knew a union of lips could be so hot, so wet, so consuming. She had trouble breathing, but more trouble pulling away from the sensations he stirred within her. Her blood ignited, burning her skin from the inside out. Despite the heat that curled around them, she pressed closer against him. His hand strayed to her throat, where she knew he felt the pounding pulse of her heart. Lower still, his fingers brushed the flesh exposed by her open-necked blouse.

His touch spread heat wherever it went, as if his fingers were tipped with fire. She should be frightened, she should be insulted that he took such liberties, but she wasn't. Not even when his hand strayed lower, sliding inside her blouse to brush the top of her breast.

"Do you want me to touch you, Lilla?" he asked against her lips.

She did. Heaven help her, she ached for him to touch her. "Yes."

"How badly do you want me to touch you?"

Pressing against his hand, she whispered, "More than anything."

He groaned and pulled away from her. The sudden absence of his heat had her reaching for him. He pinned her arms at her sides.

"Now you know about womanly urges," he said, his voice husky. "This is when you regain your senses and go inside the house like a good girl."

The ache had not abated. Her urges, she feared, were very strong. "And what if I don't?"

"You're too tempting, Lilla. And I'm too willing to help you get into trouble." He released her and stepped back. "Go inside."

Something in his eyes, a soft glow of warning, made her obey him. Once inside, she closed the door and leaned against it, less worried about his behavior than the fact that she hadn't wanted to obey him. She had little doubt now that he was a gentleman, just not the kind she was used to sharing company with. No, Grady Finch was much worse. He was dangerous.

He was the kind of man who gave a woman enough rope to hang herself. The kind who tested a woman's control, looking for weaknesses. But was he the kind to use them against her? No. And that was what made him so dangerous. His kisses were addictive. His touch, heaven. But he had more on his mind than seducing young innocents, or obviously even not-so-innocent women. He had dreams. Ambition. A purpose.

All Lilla had ever had was the fine things her father's money could purchase for her. All she'd ever dreamed of being was exactly who her father had wanted her to be.

Nothing she'd ever done had been for herself. Even her views had been carefully schooled to reflect the rules of others, as if she had no right to make her own judgments, her own decisions. She suddenly felt confused about her purpose in life, or her lack of one. She took solace in the belief that everything in life happened for a reason. What was her reason for being in Texas? To teach others, as she had thought? Or to learn about herself?

Chapter Eleven

Lilla realized a few days later that if her purpose in life was to teach, she was obviously doing a sorry job of it. Her feet were so sore she could hardly walk. She limped into the kitchen to find Maria rolling out dough for bread.

"Will that smelly liniment work on sore feet as well as blisters?" she asked.

Abandoning her chore, Maria said, "Come and sit. I will find the liniment for you."

"You're an absolute angel, Maria. I wish we had ten of you working for us in St. Louis."

Maria knelt before her, tin in hand. She glanced up, lifting a dark brow.

"Oh," Lilla breathed. "What a snobbish thing to

say. You must forgive me. I can't seem to help myself."

The woman smiled. "You will learn. As penance for your bad manners, you may scrub the floors today. It will keep you off your feet and on your knees."

Lilla frowned. "How very thoughtful."

The woman set the tin beside her and rose. "And you can doctor your own feet, miss. I will not sour my bread with the stench of the medicine which clings to the hands."

The liniment's stench did stay on a person's hands, even after a good scrubbing, Lilla recalled. Just then Grady stuck his head in the back door. Her senses immediately leapt to life. She was angry with him. He'd had the bad manners to act as if nothing untoward had happened between them the other night. He deserved to be punished.

"We'll be heading out soon," he said. "Be back around sundown again."

Lilla dropped the tin, knowing its noisy clank would draw his attention. She fumbled with her skirts, hiking them up around her ankles, then reached for the tin, which she pretended she couldn't quite reach.

"I'll get that for you."

She had him kneeling before her in seconds. Lilla fumbled with her skirts again. "It will be hard to keep my dress out of the way and apply the liniment to my sore feet. Your men are horrible dancers."

"Not to hear them tell it," he said. "Each man thinks he's better than the other."

"Well, to set the matter straight, they are all equally bad. But don't tell them I said so," she added quickly. "I wouldn't want them to become discouraged."

He glanced down at her bare feet. "Why don't you just hike your dress up over your knees?"

"It wouldn't be decent to display so much skin."

"Don't tell me you don't bathe naked like the rest of us?"

Maria giggled. Lilla suddenly imagined Grady bathing naked. It wasn't a bad vision, either. She reached down and tried to snatch the tin from his hand. "I believe you were leaving. I can manage alone."

He didn't release the medicine. "I'd be happy to help you."

"Would you?" she asked, knowing now that she had him right where she wanted him.

"Be my pleasure." His voice was deep and low, causing gooseflesh to rise on her arms.

The stench that followed ruined the moment. Lilla gagged. She held a hand over her nose and mouth. "Just hurry," she ground out.

"I'll take my time and see the job done right," he said.

The moment his hands touched her feet, she tingled all over. He rubbed harder, and her bones melted. "Oh, my," she whispered. "You do have a way with liniment."

"You're letting your dress slip down. Better pull it back up or I'll get this smelly stuff all over the hem."

Lilla lifted her dress, then leaned back and closed her eyes. His fingers slid between her toes, and she nearly moaned.

"Higher," he said.

"W-What?"

"Your dress."

She kept her eyes closed and bunched the material higher. "Is that better?"

"Just a little more."

Since he'd stopped rubbing, she complied. "Is that all right?"

"That's almost too good."

A moment later, she felt his hand brush her knee. Lilla jerked up straight. She glanced down and realized she had pulled her dress all the way up past her knees, just as he had suggested she do. She kicked out at him, landing a smelly foot right in the middle of his chest.

He stumbled back, but caught himself with his hands. Greasy as they were, they didn't help. He landed on his backside. Lilla rose, glaring down at him.

"You tricked me!"

"You tried to trick me first," he pointed out. "You're about as helpless as a female black widow spider. You just didn't want to get your hands stinky."

"If you knew the game, why did you play?"

His gaze lowered to her legs. "I may be uneducated, but I'm no fool."

"No, you're no fool," she shot back. "What you are is . . . is . . ." She tried to think in saloon terms. "As randy as a rooster with one too many peckers."

His gaze widened. Maria dropped her rolling pin. Lilla felt a blush spread over her entire body. Maria started to mumble in Spanish. Grady laughed out loud.

"Out!" Maria snapped, armed with her rolling pin. "You are stinking up my kitchen, Grady Finch! And you!" She wheeled toward Lilla. "Get yourself in the other room and scrub those floors. Scrub your mouth out while you are at it."

Lilla tried to scramble out, slipped because of her greasy feet and landed on her knees. Grady was there in a moment, helping her up. She started to thank him, noticed his liniment-smeared hand wrapped around the sleeve of her gown, and jerked away. She ran her foot over the toe of his boots.

"You have something on your face." He smeared a hand across her cheek.

She gasped and wiped the goo from her cheek. She'd ended up with the smelly liniment on her hands, after all. She placed her smeared hand upon his sleeve. "Thank you so much for pointing that out."

He glanced down. His grin faded. "Happy to have been of help." He clamped his hand over hers.

She wrestled her hand from beneath his, noting it was slimier than before.

"You need a haircut," she observed. "Your hair falls into your eyes at times." So saying, she smoothed the stray locks from his forehead, plastering then back in place with the smelly, sticky liniment.

"I prefer yours down." He reached up and stuck both his hands in her hair, shaking it so that pins scattered and her hair fell down in a clumpy mess.

"You know that liniment can turn to glue," Maria casually mentioned.

"She's right," Grady said. "I once used it on a horse's rump for a scratch. The wind blew a piece of rawhide on the horse, and it like to have never come off."

Lilla made a dash for the boiling pans. Grady made a dash for the back door.

Lilla went upstairs and stripped off her soiled clothing. The water would take a short time to warm downstairs. The stench that clung to her and the discarded gown sent her hurrying toward the window. She pulled it up and stuck her head out.

Laughter in the distance drew her attention. She started to withdraw, but noticed that no one was laughing at her. The men were ribbing Grady. Tanner Richards held his nose while he spoke to him. The foreman said something to the men and they moved toward their horses. Lilla couldn't believe he planned to spend the day without washing off. But Grady didn't follow the men, he moved toward a large watering trough inside the corral.

He stripped off his shirt while he walked and

dropped it in the dirt. The sun shimmered off his broad back. When he moved, muscles rippled. The sound of horses leaving the ranch didn't distract Lilla. Her gaze remained fixed upon the shirtless man entering the corral. He stopped before the trough, then bent and ducked his head in the water. He came up, flinging water as he smoothed his hair from his face. She had never considered the advantage of being a drop of water. Not until she watched rivulets run down his smooth, tanned skin.

She wished he were facing her instead of turned away. Of course, then he might spot her gaping at him. He stared down at the water as if contemplating something, then kicked off his boots, removed his socks and straightened. His hands moved to the front of his pants, and she knew he meant to unfasten them. She also knew that no proper lady would still be hanging out the window, hardly daring to breathe lest she distract him from his intentions.

He grasped the waist of his jeans and began to slide them down. Sweat beaded Lilla's brow. She didn't dare take the time to wipe it away—she might miss something. Lower his denims slid, down his slim hips and over firm, tight buttocks, down powerful thighs and well-muscled calves.

Lilla's knees shook, and she couldn't seem to remember to breathe. She'd been afforded this view once before—the morning she woke in a strange room with a naked man. Terrified and confused, she hadn't been able to fully appreciate the scenery. She appreciated it now.

As if he suddenly felt her eyes boring into him, he started to turn. In that same instant Lilla heard her door open.

"Here are two buckets to start with."

Lilla jerked back inside the window so quickly she bumped her head on the sill. "Ouch," she said, rubbing her forehead. Maria stared at her for a moment.

"Are you all right? You look flushed."

"Only trying to catch a breath of fresh air." Lilla moved from the window to help the woman with the buckets. "The liniment has stunk up my room."

"Sí," Maria agreed, wrinkling her nose. "Get your hair clean first."

Bending over the washbasin, Lilla allowed Maria to help her wash her hair. She was grateful for the slightly cool water to soothe her burning cheeks. Once she'd been rinsed, Lilla wrapped a towel around her head and collapsed onto the bed. Her knees were still shaking. Maria took the basin and moved toward the open window.

"What are you doing?" Lilla snapped.

"I will throw out the water," the woman explained. "Go down and fetch two more buckets up and I will bring out the tub."

The bedsprings creaked when Lilla bounded up from the bed. "I can pitch the water out."

"Do not be silly," Maria scolded. "The basin is

much lighter than the buckets. Do as you have been told."

Since Lilla could hardly make a scene over the issue of a washbasin, she scooped up the empty buckets and started toward the door.

"Aye yi yi," Maria suddenly said.

Lilla wheeled around. "What is it?"

"Mr. Grady is bathing in the water trough."

"He is?" Lilla asked, hoping to sound surprised.

"Yes, he is," Maria said. "He is like most men. No sense of modesty."

"He shouldn't be bathing in broad daylight in plain sight," Lilla agreed. "Anyone could see him."

She nearly made it to the door when Maria asked, "You were not watching Mr. Grady undress, were you?"

Lilla summoned a stunned expression before turning around. "I am offended by that question. I was merely getting a breath of fresh air. I didn't even notice Mr. Finch."

Maria smiled and turned back to the window. "That is hard not to notice."

"W-What?" Lilla stammered, forcing herself to stand still rather than try to see past Maria.

"He just stood up," Maria explained, still staring out the window.

"You shouldn't be looking," Lilla reprimanded, wanting for all the world to shove the housekeeper aside and see for herself.

Maria turned to her. "And neither should you. It is men like him who get nice girls like you into trouble. I have seen the way you two look at one another, and I do not blame you. But do you really belong here? He belongs nowhere but here, remember that."

The woman might as well have thrown a cold bucket of water in Lilla's face. Maria was right. Whatever wild attraction she felt for Grady must be suppressed. Her father would never approve of him for a husband, and Lilla had a feeling that although Grady flirted with her, kissed her, took liberties, he would never consider her marriage-worthy. Not for the life he'd forged for himself.

Shoulders slumped, she turned back toward the door.

"Oh, no," Maria worried.

Glancing over her shoulder, Lilla asked, "What's wrong?"

"Mr. Grady has just realized he has no clean clothes." She sighed. "I suppose I should fetch him some." She threw the water out the window and joined Lilla at the door. "The things I am forced to do in this house." Although she looked put out, she winked broadly at Lilla.

"Maria," Lilla squeaked.

The woman brushed past her, headed down the stairs. "I am old. I am not dead."

Later that evening, Lilla sat on the porch. Some part of her almost wanted Grady to stumble upon her again. To add to his appeal, he'd now become forbidden fruit. Someone her father wouldn't approve of, someone her social set would not approve of. A man who'd get her into trouble, and plenty of it, she imagined.

Laughter from the bunkhouse drew her attention. She'd been inside before. Been where he slept. Her dancing lessons were conducted in the structure. There wasn't much inside except bunks and blankets.

Curious, she rose and walked toward the laughter. Lamps burned inside and the door stood open. The men were dancing together. She smiled. A moment later, two men passed the open doorway and made her laugh. Grady waltzed with Sparks Montgomery. Afraid that someone might hear her giggling, she hurried back to the house. She started up the stairs when Maria stopped her.

"We have work to do."

Lilla groaned. "Not at this hour. What must we do? Butcher a hog? Wring a chicken's neck?"

"The flamenco dance," Maria reminded.

Although Lilla's feet weren't as sore as they had been, she wasn't interested in learning the dance. "I'm tired."

"You made an agreement. Mr. Grady has already had two lessons, and you will not give me time to teach you anything."

Her brow shot up. "Two lessons?"

Maria nodded. "He will show you up."

Lilla couldn't have that. "All right. Where would you like to instruct me?"

"The dining room is spacious. We can dance around the table."

The housekeeper led the way. "First, let me explain to you that the dance is one of passion. One of love. For you, the movement is with your hands, your arms, and your body. Mr. Grady has the harder part. His movements are with his feet. You are the butterfly. He is the flower."

She giggled over imagining Grady as a flower. At Maria's stern glance, she tried to take the lesson more seriously. "What am I to do?"

Maria showed her the movements, using her hands and arms. Lilla tried to mimic them.

"You have grace," Maria praised. "Your body must also move. Sway back and forth while you make the gestures with your hands and arms. And you must rustle your skirts."

Lilla stopped moving altogether. "If you mean expose my legs in the vulgar fashion I saw the dance displayed, I will not do any such thing."

The older woman sighed. "You may show your petticoats without exposing your legs. The dance is one of freedom. You must not think about anything but the movements of your body. The fire in your partner's eyes. The pounding of his feet."

Swaying while using her arms and hands made Lilla somewhat dizzy. Maria took on the male role, stomping her feet and clapping her hands.

"Dance around me," the woman instructed. "Look deep into my eyes. Look at me as if you want me like you have wanted no other before me."

Lilla laughed. "I can't."

Maria sighed again. "Mr. Grady laughs too when he must look at me as if he desires me. I will tell you what I tell him."

Interested, Lilla lifted a brow.

"I tell him to pretend that I am you."

Her brow lifted higher. "Does it work?"

"Ah, *sí*," Maria said. "That man could melt a woman with his eyes."

Lilla's imagination was not strong enough to replace Maria's image with Grady's, but she managed to get through the lesson. She planned to perform a milder version of the dance than the one she'd witnessed in her home. The one that had her father's guests fanning their faces and staring at the floor from embarrassment. The agreement was only that she dance, not that she dance passionately.

Chapter Twelve

The next week, Sally's girls had a surprise for Lilla. When she entered the saloon, they were all dressed up. The paint had disappeared from their faces, and all had arranged their hair attractively. All save one. Violet stood in the corner wearing her large clothes with her scraggly hair hanging down in her face.

"I can't believe the transformation," Lilla breathed. "Why, all of you look like—"

"Ladies?" Meg asked. "Do we look like proper ladies?"

Lilla nodded enthusiastically. "You all look beautiful."

Even the seasoned Delores blushed with pleasure. "We took a day and went to Tascosa where they have a ready-made shop. Meg had some trouble finding anything decent that fit because of those mountains of hers, but—"

"Delores," Lilla warned. "If you're going to dress like a lady, act like one as well." She strolled past the ladies, eyeing each one with concentration. Kate looked lovely with her red hair set off by a dark green gown. At least until she smiled.

"You all have excellent taste," she lied, because Lilla wouldn't be caught dead in any of the outfits, but it was a marked improvement. "Meg, maybe if you wore a pretty shawl it would detract from . . . well, your generous endowments."

With a frown, Meg glanced down. "Delores is right. It was these damn jugs that got me into trouble. Living in the streets, any scraps or offers of money were welcome. When I turned thirteen, a boy said he'd give me a nickel to touch them. It was all downhill from there. Ain't no lady has tits like these. I'm destined to be just what I am."

"That isn't true," Lilla argued. "Why, Tanner Richards and Sparks Montgomery had a fistfight over you the other night."

"So?" Meg snorted. "I've had plenty of men fight over me. Ain't never had one ask me to marry him."

"Who wants to marry a whore?" Delores sneered. "You're dreaming if you think you're ever going to do anything but grow old and die beneath some sweaty man willing to part with his money but never his heart."

Silence fell over the group. More than one sighed at the reality of their situation.

"Meg, Tanner Richards mentioned marriage and your name in the same sentence over dinner," Lilla said, stretching the truth.

The blonde's eyes lit up. "He did?"

She nodded. Delores was suddenly in Lilla's face. "Now, why would he choose Meg over me if it's a wife he's looking for?"

"Yeah, Delores could keep him much warmer in the winter," Kate said, then giggled. "She could just throw one of her legs over him and—"

"Katherine," Lilla admonished. "It isn't good manners to call attention to one's less than perfect attributes.

Delores slumped in a chair and pulled her skirts over her knees. "Hell, they're right. Look at my legs."

Lilla winced. She'd once seen a picture of a gorilla with less hair on its legs. "Delores, have you ever heard of waxing hair as a way to remove it?"

The brunette glanced up. "Waxing? What's that?"

Uncomfortable with her own knowledge about what some considered a vulgar practice, Lilla said, "It's quite popular in France. The only way I gained knowledge of the procedure was when I stumbled upon a great-aunt using hot wax to remove the dark hair above her upper lip."

"Have you ever done it?" Delores wanted to know.

Straightening her skirts, she answered, "Being a brunette such as yourself, as soon as I became a young woman, even though the hair on my legs is fine and sparse, I noticed it was dark and I thought unappealing."

"Have you or haven't you?" Delores persisted.

"Yes, I have, and I do."

"Let me see," the woman demanded.

"Right here where anyone could walk in?"

"Watch the doors, Kate," Meg ordered. "Being a blonde, I don't have that problem, but I want to see Miss Lilla's legs. Tanner Richards has hair on his back. I hate that. If I'm to marry him, I want to know how to get it off."

Oh, Lord, now she had Meg believing that Tanner Richards planned to propose to her. She'd only meant to bolster her confidence, to give them all pride in themselves.

"Okay, Kate's watching the door," Delores said. "Let's see them legs."

Even Violet moved closer, shoving her hair from her eyes to get a better view. Lilla hiked up her skirts. Kate whistled through the gap in her teeth.

"Even from here I can see they're smooth as a baby's behind."

"Lordy, them's the prettiest legs I ever seen," Delores whispered reverently. She glanced up. "I want you to do that to me. I want legs like yours."

"You ain't never gonna have legs like those," Meg said dryly. "But they'd be a sight prettier than they are without that bear coat." She turned to

Lilla. "You shouldn't hide those, Miss Lilla. One glance at your legs and I imagine you could have any man you wanted."

"She already can," Kate asserted. "And she ain't likely going to show no man her legs, neither. She's a lady, don't forget."

"I'll bet Grady Finch has seen them legs," Delores argued.

"Well, if he has, he's been polite enough not to comment upon the matter," Lilla lied. "Now let's see. I'll need some strips of clean cloth, and candles for wax." She glanced at Delores's legs again. "Lots of candles."

The women went in search of the requested items. Even Sally seemed interested in the procedure.

"Violet, you will assist me," Lilla said. "Come along to the back where we will prepare."

Since Lilla knew Violet didn't entertain men in her room, she chose to perform the waxing there. As soon as the young woman followed her inside, she closed the door.

"Why didn't you get yourself a nice dress?"

Violet flinched. "You know why. I don't care about looking pretty."

Lilla walked over and lifted her chin. "I'm not going to hit you, Violet. Just because someone raises their voice at you now and again doesn't mean you have to cower. Stand up to me."

The girl's head lifted. "Do what?"

"I said stand up to me."

"What do you mean?"

"Why didn't you get a nice dress? You look like a rag doll."

Violet's lips quivered, but she straightened. "I can look any old way I want. Mind your own business!"

"That was good," Lilla praised. "But really, you should have gone to Tascosa with the others and—"

"I said to mind your own business," Violet growled. "Do you have trouble hearing?"

Lilla promptly closed her mouth. "Okay, then, let's gather what we need to wax Delores's legs."

"I don't know why you want me to help her look prettier," Violet muttered. "You know she's mean to me."

"Let me explain the process," Lilla said, and did.

Eyes sparkling, Violet asked, "And I'm the one who gets to pull the cloth off once it's been molded to the hot wax and the hair on her legs, right?"

"Like I've said before, you are not dimwitted."

Lilla grinned. Violet did likewise, and—heaven help the girl—nothing could detract from her beauty when she smiled.

"Dancing," Grady muttered, coming from his lesson with Maria. He felt as if he had two left feet, and he figured he'd make a fool of himself at the social. Lilla would probably laugh at him, think he was clumsy at everything. And he didn't know why the hell it mattered to him so much what she thought. Nothing less than him being someone else would impress her.

He nearly tripped over the object of his thoughts as he moved down the steps of the porch. She yelped and jumped up.

"Damn, Lilla. You could tell a person when you're out in the dark."

She rubbed her backside. "You shouldn't have stormed out of the house like that. You kicked me."

"I did?" He stepped closer to her. "Where?"

Her hand immediately ceased to rub her backside. "Never mind where."

"I'm sorry."

"You should be."

"I said I was."

"Apology accepted."

They stood there for a moment. Grady remembered what had happened between them the last time they were alone in the dark. He figured she wouldn't venture outside the safety of the house come dark again. Not unless she was eager for more of the same.

"What are you doing out here this time of night?"

She straightened. "As far as I remember, it's a free country. I can come out here if I want."

"Just thought you might have learned something from the last time."

"What are you saying? That if I take a mind to get some fresh air, I can't do so without having to worry over being molested by you?"

"Only if that's what you came outside for."

Her eyes shone brightly in the dark. He'd made her angry. Grady liked her riled up. She lost a great deal of her snotty, straight-backed demeanor.

"Has it ever occurred to you to have a *conversation* with a woman, rather than simply forcing your unwanted attentions upon her?"

He laughed. "That's not what happened and you know it."

"I have little recollection of the incident," she informed him. "Now, if you'll excuse me, I'd like to sit and enjoy the evening in privacy."

"Who's stopping you?" he ground out. Didn't remember the incident, his ass.

She flounced to the porch and plopped down, not very ladylike in his opinion. Grady stomped off, made it a few feet and stomped back. He sat down beside her.

"How're the dancing lessons going with Sally's girls?"

"Why, Mr. Finch, are you attempting to make conversation?"

"Unless you'd rather do something else."

That shut her up. At least for a second.

"I'm very pleased with the progress the ladies are making."

"And the men?"

"My feet wish they would improve at a faster pace."

He laughed. "I'm surprised they haven't lynched me yet. They all have sore feet from stepping on each other, too."

She tilted her head, and the moonlight highlighted her pretty features. "And what about your feet?" She grinned. "I saw you dancing with Sparks Montgomery."

Grady swore under his breath. "Have you been spying on me?"

Her grin stretched. "I wasn't spying. I just happened to walk past and see you."

"Like you just happened to be looking out your window while I bathed in the trough the other day?"

The grin she wore faded. Even in the moonlight, he saw her blush. "I have no idea what you're talking about."

"You have a very weak memory, Lilla Traften."

"I need to talk to you about something." She suddenly looked serious.

"Talk away."

"It's about Tanner Richards."

"Did he do something to you? Or say something?"

She sighed. "No, he didn't do or say anything improper. Do you think he's in love with Meg?"

Grady shrugged. "Hell if I know. I figure most of the men in my bunkhouse are a little in love with Meg. At least come Saturday night."

"I wish you wouldn't bring Saturday nights into the conversation," she said. "Those women deserve to be treated better than they are by the men. I—"

"I hope you're not messing around in something you've got no business messing with," he interrupted. "Everyone has made their place here. Don't try to change the seating arrangements."

"Are you implying people can't change? That they shouldn't aspire to better themselves or their stations in life?"

"You can't accept them for who they are, can you?"

"Maybe not," she admitted. "Most of them really don't want the life they lead. You realize that, don't you?"

Bitter memories of the past floated to him on the night breeze. "I know that better than anyone. But it's not your place to make things the way you want them, Lilla. Some things are just the way they are."

"Would you marry one of them?"

He pulled off his hat. "I'm not in love with any of them."

"But if you were, would you?"

He gave it a moment of thought. "I guess if I loved her, and she loved me, I'd marry her."

"Then I want you to talk to Tanner about Meg. Tell him that if he has deep feelings for her, he should propose."

"Like hell I will. Tanner is his own man, and old enough to know his own mind. I'm not going to tell him who he should or should not marry."

She shifted closer to him. "I'm just saying you might let him know that if you loved a woman, her past wouldn't matter to you. He looks up to you. If he thought—"

"Lilla," Grady warned. "I'm not going to interfere, and you stay out of it. You'll only cause trouble."

Folding her arms across her chest, she said, "I should have known you'd refuse to help Meg. What the women say about you is true."

"Are we back to you watching me take a bath?"

Her brow knit for a moment. She rolled her gaze. "They think you have ice water running in your veins instead of blood."

He lifted a silky strand of her hair. "You know that's not true."

She snatched her hair from his fingers. "We have strayed from our original intent. We were discussing Meg and Tanner."

"No, *you* were discussing them. I said I wouldn't get involved."

"I assume by your attitude that you don't think much of the holy state of matrimony," she muttered.

"I don't think much about it," he said. "Doesn't mean I don't think much *of* it."

"Then you do plan to marry?"

God, the woman could turn a conversation around faster than a man could say spit. "I figure I will someday."

She started fiddling with her fingers. "But only if you can find another woman like Camile Langtry."

They'd gotten back to that. "I am not, and never was, in love with her," he informed her. "I admire her, that's all."

"Because she has spunk," Lilla bit out. "You know that sounds like some toothless cowhand's name?"

He didn't know what had stuck in her craw. Or maybe he did. "You're jealous of her."

"Don't be daft." She jumped up. "Good night."

Another thought occurred to Grady. Her jealousy might not have a damn thing to do with him. He stood. "It's because of Wade, isn't it? You're still in love with him."

She blinked. "I am not. I never was in love with him."

"You were going to marry him, weren't you?"

"I thought Wade and I had an understanding. There was never an official engagement between us."

"But you thought you were going to marry him," he persisted. "Why would you want to if you didn't—"

"I was a silly, spoiled girl," she interrupted. "I wanted to marry him because he was handsome, and because my father approved of him. Those seemed to be good enough reasons at the time."

"I hope you have better sense than that now."

She placed her hands upon her slim hips. "I have good enough sense not to stand here and discuss something with you that is none of your business. Wade is married to another woman. She is welcome to him." Lilla turned on her heels and headed toward the door.

Another disturbing thought occurred to him. "You and him. How close were you?"

Her back stiff, she turned to face him again. "What are you implying?"

He didn't like the path his thoughts took. "I know him. Before he tamed Camile, or she tamed him, whichever the case was, he had a reputation with the ladies."

"He was never anything but a perfect gentleman with me," she bit out.

Grady relaxed, having made his own conclusions after a moment of thought. "I might have trouble believing that, except you've already proven to me you haven't had much experience with men."

She lifted a brow.

"The way you kiss," he explained. "A woman who'd—"

"I'm an excellent kisser." Lilla stormed toward him, grabbed the collar of his shirt and proved it.

Chapter Thirteen

"Miss Lilla? Did you hear me?"

A hand waved in front of her face. Lilla blinked. She turned to Violet. "What did you say?"

"I've been talking about the food we want to prepare for the dance. I don't think you've heard a word I've said."

Lilla glanced down at the list she planned to make for the food selections. Sure enough, the page was blank. She'd been thinking about Grady. Thinking about the last kiss they'd shared. She had become quite the brazen since she'd been in Texas, or maybe since she'd met him, because the two events were so closely merged. She'd certainly become more aggressive than she supposed was socially correct.

"I had a Swede teach me to make meatballs when I was just a girl," Violet said. "I asked if you want me to make them for the social."

A vision came to Lilla of meat sauce staining every clean shirtfront and dress bodice in the room. "No," she answered. "What else can you make?"

Violet shoved stringy hair behind her ear. "I can make near anything if you have a recipe."

Surprised, Lilla asked, "Can you read, Violet?"

She nodded, causing her hair to fall back into her face. "My ma was a schoolteacher before my pa tricked her into marrying him. Guess he was nice to her until the wedding was over. She didn't take up for us much, because he beat her if she did, but she made sure we all learned to read, write and do figures."

"Well, that's something," Lilla said, her voice bitter. She turned to Violet. "I know you didn't get a nice dress along with the others, but beneath all that baggy material, I think we're about the same size. I'd like to give you one of my dresses."

"No, thank you," Violet responded.

Lilla sighed. "I want everyone to look their best for the dance. There is nothing wrong with fixing up and showing everyone how beautiful you truly are."

"I don't want to be beautiful." Violet stared down at the table rather than look Lilla in the eye. "I don't want to be noticed. It just causes trouble."

"That is pure nonsense." Lilla pressed her lips

together tightly. She drummed her fingernails upon the table. "Being pretty won't change your position here. Sally knows you won't entertain men. I just want you to look nice for the dance. I promise the men will treat you with respect."

Violet glanced up. "No grabbing or holding me too tight?"

"You don't even have to dance if you'd prefer not to," Lilla assured her. "You can stand behind the bar and serve the food and punch if you'd feel more comfortable."

Violet chewed her lip. "Can I have a ribbon for my hair?"

"Yes," Lilla said with a smile. "I'll even help you get ready. I planned to arrive in town early anyway to help with the final preparations."

"All right," Violet agreed. "But only because I trust your word."

Her trust touched Lilla deeply. Laughter drew her attention elsewhere. Since there were no curtains, the other women were hanging sheets over the windows to make the room look fancier. With a sheet across her shoulder and another upon her head, Meg played the bride. As she marched toward them, pretending to hold a bouquet of flowers, Lilla wanted to crawl beneath the table.

"When d'you reckon he'll ask me, Miss Lilla?" Meg asked. "I saved my whole Saturday night for him last week, and he still didn't say nothing about marrying me. Hell, I gave him plenty of time, not taking on any other customers."

"Did you . . ." Lilla's cheeks stung. "Did you demand payment for the time he spent with you?"

Meg let the sheet slip from her head. "Of course I did. You don't think I'm stupid, do you?"

"There's a question with a quick answer," Delores said, joining the group.

"Ever since she got that hair off her legs, she's even meaner than she used to be," Meg muttered.

Violet and Lilla shared a small smile.

"Are you saying I shouldn't have charged Tanner to spend time with me last Saturday night?"

Lilla tugged at the lace around her collar. "Not that I am an expert on such matters, but I would think that as a show of good faith, of your deep feelings for Tanner, you would forgo charging him for, ah, love."

"Love?" Meg frowned. "It was just business."

"That's right." Sally stepped into the circle. "Don't be giving my girls no grand ideas about settling down and turning respectable."

Sally didn't usually interfere with Lilla's lessons. She seemed content to work around the saloon, counting bottles and tending to her business.

"You wanted me to make them ladies," Lilla reminded.

"I'm paying you to teach them manners," the brassy blonde shot back. "Not to fill their heads full of nonsense. I figured if Meg learned to stop picking her teeth, Kate learned to keep her mouth shut, and Delores learned how to hide them hairy legs of hers, I might draw more customers into my place.

Maybe take some of Tascosa's business."

Lilla jumped to her feet. "Is that all these women mean to you? How much profit you can turn by using them?"

"They're whores!" Sally yelled. "Of course, how much of a profit they turn matters to me. That's half my business!"

"Hey, Sally, watch your mouth," Delores said. "That don't sound respectful."

A mumble of agreement followed.

The saloon owner narrowed her gaze upon Lilla. She took her by the arm and not so gently pulled her through the door leading to the back rooms.

"Soon as this silly dance is over with, you're finished here."

"W-What?" Lilla stuttered.

"You heard me. You've gone too far. I just wanted my girls to have some manners so they could act like them fancy whores in New Orleans. All mannerly and stuff, at least until they get a man to the back. Now you've gone and made them think they're better than what they are."

Lilla met the woman nose to nose. "I thought you had a heart, Sally. I thought you'd want a better life for these women. I see now that you didn't let Violet stay because she had nowhere else to go. You let her stay because you'd found someone to do all the work around here. I bet you don't even pay her."

Sally lifted her multiple chins. "I give her a place to stay, don't I? I buy the food she cooks and them old dresses she likes to wear. She has a bed to sleep in at night. I think that's pay enough."

"I am in jeopardy of losing my temper," Lilla said in a tight voice, her fists clenching at her sides. "I think it would be best if I leave until I regain my composure."

"Yeah, go on and get out of here," the woman said, dismissing her. "I'd hate you to bust your buttons."

Never had the urge to strike someone been so strong in Lilla. She would not stoop to such measures. Instead, she fought the only way she knew how. "Your hair is too brassy, your brows are too dark, your teeth are yellow, that mole on your fat chin is ugly, and your nose is too big. So there."

She stomped out, noticed the girls scatter and paused. "I will see you ladies next week for the dance." She made it outside and to the buggy, having earned the right to drive it herself the day she nearly ran Grady over in the streets of Langtry. Violet came rushing out with her supplies.

"You forgot these, Miss Lilla."

Lilla took a deep breath. "Thank you, Violet."

Delores appeared, carrying her parasol. "Wouldn't want you to be without this. This dad-burned sun will ruin that pretty pale skin of yours."

Taking the parasol, Lilla thanked the brunette.

Meg strolled out next.

"Don't tell me I've forgotten something else," Lilla muttered.

The blonde smiled. "No. I just wanted to thank

you for standing up for us to Sally. We heard what you said, and ain't no one cared about our feelings for a long time. No one sure as hell has stood up for us the way you do."

"She's right," Delores mumbled. "You're a fine lady, Miss Lilla."

Tears misted Lilla's eyes. She was so overcome she could only nod and slap the reins, sending the buggy down the rutted street of Langtry. How could Sally look upon the women who worked for her the way one might regard a herd of sheep? The question caused Lilla a slice of guilt. She herself hadn't seen the women as people when she'd first met them.

They were beneath her, or so she'd believed. As if being of a lower station, or having few choices in life, made them hurt less over an unkind word, or feel less guilt over a wrong turn taken. If Lilla had any say in the matter, she'd make sure that all of Sally's girls found husbands and lived respectable lives.

Feeling rather proud of herself, she hummed as she drove the buggy. The sound of a horse's hooves made her turn her head. A lone rider trailed her. She didn't recognize the horse as a WC animal, nor did she recognize the man as one of the WC ranch hands. She almost pulled up; then she remembered she was not in St. Louis but in the rugged, untamed land of Texas.

"Yaw!" Lilla yelled, smartly slapping the reins and startling the horse into a full run.

* * *

"Finch. Hey, boss man, I'm talking to you."

Grady glanced up from checking for rocks in his horse's hoof. "What?"

"Hell, Grady," Tanner said. "I been asking you if your horse has gone lame for the past ten minutes."

"You have?"

Tanner nodded. "Your mind must have wandered off somewhere else."

Yeah, it had gone somewhere else all right. To a woman he had no business thinking about. Lilla surprised him at times. She'd play the snooty miss one day, and grab him and kiss the fool out of him the next. He didn't understand women, that was all there was to it.

"So is he lame or isn't he?"

"Looks that way." Grady rose, stretched his back, then removed his hat to wipe a sleeve across his brow. "Go find the others. Tell them to check those poison baits we set out for the coyotes and then head on in."

"Sure thing."

Tanner started to move away, until Grady cussed softly. "Hold up a minute."

The ranch hand turned his horse around. He sat, a brow cocked in question, as Grady fiddled with his hat.

"Yeah, boss?"

Grady cleared his throat. "Ah, Meg, over at Sally's place. You sweet on her for real?"

Red crept up Tanner's neck. "Why are you asking? You figuring on having her for yourself?"

Shaking his head, Grady said, "No, not thinking of trespassing. Just wondering if you have feelings for her that go deeper than what happens between you on Saturday nights."

Tanner glanced around. "You ain't gonna tease me about it like the other men, are you?"

Grady stuck his hat back on his head and walked toward him. "No. Nothing funny about a man in love."

"Ain't so sure it's love," Tanner confessed. "I know I sure like to spend time with her, and it eats at me awful to think of her spending time with someone else. But . . ."

"But what?" Grady prompted.

"Well, you know. She's a whore."

"Really?" Grady tried to act surprised. His antics made Tanner snicker. "If you hadn't outright told me, I might not have known. Don't expect other folks would know, either, if she were your wife instead of down there working at Sally's."

"But that's just it," Tanner said. "Folks around here know what she is. The men—"

"To hell with them," Grady cut in. "Who are you going to please? Them or yourself? And are your feet stuck to WC ground? If it bothers you that much, you could take her and move on. Start over fresh somewhere."

Tanner scratched the whiskers on his chin.

"Guess I could. I mean, if that's what I took a mind to do."

"Hey." Grady lifted his hands. "I'm not trying to sway you one way or the other. The choice is yours to make. I didn't want someone else minding your business for you."

"Damn straight," Tanner agreed. "If I take a notion to marry Meg, I won't have no one telling me I can't."

"Except maybe her," Grady pointed out. "You do know she has to agree?"

Tanner laughed. "Sure, she'd agree. Marrying me would have to be better than making a living on her back."

Grady turned toward his lame horse. "I would advise you to keep that opinion to yourself, Richards." Mounting his horse, he turned the animal toward the WC. He'd keep to a slow walk. It would give him time to beat himself up over doing exactly what he told Lilla he wouldn't. He'd gone and gotten involved in matchmaking.

She had a way of making him do things he said he wouldn't. Dancing, matchmaking, kissing her when he'd told himself a hundred times that nothing but trouble could come of chasing her skirts. He knew the code of conduct for respectable men and women. A decent man didn't ruin a nice girl, at least not without marrying her or getting himself hanged.

With Lilla, he figured that only the latter would suit her father. And this dance she had planned for next Saturday night—he had a bad feeling about it. Grady had half a mind to tell Lilla she couldn't have her silly dance. Hell, he had more than half a mind to give her the money she needed to return to St. Louis and send her packing.

Then everything around Langtry would return to normal. Maybe he'd return to normal, too. He sure as hell wouldn't be thinking of his future spread and her in the same crazy thought. He wouldn't lay awake at night to the tune of the men snoring and think about kissing her again, dream about doing more than that with her. She was an itch he couldn't scratch. A cactus needle he couldn't pluck. Forbidden fruit, and it was sure as hell true that it tasted sweeter than all the rest.

Grady was still making a mental list of all the things Lilla was when he rode up to the ranch. He'd have to rub that smelly liniment on his horse to help with the swelling. He thought it'd be a lot more fun to rub it all over Lilla and see how much of it she could get on him. He smiled, then frowned when he noticed a thick spiral of dust heading toward the ranch.

He dismounted and tied his horse to the corral pen. Whoever it was, they had to be riding hell for leather to raise that much dust. He walked to the trail he and the men had made from so many trips to town on Saturday nights, and squinted into the sun. A buggy came into view. At the reins was the proper Lilla Traften, snapping the reins and yelling "Yaw" like a seasoned mule skinner.

He didn't realize how fast she was flying until she nearly ran him over. The way she drove the buggy, she might kill the horse and break her pretty neck in the bargain. He wheeled around, surprised that she maintained the strength to bring the horse to a stop. She jumped down from the buggy seat, but instead of running for the safety of the house, which she would have done had she known how mad he was, she ran toward him.

"What the hell—"

"There's someone chasing me," she said, out of breath. "He's been on my tail since I left Langtry."

Putting his anger aside, Grady turned back to the road. A man on horseback appeared on the horizon. Grady couldn't see him closely, but he didn't recognize the horse, and all his men were out working.

"How'd you manage to outrun him with a buggy?"

"He doesn't ride very well," she answered, still gasping for breath. "I saw him nearly fall off his horse a couple of times."

"A greenhorn?"

"What do you think he wants?"

Grady squinted at the rider again. "Don't know, but if he's not looking for trouble, he'll ride in here and tell us."

They waited. The rider turned away from the ranch and took off.

"Damn," Grady swore. "My horse is lame, and by the time I saddle another one, he'll be long gone."

"Do you think he meant to harm me?"

He glanced at Lilla. Her hair had fallen down and she wore a coat of dust. Her eyes were round with worry.

"I think if he couldn't ride in here with me standing beside you, he was up to no good. Probably just roaming when he spotted you and thought you'd be easy picking."

She shivered. "I don't even have any money on my person for him to rob. That might have made him angry enough to shoot me or something."

"Or something," he agreed. "You're not going anywhere from now on without me beside you."

For once, she didn't argue with him.

Chapter Fourteen

Lilla could hardly contain her excitement. The day of the dance had finally arrived. Even dark thoughts of the stranger who'd trailed her back to the ranch didn't dampen her spirits. Tonight she would see the results of her hard work. Langtry would have a social, and she would preside over the affair. The dance was an opportunity for her students to shine, and for her to shine, too. Only one thing cast a shadow on her enthusiasm.

She glanced at Grady, sitting beside her on the buggy seat. He was driving to town early so she could help with preparations for the dance. "About our agreement," she began.

"Which one?" he asked dryly.

"This silly flamenco we must perform."

He lifted a brow. "Are you trying to back out on our deal?"

"Of course not," she snapped. "I'm saying that if you have any qualms about doing the dance, I will most happily go along with your decision."

He smiled. "I'm sure you would. When I give my word, I keep it. I told my men I'd dance with you, and I will."

At times, she really hated the fact that Grady was a man of his word. "All right," she muttered. "But I would like to start the evening with our performance and get it over with."

"Nervous?"

"Not in the least," she lied. "You will make certain the men are presentable this evening? That they've shaved their whiskers and combed their hair?"

"I'll suggest they make an effort. Maria will probably give them the once-over before we leave."

"I wish she had wanted to join us this evening." Lilla turned to him. "She should get out more than she does."

"I imagine she'll enjoy having a quiet night at the ranch. No one to cook for or clean up after."

Lilla sighed. "I suppose so. Still, it would be nice if she had more opportunities to socialize. If she met a nice man—"

"Don't go matchmaking Maria now," Grady interrupted. "Do you always mind everyone's business but your own?"

"I like to see people happy. Is there anything wrong with that?"

He looked at her. His eyes were more blue than gray this afternoon. "What about you? What makes you happy?"

At one time, she might have unthinkingly said a new hat, or a pretty dress, hosting a lavish party for her father. Those things suddenly seemed trifling. The awful truth had caught up with her in Texas.

"I don't know," she answered truthfully.

"Hell, don't you think it's time you found out?"

Lilla shrugged. "I imagine some people spend their whole lives searching for happiness. Looking for something, or someone."

Grady pulled the buggy to a halt. "I pity them. Happiness is all around if a man, or a woman, will stop long enough to notice."

After a moment's study of her desolate surroundings, she said, "I don't see it."

"That's because you're not looking hard enough."

"Show me."

He pointed. "There."

It took her a moment to distinguish a cottontail among a pile of brush. "I only see a rabbit."

"Look closer."

After staring at the rabbit a moment longer, she made out the shapes of the little ones and smiled. "It has babies."

"See the sky?"

She glanced up. The sky was indeed beautiful. Clear blue with hazy, long clouds that looked as if they rippled all the way to the ground in the distance.

"I figure that's how the ocean looks," Grady said.

"Somewhat," Lilla agreed.

"You've seen the ocean?"

His envious expression made her laugh. "Father took me to Europe three years ago. We had to cross the ocean, and I was never so sick in my life. I spent the entire trip hunched over a basin in my cabin."

"But when you first saw it, didn't you think it was something special?" he persisted.

Lilla easily recalled the scene. "Yes. I remember staring at the endless water, watching the waves crash on the shore, and thinking how huge it was, and how small it made me feel."

"Were you happy in that moment?"

She tried to recall. "I was frightened. It was so vast, so strange to me. Beautiful, but menacing at the same time. I was afraid it would swallow me up and I'd disappear."

He turned toward her on the buggy seat. "Tell you what I would have done. I'd have walked right out into that ocean, let the waves hit me in the face and yelled with the sheer joy of being included in it all."

"Included in what?"

Grady shook his head as if she were missing the point. "The grand scheme of life. The sunrises and the sunsets. The day-to-day miracles. The good and the bad. I'm happy just to be a part of it all, aren't you?"

Had he not put it so simply, so eloquently, she probably wouldn't have given the notion any real thought. She supposed it was a miracle to be alive, at this moment, at this second in time. And she did find pleasure in the simple joy of sitting beside him beneath a Texas sky, the blue backdrop turning his eyes the color of that strange ocean. His gaze lowered to her mouth. The quick leap of her pulse, the sudden anticipation she felt over the possibility he might kiss her, were also reminders that she was very much alive.

When he glanced away and took up the reins, Lilla acknowledged her feelings of disappointment as further proof that she lived. He set the horse into motion, but this time, the drive into Langtry wasn't just a long, hot trek to town. Lilla spent the journey looking for happiness.

A few hours later, she found a great measure of joy when Violet stood before her a changed woman. Lilla had washed and dried the girl's long hair, marveling over the gold that leapt to life in her usually brown, stringy strands. She'd tied the glossy mane back with a dark orchid ribbon, one that matched a fancy dress Lilla had brought along before she realized she had no place to wear such finery. The gown accented Violet's soft curves and slim waist perfectly. She was beautiful, even more lovely than Lilla had suspected.

"I can't wait to see the look on Delores's face," Lilla said with a grin.

Violet did not smile back. "I'm not sure I can go out there looking like this."

"What?" Lilla steered Violet toward the mirror. "How can you say that? Look at yourself. You're an absolute vision."

Violet glanced everywhere but at herself. "I feel like it's a lie."

"A lie?"

The girl turned to her. "I look like a pretty red apple. All shiny on the outside, and eaten up with worms on the inside."

Grasping Violet's slender shoulders, Lilla said, "What happened to you wasn't your fault, Violet. You were a child thrust into an adult situation. You must stop blaming yourself."

"I could have done more about it than I did," she said. "I could have killed myself instead of allowing that foul man to keep using me. I didn't have the courage. That makes me deserving of what I got, of what I am."

Lilla released her and sighed. "It's easy enough for someone else to say what they would have done in the same situation, but no one really knows until they are faced with such a trial. You did what you had to do in order to stay alive. Take pride in the courage you showed, pride in the strength you have within. If you crawl into a hole and hide, or if you can't see your own worth, you give the man the power to still control you—to control you for the rest of your life. He will have won."

Violet lifted her head. "I won't let him do that to me. I won't let any man do that to me. Not ever again."

Although a novice at showing affection, Lilla leaned forward and hugged the girl. "Live, Violet. Put the past behind you and move forward. Know that you can be anyone and anything you want to be, if you have faith in yourself."

"I'll try, Miss Lilla," Violet promised. "I'll try for you."

Pulling back, Lilla smiled sadly at her. "Don't do it for me. Do it for yourself." She straightened. "Now we must move forward and get our dance under way."

The girl nodded. Hand in hand, they strolled from the back rooms to the saloon. When they joined the other women, the room's noisy chatter died a quick death.

"Who the hell is that?" Delores finally asked.

"It's Violet," Meg whispered. "Good Lord, girl. Where you been hiding all that?"

"Isn't she lovely?" Lilla felt as pleased as a new mother.

Kate whistled through the gap in her teeth. "She looks like a regular lady. Near as pretty as Miss Lilla."

Delores put her hands on her hips and glared at Lilla. "Ain't none of the men gonna notice the rest of us with her all gussied up like that. She'll be fighting them off with a stick."

At the fear that entered Violet's eyes, Lilla gave her hand a squeeze. "Nonsense. All of you look lovely in your new clothes. Besides, Violet has agreed to tend to the food and punch. She won't have much time for dancing or socializing."

"Good. Keep her behind the bar," Delores grumbled.

"All right, ladies," Lilla said. "The men should arrive shortly. Let's get the food set out and the punch made. Where is Sally?"

"She's in the back," Meg answered. "Said there wasn't no point in coming out if she can't serve liquor and none of us are working tonight. She ain't too happy about this dance. Said the social is cutting into her profits."

"It's just as well if she stays out of the way," Lilla said. "Tonight you are all ladies, and I won't have her telling you otherwise."

"Come tomorrow, we'll all be back to being whores," Delores pointed out.

"Some of us might not be," Meg argued. "I'm hoping Tanner Richards will propose to me tonight."

Lilla's stomach twisted. She really shouldn't have meddled in the relationship between Meg and Tanner. "I wish we had musicians," she fretted, hoping to change the subject. "A dance isn't nearly so nice without music."

"I have found musicians," Rosita, the pretty

Mexican woman, spoke up. "Pedro, he is one of my regular customers, he knows a few men who play instruments together. Only a guitar, a flute and a violin, and Pedro himself can play the piano. They have agreed to provide our music."

Dancing a waltz without a proper orchestra might prove difficult, but Lilla was pleased there would be some type of music. "That will be wonderful, Rosita. Thank you."

Grady had stayed long enough earlier to move the tables and chairs. They'd all been lined up on one side of the room, leaving the other side open for dancing. The food and punch would be placed upon Sally's worn bar. Lilla had brought food that she and Maria had prepared. A small kitchen area was behind the bar. The women bustled in and out of the kitchen, taking dishes.

Lilla supervised where each dish should be placed while Violet and Meg made the punch. The excitement built when the men who were to play arrived. With Rosita's help, Lilla offered them food and drink, then instructed them as to where to set up. Then the waiting began—the anticipation of the men arriving. Meg walked past Lilla, took one look at her and handed her a glass of punch.

"Here, honey. This will help you relax."

Grady had never heard so much complaining at one time in one place in his life. Maria had given haircuts all around, and insisted that Sparks Montgomery shave his whiskers even though the man was growing a beard. She'd told him he could grow it tomorrow. She'd made Smitty White bathe twice, because he was prone to body odor.

Tanner Richards had made the mistake of trying to wear a shirt with a missing button. Problem was, it was his best shirt, so they'd all had to wait while Maria found another button and sewed it on. No one owned a suit. Cowhands didn't have use for fancy clothes. They'd done the best they could, even scraped the manure off their boots and given them a good polish.

"It's just plain silly," Smitty grumbled. "We could be drinking, playing cards and doing more than dancing with the women tonight, but we got to please Miss Lilla. We got to please the boss man so he can please Miss Lilla."

Grady had been only half listening to the complaints as the men rode toward town. "What was that, Smitty?"

The cowboy looked momentarily startled, as if he'd spoken private thoughts out loud. Because the other men were staring at him, obviously daring him to repeat himself, Smitty straightened in the saddle. "Hell, it's the truth, Grady. You been falling all over yourself to please that woman since she showed up."

"Yeah, he's right," Tanner said. "It's 'cause of Grady we all have to go to this shindig."

Grumbles of agreement followed.

"You're the one who thought it might not be such a bad idea, Richards," Grady reminded Tanner.

"And you men are the worst bunch of bawling calves I've ever heard. It won't hurt any of you to go to the dance—to treat the women nice and respectful, behave like gentlemen for a change."

"I do believe you've gone soft on us, boss," Sparks muttered. "I think Miss Lilla Traften from St. Louis has gelded you."

Tanner laughed like a hyena. He sobered when Sparks said, "I wouldn't be laughing, Richards. Rumor has it you're all set to marry yourself a whore."

"Who said that?" Tanner demanded. "I never said that."

Grady shot Tanner a disgusted look. The man was a coward if he couldn't own up to his feelings for Meg. He also didn't care for Sparks's comment. Gelded? The men thought he behaved like a cut bull? He knew all his parts worked fine, and it was because of Lilla he knew they worked. Hell, they'd started working overtime the moment he saw her and hadn't stopped working since.

Soon enough the sound of music drifted to them. The hazy image of Langtry appeared.

"Remember, men, no fighting, swearing or spitting."

"Can't wait to have me a dance with Meg." Sparks cut his gaze toward Tanner. "Ain't no way those big teats of hers can't rub up against a man."

"You're not dancing with her," Tanner growled. "All of you best keep your distance from my Meg."

"She's not yours," Smitty argued. "She ain't got a ring on her finger."

"Men," Grady warned. "We're not even there yet and you're all itching to get into a fight. Try to exercise some self-control."

" 'Spose you want us to follow your shining example," Tanner muttered. "We do that and none of us will ever get between a woman's legs again."

The insults were starting to annoy the hell out of Grady. "Did it ever occur to any of you that a man can still get what he wants from a woman without tossing down a few coins and throwing her on her back?"

Sparks Montgomery urged his mount up beside Grady. "What do you mean?"

Grady had started to dig himself a hole. He dug a little deeper. "I'm saying that any woman can be wooed into giving freely what the rest of you are willing to pay for. A man just has to know how to go about it."

"And what way would that be?" Tanner demanded.

"By using good manners," Grady answered. "Being gentlemanly. Treating her special."

"Sheshus," Sparks scoffed. "I haven't seen where your gentlemanly ways are doing you one bit of good with Miss Lilla. It'll take more than fancy words and fancier footwork to woo that one out of her corset."

"Care to wager on that, Montgomery?" Grady wanted to bite his tongue. He'd let his pride outrun common sense. He'd allowed the men to goad him into feeling as if he had something to prove. And proving anything with Lilla wasn't a good idea.

"I sure do care to wager on it," Sparks answered, grinning.

"I'll take part of that bet," Tanner piped up.

Smitty joined in. "A day's pay says you can't loosen her corset strings before the night's over."

Grady felt as if he'd just lost ten years of living. Bragging rights were usually reserved for young fools whose balls were too big and whose brains were too small. But the men were right. Lilla had led him around a bit. Dancing, matchmaking, making him keep his urges under control even when she sent him signals that he didn't have to behave himself.

"We shouldn't be discussing her," he said. "It's disrespectful."

"Are you backing up now, boss?" Tanner teased. "Afraid you've lost it with the ladies 'cause you ain't used it in so long?"

The laughter that followed was tough to swallow. Grady could have Lilla if he wanted her. Well, he did want her. Physically he wanted her. But he wasn't one to seduce virgins. Women who made their living pleasing men, who knew what they wanted when they invited a man into their beds, were one thing. An innocent young thing of good breeding from a respectable family was another.

"How about it, Grady?" Sparks goaded. "Are you gonna show us how it's done? Or are you gonna turn chicken 'cause you don't think you have what it takes to woo that prim-and-proper miss?"

The bet was only that he could loosen her corset strings, Grady told his guilty conscience. He didn't say he'd get her on her back, take anything that didn't belong to him. She'd wanted him to touch her the other night when he'd sent her into the house. And he'd wanted to take advantage of the fact, but he hadn't. There wasn't much wrong with loosening her corset strings, having a feel of her smooth, soft skin. As long as he kept things from going any further.

"I know you have a bottle with you, Smitty," he said. "Give me a swig."

"I ain't got no l-liquor," Smitty stuttered. "You said there was to be no drinking tonight, boss."

Grady pulled his horse to a stop. He turned to the cowhand. "Give me the damn bottle, Smitty."

Chapter Fifteen

"Here they come!" Kate shouted.

Girlish squeals followed the announcement. Lilla felt a little like giggling as well. Odd, but the punch seemed to have relaxed her. After two glasses she felt much calmer, as if her bones had turned to liquid. She remembered feeling like this under two other circumstances since her arrival in Texas: each time Grady had kissed her, and the time she'd sipped water from a whiskey-tainted canteen. She glanced at her cup and frowned.

"Meg. Did you put something in the punch?"

The buxom blonde patted her hair into place. "Just a touch of rotgut." She winked. "Can't see how anyone can call it punch if it doesn't have one."

Lilla bristled. "I sepsifi-specifically said, no liquor tonight."

"I only poured a little into it when Violet wasn't looking," Meg defended her actions. "My nerves are raw from wondering if Tanner will ask me. I needed a little something. Figured we all did."

Since the punch had helped calm her own jumpy nerves, Lilla had to agree. "I suppose a little won't hurt." She glanced at the other women and groaned. "Ladies, do not hang out the door like cats waiting to be thrown dinner scraps. Remember, tonight we are trying to achieve an air of sophistication."

"Delores has just achieved an air, but it ain't sophistication." Kate waved a hand in front of her face.

"Hell, Delores," Meg complained. "Couldn't you have gone somewhere else to do that?"

To her credit, Delores had the manners to blush. "I can't help it. I pass wind when I'm nervous."

An unpleasant odor filled the room. Lilla wanted to curse. "Meg, get Delores a glass of punch," she bit out. "The rest of you, find perfume. Quickly!"

The first thing Grady noticed when he strolled into the saloon was the overwhelming smell of cheap perfume. The second thing was how beautiful Lilla looked. She'd brought a change of clothes with her. Her deep blue gown set off her violet eyes. The fabric looked like silk, and the gown displayed her womanly curves to perfection. The skirt billowed out, suggesting she wore several petticoats beneath.

Realizing he stared, he tried to give the other ladies equal consideration. They looked nice, but they all seemed to be out of breath. Or maybe they just couldn't breathe because of the perfume. Then he noticed that none of his men were looking at the women. They were all gaping at the bar . . . or rather, at a woman who stood behind the bar.

"Holy moly," Smitty White managed to rasp. "Where'd she come from?"

A migration started in the direction of the bar. The beautiful young woman behind it turned as pale as the white sheets draped across the windows. Lilla was there in an instant, barring their way.

"All of you know Violet. She helps Sally around the saloon. And it is not polite to gawk with one's eyes bulging and one's tongue flapping. I promised Violet she would be treated with respect and kindness tonight. Any man who doesn't mind his manners will answer to me."

"And me." Grady joined Lilla. He had trouble believing that the woman behind the bar was the same unkempt girl he'd seen working around the saloon. He'd always felt a little sorry for her. Now he could plainly see that she was terrified by the attention she received.

"That's Violet?" Tanner asked, his eyes still wide.

Meg flounced to Tanner's side. "She's just the same as she was before, afraid of her own shadow, so don't be thinking she'll give an ugly cuss like you the time of day."

"Or night," Delores added. "Why are you all slobbering over her, anyhow? Don't anyone want to see my legs? I got the hair off of them."

All male heads swung toward Delores. Lilla groaned again. "I have an idea." She stepped between the men and Delores. "Why don't the gentleman all go out and come back in again."

"Go out and come in again?" Sparks asked, scratching his head.

"Yes. Give me a few moments with the ladies, please."

Of course they all looked to Grady. He nodded, and the men shuffled out. Lilla took Delores by the arm and led her to the back.

"A lady does not offer to show men her legs!"

Delores huffed up. "It distracted them from Violet, didn't it? I had to do something. She looked like she was about to faint."

A little of Lilla's ire drained away. "Well, yes, I suppose it did." She narrowed her gaze upon the brunette. "But don't tell me you did it for her. You don't care one whit about her."

"I do so," Delores shot back.

"You treat her horribly!" Lilla snapped.

"Yeah, and one of these days I figure I'll bait her until she rears up like a mean old bear and stands up for herself for a change."

Lilla blinked. Her brow knit. "Are you telling me

you say mean things to her in hopes of making her angry?"

Delores glanced around, as if to make certain they were completely alone. "Something has to work on her. The other girls are nice to her, and that don't seem to help. I reckon she needs to squeeze all that poison inside of her to the surface so she can spew it out."

The vision that came to mind was not pleasant, but for the first time, Lilla had a feeling she might have misjudged Delores. "Then you don't hate her because she's pretty?"

The brunette waved a hand in the air. "Hell, no. That girl doesn't belong here. Never has and never will. She can't find the sense to see that. If it takes me baiting her into leaving, then I will. There was a time I could have gotten away from this nasty business. I didn't take it. I didn't think I deserved it. I don't want her making the same mistake."

Maybe it was the effects of the punch, but Lilla felt a warm tingle in her belly. Delores had always seemed the most hardened of Sally's women. Who would have guessed she had such a soft heart? Lilla leaned forward and hugged her. "You're very kind, Delores."

The saucy brunette squirmed from her embrace, her gruffness firmly fixed back in place. "Don't go gushing over me. It makes me nervous. And you know what happens when I get nervous."

Lilla quickly stepped away from her. "All right.

I'll go out and talk to the men for a moment. Make sure Violet doesn't bolt."

"I'll keep her put."

They hurried back into the saloon.

"I need me another cup of punch, Mouse," Delores called, moving toward the bar.

Once outside, Lilla confronted the men. They all looked clean and polished. Grady always looked good, but the trim to his hair added to his appeal.

She came right to the point. "Violet is afraid of men. It took a small miracle to get her to let me fix her up tonight. I promised her that all of you would show her the proper respect."

"We didn't mean nothing by staring," Tanner said. "We were just surprised. Didn't know she was so pretty."

"Well, she considers being pretty a curse. Please be kind, but not overly friendly."

"What's that mean?" Sparks asked.

"It means smile and compliment her but keep your tongues from hanging out of your mouths," Grady answered. "Now go back in and pay proper respect to the other ladies."

The men shuffled back inside. Lilla took a moment to catch a breath of clean air. Grady stood staring at her.

"What?"

He smiled.

"What?" she demanded. "Is there something in my hair? On my face?"

"No, you look beautiful. I'd have never thought

Miss Lilla Traften from St. Louis would take a soiled dove under her wing, much less a whole flock of them."

She made a pretense of smoothing her gown, pleased that he'd said she looked beautiful. "Has it ever occurred to you that you might not know everything about me?"

"It's beginning to," he admitted. "I'm also thinking that you might be learning some things you didn't know about yourself."

"I suppose I am." She glanced up at him, wondering what color his eyes might be this evening. They were smoky gray. Their gazes held for an uncomfortably long time. Lilla shook her head. "We should go inside. I am neglecting my duties as hostess."

She started to move forward, but Grady stepped in front of her. His face suddenly looked flushed. If she didn't know him better, she'd swear he was blushing.

"I-I did something stupid on the way to town."

Lilla lifted a brow.

"I, ah, well . . ."

"Spit it out," Lilla said.

He smiled, but it was an uncomfortable one. "The men were teasing me about being too much of a gentleman with you."

"Oh?"

His collar must have been too tight, because he kept tugging at his shirt. "One thing led to another, and I did something I shouldn't have."

Lilla felt a moment of alarm. "You didn't tell them about . . . that you and I have—"

"Oh no," he quickly assured her. "I wouldn't do that."

She sighed with relief.

"I bet them I could loosen your corset strings before the night was over."

"You what?"

"It was a stupid thing to do," he grumbled. "I feel bad about it. I'd never try to seduce you."

Lilla wasn't sure that was a compliment. "Never?"

"Well, no. There wouldn't be any point to it."

Her hands went to her hips. "Are you implying that I am undesirable? That if given the chance, you wouldn't—"

"Oh, I'd want to," he assured her. "I'm just saying I *wouldn't*. I . . . well, hell, I guess I respect you too much."

A hot flush coated her entire body. "You do?"

"Seems so."

She narrowed her gaze on him. "And this bet you made. What were the stakes?"

"A day's pay."

"A day?" she huffed. "I would think I would be worth at least a week's income."

"You're mad because I didn't bet enough on you?"

Her reaction was rather embarrassing. "Just a little insulted," she admitted. "So, you let the men goad you into bragging about your manly abilities?"

"Yes. And I apologize."

She had to wonder if his admission wasn't part of the plan to seduce her. "At least you were honest with me."

"I believe honesty is important."

Lilla agreed. "I don't think I've had a single relationship with a man who was honest with me. Mr. Langtry failed to mention to me that he had once been a hired gun of considerable reputation. And later, of course, he fell in love with someone else. Gregory Kline only paid me court because of my father's money."

"I've never been nothing but a cowhand with big dreams, and I don't care about your father's money. But I do care about being deceitful."

She liked that about him. She liked it a lot. "I think the men should be punished for goading you into making such an improper bet."

"I don't see why, when I was fool enough to let my pride get the best of me."

Lilla smiled. "A day's pay should be punishment enough for them."

His dark brows drew together. "What are you planning?"

Turning toward the door, she said, "Come along, Mr. Finch. We have a dance to perform."

The men were talking politely with the women when Grady and Lilla reentered the saloon. Delores wasn't showing off her legs, and Violet seemed to have settled down now that the men weren't crowding her.

Grady wondered what Lilla was about to do. He'd thought he'd have to hog-tie her into carrying out her agreement. Truth was, he felt damn uncomfortable about doing the dance. He still thought dancing was sissified.

"Could I please have everyone's attention?" Lilla called. "I know this was to be a waltz, but Mr. Finch and I have agreed to show you a flamenco."

"What's that?" Meg asked.

"It is said to have originated in Spain, but the Gypsies, I believe, first introduced it there. The flamenco is a passionate dance, not usually performed among polite society."

"And you're going to do it?" Delores asked, her brow raised.

Lilla twisted her fingers together. "Well, yes. It was part of an agreement Mr. Finch and I made, and we all know that bargains are to be kept, correct?"

It didn't escape Grady's notice that she seemed to focus on the men rather than the women. Murmurs of agreement followed. Posture stiff, she moved to the middle of the dance floor and nodded toward the musicians.

The soulful strums of a guitar began as Lilla stood proudly. Grady knew she was uncomfortable, and he silently praised her courage. Wearing a smile, he sauntered toward her. They faced each other, placing their hands palm to palm. The soft strums continued while they stared into each other's eyes; then the guitarist strummed harder, louder, and Grady began his movements.

He wasn't much for fancy footwork, but the dance was more like stomping than dancing, so he managed the heel-and-toe repetition. Lilla began to snap her fingers, to move her arms and sway to the music. Their gazes remained locked upon one another.

Her features were perfect. Her skin flawless. He could stare at her for hours, and now he'd been afforded a brief opportunity to look to his heart's content. Her cheeks flushed as she swayed around him, her fingers snapping, arms waving gracefully in the air. Her hips moved in sensuous rhythm to the guitar strums. She rustled her skirts, teasing him with a glimpse of her frilled petticoats. Grady had trouble concentrating on his steps.

The music intensified. He stomped to the beat, clapped his hands and kept his gaze locked with hers. He knew the moment the dance claimed her—the second she forgot who she was, and only felt the passionate strums of the guitar seducing her.

She twirled and danced with reckless abandonment, her lips parted in invitation. Closer she danced, teasing him, tempting him, driving all thoughts from his mind but her. Lilla's eyes glittered like twinkling stars. Her body brushed against him, pulled away, her movements as blatant as the act of love. He grew hard, ached with desire for her.

The heat in her eyes flared—issued a challenge. When next she brushed against him, he reached out and pulled her close. She had broken him, shattered the control he'd tried to maintain since the moment he saw her. Time stopped; the music faded. There was only her, only him, and what pulsed between them. He twisted his hands into her hair. Slowly he lowered his mouth to hers. He felt the warmth of her breath, almost tasted the sweetness of her lips. Then a roar of shouts and clapping startled him sane. With difficulty, he glanced up. A small sea of cowhands and soiled doves grinned back at him.

As if he held a flame, he released her. She swayed, might have fallen had he not quickly steadied her. The fire in her eyes banked to a soft glow. She straightened and pulled away from him.

"Oh, dear," Lilla said, fanning her face. "I fear I've overexerted myself. Please escort me to a chair immediately."

Grady helped her to a chair. Everyone gathered around. She gasped as if she couldn't breathe. Grady became alarmed until she glanced at him from beneath her lashes and smiled.

"I fear my corset laces need loosening." She rose. "Mr. Finch, could you assist me?"

He blinked. "Excuse me?"

She glanced over her shoulder and smiled, then walked through the doorway leading to the back rooms. Dead silence accompanied him to the door; then he heard one of the men mutter, "There goes a day's pay, boys."

Grady found Lilla giggling on the other side of the door. He laughed, surprised she'd do anything so daring to teach the men a lesson.

"You know you've just compromised your reputation?"

Her eyes still dancing, Lilla said, "When you consider the reputations of those present, I don't believe I've done much damage."

His smile faded. "That's where you're wrong. You've done plenty of damage." He backed her up against the wall. "You've placed yourself in a dangerous situation, Miss Traften."

"Have I, Mr. Finch?"

She knew damn well she had. Dancing with him the way she did, teasing him, testing his control . . . If she'd looked one bit frightened of him now, staring up at him with her face flushed and her lips parted, he would have released her. But she had the look of a woman who understood what was coming. One willing to meet it head on.

"Big mistake," he said, then lowered his lips to hers.

Chapter Sixteen

Lilla never knew a woman could burn for a man. For his kisses, his touch, the very feel of his strong, hard body pressed against hers. She kissed him back. Gave him all the fiery passion the dance had built within her. Their tongues touched, teased, began a dance of their own. Her fingers twisted into his hair, pulling his lips back to hers.

The bold thrust and withdrawal of his tongue spread flames to the deepest pit of her soul. She strained against him, felt the fire spread to her most secret parts. His hand closed over her breast and her nipples tightened in response. She wanted to feel his skin against hers. She'd been denied physical closeness with another human being all her life.

Her body craved it; her mind allowed the weakness.

"Lilla," he groaned. "Stop me. Stop me before I drag you into one of these rooms and there'll be no turning back."

She should stop him, but she couldn't. Nothing could slow the passion she felt for him, the need for whatever contact he would give her. He broke from her, took her hand in his and started for the closest room. The door leading to the hallway suddenly creaked.

"You'd better get out here, boss," Smitty White said. "I think trouble might be brewing."

Only a sliver of light slipped through the door, but it was enough to startle Lilla with a splash of reality. Good Lord, what had she done? Or almost done? Grady didn't allow her time for self-recrimination. He pulled her in the opposite direction. They stumbled upon a scene that had trouble written all over it. Four men stood at the bar. Lilla didn't recognize any of them.

"You men are a ways from Tascosa," Grady said.

"Finch." One of them nodded. "Figured we'd find us new doves to socialize with tonight. We've already been too many rounds with the gals in Tascosa."

"We're not working tonight," Delores piped up. "We're dancing."

The strangers snickered.

"Dancing?" the man who'd addressed Grady repeated. "Hell, Saturday nights ain't for dancing.

They're for drinking and whoring. Do you boys have rocks for brains? Or are the rumors floating around about you true?"

"What rumors?" Tanner Richards demanded.

"Word around the area is that you boys are taking charm lessons."

Judging by the way the WC men responded, with blushes and shuffling of feet, Lilla suspected that not one man would step forward and admit to the charges.

"There's nothing wrong with a man having manners." It was Meg who spoke up. "You boys don't have any, and you're not going to get anything you want here, so you'd better move on."

The man who'd done all the talking glanced at Meg. His eyes nearly popped out of his head when his gaze lowered to her breasts. "Heard there was a gal here who'd put an old milk cow to shame."

"Watch your mouth." Tanner stepped forward, shielding Meg from the man's sight.

"No matter," the man said. "I think more than a good handful is a waste." His gaze darted toward Violet, who stood pale and frozen behind the bar. "Now, that one looks like she'd be to my taste."

"I want her after you're done, Slate," another of the strangers said, grinning lewdly at the girl.

Lilla saw a tremor of fear shake Violet's slim form. Something inside her snapped. Maternal instincts perhaps, since Lilla felt like a mother bear defending her cub.

"Leave her alone," she ordered.

The stranger's head swung around. His eyes took on a wicked gleam.

"Now there's a prime piece. The ride over here and back was well worth the trip."

Lilla opened her mouth to protest his rude comment, but Grady stepped in front of her.

"You're insulting a lady."

Peeking around Grady, Lilla noted that the statement clearly had no effect upon the man. He ran a cold glance over her protector.

"By the look of her, seems to me that you must have been insulting her just before you came busting out of the back rooms. She looks freshly plowed to me. I don't mind taking sloppy seconds."

Lilla was at a loss to understand the conversation, but Grady tensed, then took a step toward the man.

"She ain't one of us," Kate interrupted. "She's our charm school teacher."

The man laughed. "I wouldn't mind her teaching me a thing or two."

"I'll teach you a thing or two." Grady lunged for the man.

Barroom brawls were certainly a thing whispered about among polite society, but Lilla never dreamed she'd one day find herself in the middle of one. Nor would she have imagined that a man with such a gentle touch could pack such a wallop. Grady punched the stranger and sent him reeling backward against the bar. Several plates of food went crashing to the floor. The stranger's companions were on Grady in an instant. Two of them held him while the other one delivered a blow to his middle.

Frantic, Lilla glanced toward the WC men. They were just watching.

"Help him!" she shouted.

Tanner shrugged. "Hell, there's only four of them. He can handle it by himself."

To her astonishment, the musicians struck up a waltz. Her students began dancing together. Lilla felt as if she were in the middle of a bizarre dream. She glanced back at the struggle by the bar. Grady kicked the man who punched him, and in a place that seemed to cause great damage. His assailant doubled over and fell to the floor, clutching himself in what she considered a crude manner.

The man who'd insulted her and started the trouble roused himself. Grady had almost managed to struggle free from the two men holding him. He'd popped all the buttons from his shirt in the process, baring a good portion of his muscular chest and flat stomach. She took a moment to appreciate the scenery, and then the sound of a fist connecting with flesh brought her from her dazed state. The man who'd started the trouble landed a solid blow to Grady's jaw. Lilla wouldn't stand still for further abuse. She marched up to the stranger.

"How dare you hit a man while he's clearly at a disadvantage! Have you no honor?"

The man grinned. "No," he answered, then grabbed her and kissed her.

"Get your filthy mouth off of her!" Grady yelled.

Lilla struggled, repelled by the man and the touch of his lips. She heard a crash, felt liquor spew over her face and hair. The man drew back, a glazed look in his eyes. He released her and fell to the floor. Violet stood behind the fallen man, the remains of a broken bottle clutched in her fist.

The girl smiled at Lilla. She smiled back.

"Hey, whore!" One of the men holding Grady released him long enough to step forward and shove Violet backward. She cringed, and the sight of Violet trembling before yet another abusive man sent rage rushing through Lilla. She went for the man's face with her nails.

More punching and swearing noises sounded behind her. The man captured both of her wrists in one hand, then drew back a fist. She squeezed her eyes closed, waiting for the blow to fall. It never did. She opened her eyes. Grady had wrapped his hand around the man's fist, and the look on his face was enough to freeze hell itself.

"Does it make you feel big to hit a woman?"

The man's Adam's apple bobbed. "Hell, I wasn't gonna hit her."

"You got that right," Grady said, his voice soft, deadly. His grip visibly tightened upon the man's fist. A second later he pulled it down and back, causing a loud snap. The man screamed in agony as he fell to his knees.

"You broke my damn arm!" he yelled.

"Be thankful I didn't kill you," Grady spat. "I

have no tolerance for men who hit women . . . or children," he added bitterly.

Something Lilla had never seen in Grady blazed in his heated stare. Maybe some long-ago memory held him. Whatever it was, it chilled her to the bone.

"You've all outstayed your welcome," he said.

The music had stopped. Sparks Montgomery and a couple of other men came forward and helped remove the intruders. They dragged them from the saloon. Broken dishes and food littered the floor. The mess didn't concern Lilla. The sight of Violet still crouched down, her hands held over her head protectively, did. She went to the girl and knelt beside her.

"It's all right, Violet," she said softly. "He's gone."

"He'll never be gone," she sobbed. "He just gets a different face."

Lilla tightened her arms around the girl, but she couldn't offer comfort beyond that. She feared that if Violet continued to live and work in surroundings like Sally's Saloon, the man her father was, and the man he'd sold her to for a case of whiskey, would continue to resurface in the form of other men.

"What the hell is going on in here?"

Sally had emerged from the back. She nodded toward the broken dishes and the food smeared over the floor.

"There was some trouble," Delores explained.

Grady and the other men came back in. From

the looks of the foreman, no further explanation was needed. Lilla winced at the bruise forming along his jawbone.

"You know I don't allow fighting in my saloon, Grady Finch."

"He was protecting Violet and me," Lilla said, rising.

The brassy blonde sashayed toward her. "My first mistake was allowing you inside my place. All you've done is cause trouble."

"That ain't so," Delores argued. "She's taught us some manners. Made us feel like we're more than women who are gossiped about and looked down upon."

"She's given you fool notions, all right," Sally agreed. "For all your fancy clothes and fancy manners, it hasn't changed a damn thing. There still ain't a man present who'd consider any of you good enough to marry."

All eyes strayed to Tanner Richards. Meg stared at Tanner, too, and the hopeful look on her face nearly broke Lilla's heart. Tanner glanced at her, flushed, and glanced away.

"Is that how it is, Tanner Richards?" Meg asked. "Am I good enough to bed but not good enough to marry?"

"I won't be hog-tied into taking a . . ."

"A what?" she demanded.

He turned to her. "You know what you are, Meg. Hell, everyone knows what you are. Do you think I'd want to spend my life having men snicker behind my back? Do you think I'd want to spend it wondering if every man we pass on the street has been in your bed? Do you think I'd want my children to have a mother who was once a whore?"

Meg's eyes filled with tears. She ran from the room and into the back.

"I'd like to kick your ass, Richards," Grady said. "This may come as a surprise to you, but whores make wonderful mothers."

Lilla's gaze slid toward Grady. He had that look about him again. As if he were somewhere else. Reliving another time in his life.

"*I'd* like to kick your ass, too, Tanner," Delores said. She moved toward the back rooms. "Meg didn't have much choice about who or what she became. You could have changed that for her." She paused before stepping through the door Meg had left open. "I hope you've had your fill of her, 'cause I can guarantee you won't be crawling between her legs again. Or mine." Her gaze included all of the men. "None of you."

"What are you saying, Delores?" Sally demanded. "Are you and Meg quitting?"

The brunette drew herself up proudly. "We're going on strike like those cowboys up Tascosa way. When Tanner reconsiders marrying Meg, I might reconsider returning to regular work."

"I'm striking, too," Kate said, grinning with her gap-toothed smile.

The other women nodded in agreement.

"See what you've done!" Sally shouted at Lilla. "This is all your fault!"

"And his," Tanner grumbled, looking at Grady. "He should never have made us take those silly lessons. You heard the men in here earlier. We're laughingstocks."

"Tanner is right," Sparks said. "Now them lessons have caused trouble with our women. Meg probably wouldn't have considered marrying Tanner if Miss Lilla hadn't put the notion in her head."

"The fact that Tanner isn't man enough to marry the woman he wants is not Lilla's fault," Grady argued. "And if he was any kind of man at all, he'd go and apologize to her for what he said."

"Like hell I will," Tanner shot back. "I ain't taking orders from you no more, Finch. Fact is, if the women are striking, so am I. When they come to their senses, I might reconsider."

"Are you saying you're hanging up your saddle until the women let us back in their beds?" Sparks asked.

"Yeah, that's what I'm saying," Tanner answered. "Who's with me?"

Lilla was more than distressed to see the men rally behind Tanner. Grady would probably hate her for this.

"You men better think twice," he said. "If you leave, I can't promise you a job when you want to return."

Thank goodness the threat of losing their positions at the ranch seemed to cause more than one man to pause.

"Tell you what," Sparks said. "You make Miss Lilla go talk sense to the women, forget these silly lessons, and we'll forget about striking."

Grady glanced at Lilla. She didn't believe she could tell the women they had no right to take pride in themselves, no right to want more from life than what they'd been handed. Grady spared her the dilemma.

"No," he said. "I won't do that. I can't do that. The lessons are negotiable, those women's feelings aren't."

A stare-down ensued, Grady against his men. Tanner made the first move, toward the doors leading outside. Every WC ranch hand shortly followed him.

"If you reconsider, we'll be waiting in Tascosa, where there are women who know their place," Smitty White muttered in parting.

Grady made no comment, but Lilla saw his bloody knuckles clench. She felt horrible for him, and for Meg.

"You two get on out of here," Sally said, glaring at Grady and Lilla. "You've caused enough trouble for one night."

"I'd like to talk to Meg," Lilla said.

The brassy blonde shook her head. "You've talked to her enough. Now I have to go back there and try to make her see reason—make them all see reason. Leave like I told you to do. This is still my saloon."

Lilla wanted to argue, but Grady took her hand. "Come on, Lilla. Let's go home."

They started for the door, but Lilla noticed Violet still hunched on the floor. She stopped and held out her hand.

"Come on, Violet."

The girl stared at her hand, then up at her. Confusion clouded her wide blue eyes.

"What do you think you're doing now?" Sally huffed.

Lilla lifted her chin. "I'm taking Violet with me."

"Taking her where?" the woman demanded.

"Anywhere but here," Lilla answered. "Take my hand, Violet."

"B-But I can't leave," she whispered. "I belong here."

At Sally's gloating smile, Lilla felt tempted to bruise her own knuckles against the woman's painted face.

Grady stepped up beside Lilla and offered his hand. "You don't belong here. Come with us."

Slowly, cautiously, Violet slid her small hand into Grady's large one. He helped her up.

"Do you need to collect your things?" Lilla asked.

"She ain't got any things," Sally answered. "If she's running out on me, I figure what little she has is mine."

Lilla wanted to argue that Violet had worked for

what little she owned, but the girl placed a hand on her arm.

"Let's go before I lose my nerve."

Casting Sally a dark look, Lilla swept Violet out of the saloon. Grady helped the women into the buggy and tied his horse to the back. They rode in silence toward the ranch. Once, Violet's head started to turn toward town.

"Don't look back," Lilla said softly. "Don't ever look back, Violet."

Chapter Seventeen

Grady's ribs hurt by the time they reached the ranch. Worry had also set in. What in hell would he say if Wade and Camile returned to find he'd lost all their hired help? He couldn't single-handedly run a spread the size of the WC. He might get by for a few days, but this thing with the men might not blow over as quickly as he hoped.

If worse came to worst, he could ride to Tascosa and hire on a new bunch, but he didn't want to. Most hands without a job were out of work for a reason. Either they were lazy, had a price on their heads, or were too fond of a bottle. He'd grown comfortable with the outfit he had, and didn't want them out of work when or if they came to their senses and returned to the ranch.

Lilla, he suspected, would try to shoulder the blame for the trouble. He wouldn't let her. If anyone was to be blamed, it should be him. He should have never gotten her mixed up with the women at Sally's. He should have sent her home the minute she realized she had no real students. He'd been stubborn about the matter—had wanted her to suffer a little, he figured for his mother's sake. Now he had no choice but to give her the money and send her on her way. Send her back where she belonged. Far from him and forbidden encounters in dark hallways.

She'd been quiet the whole trip home. Maybe she'd been thinking about their interrupted encounter. Maybe she was embarrassed that she'd let passion rule her head with a man like him. A man he figured her father wouldn't approve of—a man who had nothing but a little stretch of land he hoped to grow into a full-blown working ranch.

It was settled in Grady's mind. Lilla was going home as soon as he could get her on a stage. He wondered what he was supposed to do about Violet. No doubt the girl wondered what had possessed her to leave a roof over her head and a meal at the table for an unknown future. He was curious to see what Maria would have to say about Lilla bringing home one of Sally's girls. Real curious.

The housekeeper had plenty to say. Grady had barely gotten Lilla and Violet into the house when Maria bustled into the foyer wearing her nightclothes. She took one look at Grady, started muttering in Spanish, then noticed Violet.

"Who is this?"

"This is Violet," Lilla answered. "Violet Mallory. Violet, this is Maria. She runs the Langtry household. Violet will be staying at the ranch for a while."

Maria's brows shot up. "Where did she come from?"

"Town," Lilla answered vaguely.

Maria sniffed the air. "You smell like liquor." Her gaze narrowed. "Have you been drinking, Miss Lilla?"

"No," Lilla assured her. "Well, a little rotgut in the punch, but I smell this way because Violet broke a bottle over a man's head and the liquor got all over me."

Frowning, the woman turned her gaze to Grady. "I see you have been fighting."

"We had a little trouble at the dance," he admitted.

"Maria, why don't you take Violet upstairs and get her settled?" Lilla suggested. "She may stay with me in my room. Oh, and I have plenty of nightclothes she can borrow."

"She has no clothes?" Maria asked, eyeing Violet up and down. "Why does she have no luggage?" Her nose twitched as if she'd gotten wind of more than the smell of liquor. "Is she from the saloon?"

"No—"

"Yes," Violet interrupted. "I worked there. Miss

Lilla was kind enough to offer me a place to stay, since I no longer work at the saloon. But this fine house is not for the likes of me. I'll return to Sally's if Mr. Finch will drive me back."

The girl turned as if to leave, but Lilla blocked her exit. "Nonsense." She turned a reproachful gaze upon Maria. "We have no formal places in this house, do we, Maria?"

Grady watched the exchange between Lilla and Maria. He was surprised when the housekeeper lowered her gaze. "No, there are no places in this house. We are all equal here. Come, Miss Violet. I will see you settled for the night."

Violet allowed herself to be led away, glancing gratefully over her shoulder at both Lilla and Grady.

"That was a nice thing you did for Violet tonight," he said. "But have you thought of what you're going to do with her come morning?"

"No. I'll figure out something." She glanced up at him and winced. "Come into the kitchen and let me clean you up. Maria keeps bandages in stock for emergencies. I've seen the way you flinch when you move. I suspect you have a cracked rib or two."

He started to tell her he could tend to himself, but he needed to talk to her anyway. No use putting off till tomorrow what he could settle tonight. He sat in a chair while she scurried about the kitchen. He liked the graceful way she moved, the way her petticoats rustled beneath her skirts, the soft, flowery scent of her that even the liquor couldn't overpower. He was beginning to like too much about her, and that was a problem for him.

"I'm sending you home."

Lilla stood at the dry sink. She'd just finished dipping a cloth into a bucket of water and wringing it out. She turned to him. "What?"

"I've decided you're going home."

Her heart leapt, but she wasn't positive it was with joy. And she didn't much care for the way *he'd* decided she would do anything.

"What about the money? I haven't earned enough—"

"I'll give you the money."

She walked to him, kneeling so she could wipe the blood from the corner of his mouth. "But you said I should earn my way. You said—"

"Forget what I said. I've made up my mind. After . . . well, after all that's happened tonight, you'll be safer away from here. Back home where you belong."

A lot had happened during the dance. She suspected he didn't refer only to the fight with the men from Tascosa. Her face started to burn as did other parts of her. She'd been brazen with him in the back hallway, had come close to going into one of the rooms with him. She could only speculate about what would have happened if they had not been interrupted. Over and over again.

Dabbing at the blood on his lip, she said, "I don't believe whether I leave or not is your decision to make."

He placed a hand over the one she held to his mouth. "Lilla, you are going to be reasonable about this, aren't you?"

It sounded like a question her father would ask her, had in fact asked her several times throughout her life. She'd always been reasonable. Always done what she was told, thought what she was supposed to think. Behaved like a lady.

"I don't think I'm going to be reasonable," she admitted. "I've grown fond of the idea of earning my own way home."

"You're not serious?"

She gave it a moment of thought. Not long ago, she would have given anything to go home. She would have taken his money, and without an ounce of guilt. After all, it wasn't as if her father wouldn't return the money to him. That was the problem. As long as she allowed her father to support her, she felt that she must abide by his rules, be the daughter he wanted her to be instead of the woman she was. She felt as if she were just now finding out who Lilla Traften might be, and wasn't ready to give up the journey. Not yet. Besides, there was the problem of Violet. Lilla felt responsible for the young woman.

"I am serious," she decided. "I simply can't go yet."

He took the rag from her hand and wiped his face. "You sure as hell can't stay."

"Why not?" she demanded.

"Lilla," he began, then sighed. "For one thing,

you can't earn your way home now, anyway. Sally said your lessons were finished, the men have all run off, and there's nothing for you to do here."

Grady had presented a good argument. Maria wouldn't need her help with all the men gone. There was nothing at all for her to do . . . except one thing.

"I can help you run the ranch until the men return."

She got a nice view of his straight teeth because he laughed. He continued to laugh until he realized she hadn't joined him in the joke.

"You're not serious?" he repeated.

Lilla lifted her chin. "You said yourself that I am very teachable."

"Yeah, that's what I'm afraid of," he muttered.

Her cheeks flushed again. He'd made the remark after he'd kissed her upstairs. "What is that supposed to mean?"

His eyes turned a dark shade of smoke. "You know what it means. If Smitty hadn't interrupted us in the hallway, we'd still be in a room at Sally's doing what neither of us has any business doing together."

She suspected he was right, and had to bow to his experience in matters he knew more about. How long did it take for a man and woman to complete the act? Surely not this long. She supposed that to simply ask him would not further her goals at this point. Instead, she'd lay the blame for her banishment from Texas upon him.

"So, what you're saying is that because you lack control over your manly urges, I cannot stay and fulfill my obligations?"

He blinked. "I didn't say that."

Lilla rose. "Yes, you did. In so many words."

Grady stood too. "Words you're putting in my mouth. And *your* control isn't anything to brag about. I expected better from you."

"You expected?" Rage washed over her. Lilla was damned tired of expectations. "Am I not allowed to feel passion? Am I not allowed to make mistakes like everyone else?"

"Yeah," Grady answered. "Just do those things far from here."

Instead of venting her anger by hitting him over the head with a skillet, Lilla burst into tears. The fact that she would succumb to such weakness in front of him made her cry all the harder.

"This isn't a trick, is it?" Grady asked.

She paused long enough to look at him. "A trick?"

"The crying," he explained. "I can't stand to see a woman cry."

She sniffed loudly. "Then you'd better leave."

"That wouldn't be polite."

If she weren't in the process of crying, Lilla would have laughed. "You are not polite, Grady Finch, so why worry about it now? I thought you might understand, that you could see where earning my way has become important to me, but you're just like my father."

"Considering what all we've done together, I wish you wouldn't say that," he mumbled.

Lilla cast him a dark glance through her tears. "I mean in your desire to ride roughshod over me and tell me what I can and can't do. In every other aspect, I assure you that you and my father are nothing alike."

"That's good," he said. "Except maybe the part where he has a lot of money and I don't."

"Which is exactly why you should let me help you run the ranch. Wouldn't it stand to reason that if the two of us are doing the work of nine men, we should be paid their income?"

He rubbed his bruised jaw. "I suppose."

"Just think how much faster I can earn my passage home and you can buy your land."

"There's a problem with your reasoning. I can do the work of nine men. You'll do good to handle the load of one."

"But you'll give me a chance?"

Grady stared into her eyes for a long moment. He finally glanced away.

"What about the other thing?" he asked.

"What thing?"

He glanced back at her. "The thing between us."

"Oh, that thing." She straightened, prepared to be rational regarding the matter. "We shall take turns. One week it will be my turn to exercise control, the next it will be yours."

His smile almost broke the deal. "And you think that's going to work?"

"I have no doubts concerning myself, but if you—"

"I can control my urges," he assured her. "Regardless of what you've probably been told countless times by men, you're not that irresistible."

Lilla couldn't recall being told even once that a man found her irresistible. Well, not unless she'd known for certain that it was her father's money the man found hard to resist.

"Then we have an agreement?" she asked.

He shook his head and laughed. "I'd be crazy to say yes."

"And if you say no, I'll be forced to return home by means other than my making. Please don't do that to me."

His smile faded. "Why? So you can prove something to your father?"

She took a deep breath. "No. So that I can prove something to myself. I find I enjoy being independent. I suppose I never thought I would because no one has given me the chance until now."

Grady rubbed his forehead. "I don't know, Lilla."

"Please," she whispered. "Just let me try."

"You know, the men could wise up tonight and be back here before morning."

"Then I will simply go back to our prior arrangement of helping Maria."

His boots seemed to suddenly become of great interest to him. Finally, he said, "All right. We'll give it a try."

Lilla wanted to throw her arms around him. She refrained, but couldn't control the smile she felt bursting out on her face. "I will see you bright and early in the morning."

"Get some sleep. You'll need it," he said, moving toward the door.

If he hadn't placed a hand on his ribs as he walked, Lilla might have forgotten about his injuries.

"Wait," she called. "Let me bind your ribs. What with all the riding, roping and stuff we'll be doing tomorrow, you'll need them bound up tight." She'd thought she heard him groan and assumed it was because of his injuries.

Lilla retrieved the bandages. He pulled his shirt from his pants. The shirt buttons were missing because of the fight and his skin felt warm to the touch. She started by placing a bandage under his arm, which meant she had to brush against him while she wound it around his back. His breath stirred the tendrils of hair on her forehead. He must remove his shirt on occasion while he worked or his skin wouldn't be the dark color it was, she reasoned.

He looked smooth and muscled, and his nipples were a dark copper color. She brushed one by accident, and like hers did on occasion, it hardened. She couldn't stop staring at it.

The other one hardened as well. They were like small pebbles, but perfectly round. She found herself wanting to trace their shape with her fingertips.

And she suddenly remembered something else that had pressed against her in the hallway of Sally's back rooms.

Grady shifted, and she realized her hand rested on his stomach. It was hard, too, but flat—not hard and round, or hard and big. Lilla shook her head and tried to dislodge the wicked thoughts running rampant through her mind. A question came to her. One that Grady expressed a second later.

"Is this your week or mine?"

Chapter Eighteen

Grady had spent a restless night. He called himself all kinds of a fool for allowing Lilla to stay and help him with the ranch. His opinion didn't change in the morning when he saw her moving toward him, her cheeks flushed with excitement, her long hair tied back with a pretty bow. The old buckskins she wore contrasted with the bright bow, and she carried her parasol. She also wore the dainty lace-up boots that put blisters on her feet.

"What's that for?" he asked, nodding toward the parasol.

"I haven't a hat that will properly shade my face from the sun," she explained. "If we're going out on the . . ." She glanced toward the distance. "Out there, I'll need protection."

"The range is what it's called," he provided. "But first things first."

"Oh, I've had breakfast," she assured him. "I had to fix my hair while you were eating, and of course Violet is at a loss as to what to do while I'm working, so I turned her over to Maria. I believe they plan to tidy up the bunkhouse. I said since the men are gone, the cots should be stripped and—"

"Lilla," Grady interrupted. "There's something you should know about me right off."

She squinted at him, seemed to realize what she was doing and widened her eyes. "And what is that?" she asked, popping her parasol open and perching it over her head.

"I'm not one for chitchat first thing in the morning. It grates on my nerves."

"Oh. All right, then. I'll try to refrain from prattling."

"I'd appreciate it."

"That settled, what should we do first? Wrangle some cattle? Break a horse or two? Put a little mark on their hides?"

"Branding is what it's called," he said, thinking he'd have a headache before noon. "And no, we're not doing any of those today."

She frowned. "We're not?"

Turning, he motioned her to follow him. "I figure that before we can do anything else, I need to teach you to ride."

Lilla fell into step beside him. "I've been watching you and the other men ride around every day. It doesn't look all that difficult."

Grady tried to keep from rolling his eyes. "That's because most of them were born in a saddle. There's a skill to good riding. Just like it takes skill to rope and cut cattle from a herd, and countless other things we all do around the ranch."

"I know I'm a gentlefoot, but I'm sure I'll learn quickly."

"Tenderfoot," he muttered darkly. "And speaking of feet, couldn't you find a decent pair of shoes to wear?"

She glanced down. "These are the most sensible shoes I brought along. Granted, they're too tight for walking long distances in the blazing hot sun, but since I figured we'd be riding instead of walking—"

"All right," he cut her off. "But they're going to get ruined."

"Ruined?"

Rather than explain, Grady swung the barn doors open wide. There were several stalls where the men kept the horses they planned to ride the next day. It saved time from having to rope them or round them up. Most of the time, the rest of the horses were left to graze, or a few were put in the corral in case one needed to be saddled quickly during an emergency.

"Oh, dear." Lilla placed a hand against her face. "What is that smell?"

"That smell is our work this morning."

Her eyes widened. "Our work?"

He moved inside and grabbed two shovels. "We have to muck out these stalls."

"Muck out?" she repeated weakly.

"Shovel the manure out into the center, then shovel it into the back of a flatbed so we can haul it off and spread it over the ground. Helps the grass." When she didn't respond, Grady glanced at her. She looked horrified.

"Independence is stinky, messy, sweaty work. Care to reconsider? I could take you to Tascosa today and probably have you on a stage home by the end of the week."

She removed her hand from her face, nibbling on her bottom lip as if considering his offer. After a moment, she snapped her parasol closed and hung it on a peg inside the barn. "I'm ready to begin," she said primly.

Grady had purposely chosen one of his least favorite tasks around the ranch to start off the morning. He figured Lilla would bolt at the first sign that she'd have to do distasteful work. Since they hadn't gotten started yet, he refrained from being surprised that she had the determination to jump in with both feet. He handed her a shovel, then pulled a pair of sturdy gloves from his back pocket.

"Wear my gloves or you'll have blisters on your hands, too."

"But won't you need them?"

He shook his head. "My hands are callused and used to hard work."

She slid on one of his gloves. It swallowed her dainty hand. "You have big hands, too," she mumbled, then glanced up, her cheeks turning red. "Which I suppose only makes sense because you're big . . . that is, tall."

He shrugged, hardly listening because she tended to prattle. "I can tie some rope around your wrists to help you keep them on. And I have an idea about your shoes, too."

Lilla thought she looked like a scarecrow. Her gloves were tied to her hands with thin ropes, and her shoes were covered in burlap, with ropes tied around her ankles. Her ensemble was not in the least fetching, but then, neither was the thought of shoveling manure all morning.

"We'll start at the back and work our way forward," Grady said. "Follow me."

The stalls lining the barn were not the only grounds covered in horse dung. Lilla picked her way carefully through the mess. Grady swung a stall gate open. Flies swarmed, and the stench was almost overwhelming.

"Are you sure you want to continue?" Grady asked.

She knew he meant with the whole agreement, not just the stalls, or she would have quickly answered no. Afraid she'd gag or, worse, swallow an insect if she opened her mouth, she nodded. He grabbed a bandanna from his back pocket.

"Tie this around your nose and mouth. It'll help."

He pulled the bandanna tied around his neck up over his face. Lilla had trouble manipulating the material while wearing her oversized gloves. Grady did the job for her.

"Grip the handle of the shovel like this, dig, then scoop." He demonstrated. He threw a large pile of manure from the stall into the middle passageway of the barn. Disgusting as the job was, Lilla didn't think it looked too difficult. She followed his example. Her shovel came away with a small portion of manure.

"You'll have to put your back into it," he said. "Use the strength you have in your arms."

Only a short time later, Lilla's back and arms were screaming in protest. Needlepoint, she realized in that moment, did not count as exercise. They'd only managed to do two stalls, with Grady doing the major portion of the shoveling, and she sorely needed a rest.

"I must stretch my back," she finally blurted. "I fear I will be hunched over from this day forward."

He nodded toward a stack of hay. "Rest for a minute."

She leaned her shovel against the stall gate and hobbled to the haystack, where she collapsed, grateful he hadn't complained about her lack of stamina. He, to the opposite, seemed to have a great deal of stamina. His shoveling had an almost appealing rhythm to it. She found herself mesmerized by the grace with which he moved, the determined set of his jaw, the slight sound of exertion that his breath made when he plunged the shovel into the manure, then withdrew.

He plunged and withdrew, over and over again with a steady stroke, an unwavering rhythm. She tugged at her shirt collar, feeling as if it were strangling her. Snatching the bandanna from her nose and mouth, she tried to breathe. The stench made her cough. Grady stopped shoveling.

"Maybe you should go outside for a few minutes," he suggested. "Breathe some fresh air."

Lilla thought that was a good idea. She started to rise, then noticed an odd contraption in a corner of the barn.

"What's that?" she asked.

His gaze followed the direction of her nod. "It's an old plow."

"What does it do?"

Grady wiped a sleeve across his brow. "It levels the ground with that board attached to the back. Wade used it when he planted the garden."

Lilla had an idea. "Can you attach it in some way to a horse?"

"Yes. Why are you asking?"

Sudden excitement churned her blood. "I'm thinking we could attach it to a horse, back it into the stalls and scrape the manure out with the board."

Glancing at the plow, he said, "That might work,

but there'd have to be some weight applied to the board."

"Couldn't one of us stand on it?"

"Maybe," he admitted. "That never occurred to me, I guess because with the men, it doesn't take long to clean up the stalls."

"Well, we don't have the men," Lilla said. "And if it could cut our work time in half, we could move on to something more pleasant."

"Already had your fill of ranch work?" he asked, pulling down his bandanna to display a smug smile.

"No, I'm perfectly willing to resume shoveling. I just thought it would save us time."

He stared at the plow, as if calculating whether or not he thought her plan would work. "I guess we can give it a go."

Preparations were soon under way. Lilla watched Grady rope the horse he usually hitched to the buggy. He made that look simple, too. With more than a little effort, they harnessed the horse to the plow. Although Lilla could manage nicely with a horse and buggy, she felt nervous about guiding a horse and a plow. Grady argued that her slight form wouldn't be sufficient to weigh the board down, so he assumed that role.

Their first attempt was disastrous. The horse, used to exerting the strength needed to pull the heavier buggy, lunged forward at the slightest touch of the reins on his rump. The jolt sent Grady flying off the plow to land in a particularly mushy stall of manure. It coated his back from head to foot.

He rose, plucking manure from the shoulder of his shirt. "That didn't work."

Lilla wasn't about to take a shovel in hand again. "The horse doesn't understand that not as much strength is required, is all. Give me another try."

"One more," he agreed. "If it doesn't work this time, we go back to shoveling."

It actually took three more tries, and Grady looking more like a pile of manure than a man, to prove that her idea would work. Once they all got the hang of it, the horse included, the process went much smoother. In a short time, they had the stalls clean. A while longer and they had dragged the manure outside into some semblance of a pile. The sun had become merciless. Lilla wasn't enthused about the prospect of shoveling the manure onto a flatbed wagon.

"The manure needs to dry out," Grady said. "I suppose we can wait a couple of days before we shovel it onto the flatbed."

Those were almost the sweetest words Lilla had ever heard. She was hot, dirty, tired and starving. She glanced toward the house, longing to be inside where the heat wasn't as stifling. Wishing to be clean even if it meant sweeping floors or feather dusting.

Violet appeared on the porch waving for them to come.

"Maria must have the noon meal ready," Lilla said, her stomach grumbling in anticipation.

"We can't go inside like we are," Grady informed her. "Maria will have our hides."

Lilla wasn't much cleaner than Grady. Manure had splattered her clothing, probably her face as well. All that was visible of his features were his eyes. She couldn't help but giggle.

"I must look pretty bad," he said.

She started to cover her mouth and giggle again, but when she brought a dirty glove to her face, she almost choked instead.

"Let me take those off for you." Grady stepped forward and untied the ropes securing her gloves. He bent and removed the ropes around her ankles. "Do you know what we do when we're too dirty to go inside the house and eat?"

Lilla had never seen the men get as dirty as the two of them. She had no idea what they did, or why Grady unlaced her dainty boots.

"You should slip those off," he advised.

"B-But the burlap kept them from getting ruined," she stammered. "And how do I walk to the house?"

"I'll carry you."

Before Lilla could respond, he grabbed her around the knees and slung her over his back. Her unlaced boots fell off when she tried to kick him. He started walking, carrying her.

"Put me down!"

"What?" he asked.

She struggled. "I said put me down. I'm not a sack of supplies. This is highly improper behavior!"

"Did you ask me to put you down?"

Lilla saw the brightly colored ribbon she'd tied in her hair hit the ground. It was sprinkled with manure, so she wasn't overly upset by the loss. She was upset about having to hang over Grady's filthy back.

"Yes! Put me down this instant!"

He did. Cold water hit her backside, then she sank, her whole body going under. She came up sputtering. He'd carried her over to the horses' water trough and dropped her in!

"You son of a bitch!"

Grady's eyes widened. "What did you call me?"

In the process of shoving her dripping hair over her shoulder, she froze. Lilla did not curse. She'd been taught better, had hardly even heard any cursing until she journeyed to Texas. Swear words grew about as rampant in the Panhandle as prickly pear cactus. The men watched their manners to an extent in her company, but that didn't keep her from hearing them at night inside the bunkhouse, swearing every other word. She supposed she'd picked up some bad manners.

"I believe I called you a son of a bitch."

"I believe you did," he agreed. He smiled a little.

It was difficult not to smile back. The cold water felt wonderful, and her clothes were certainly of no consequence. Camile might disagree, but Lilla wasn't concerned.

"A gentleman should ask a lady if she wants a bath before he sees that she gets one."

Grady stepped closer and stared down at her. "It wouldn't be proper to ask such a question."

He couldn't look innocent if his life depended upon it, Lilla decided. She blinked up at him. "Could you at least give me a hand up?"

With a nod, he extended his hand. Lilla grabbed it and pulled with all her might. She hardly budged him.

"You didn't think I would fall for that old trick, did you?"

Irritated, she splashed water at him. She only managed to make the muck covering him slimier. He wiped a hand across his face.

"If you wanted me to join you, you should have just asked."

Her mouth dropped open when he climbed into the trough with her, boots and all. She quickly closed it, worried she'd get a taste of something foul. Even though they were both dressed, Lilla considered the two of them together in this trough highly improper. Even as slimy as the water was, it led the way to visions of herself and Grady in a tub together without clothes.

"What if someone sees us?" she asked, glancing around.

"Sees us what?" He didn't wait for an answer, but dunked his head beneath the water. Lilla waited for him to resurface.

"Together like this," she stressed.

Grady laughed. "Who is going to see us? No one is here but Maria and Violet, and they're both in the house getting the meal set out. Besides, it isn't as if the two of us were naked."

His last statement hung in the air like the cheap perfume at Sally's place. Lilla tried not to stare at the way his shirt molded against him, or imagine him without it.

She glanced down and realized that her own clothes were clinging to her skin. Her nipples were embarrassingly erect. She ducked further down into the disgusting water; it was better than being seen in such an embarrassing state. His smile said he noticed her problem.

"Would you please get out so that I may get out?" she asked.

He didn't argue. Grady climbed out of the filthy water and extended his hand. "I'll help you."

She frowned at him. "You don't think *I'm* falling for that old trick, do you?"

"I'm only being polite."

If his eyes hadn't been dancing with mischief, she might have believed him. "Your politeness is impolite, Mr. Finch. Please go away."

"All right." He sighed. "But I should warn you, the bottom of the trough is slippery with moss. It hasn't been cleaned out in some time. I thought that would be one of our chores today; otherwise I wouldn't have thrown you in. The water's not fit for horses to drink now."

"Warning noted. Good day."

He shook the water from his hair and walked toward the bunkhouse, where she assumed he would shed his wet clothing. Lilla waited until he'd disappeared inside before trying to rise. She had a horrible time getting any grip with her bare feet. It took her three tries to climb from the trough without falling down. Her feet were sensitive to the rocky ground. She snatched up her shoes and hobbled toward the house, cussing the whole way.

She felt like cussing again that evening. Lilla sat with Violet on the porch, watching the sun set. The afternoon had not gone as she'd planned. After her bath, and having her meal brought upstairs, she'd only meant to rest for a moment. The next thing she'd known, Maria had been shaking her awake for supper. Grady had already finished and disappeared before she made it downstairs. She felt horrible, mentally and physically. Her shoulders and arms ached, but, much worse, she'd slept the afternoon away while he worked. Some ranch hand she was.

"I saw you today," Violet said quietly.

"Saw me?"

"With Mr. Finch. In the water trough."

Lilla inwardly cringed. "We were—"

"Laughing," Violet interrupted. "And from what I could tell, flirting."

"I don't recall that we were flirting," she said. "Mr. Finch and I are . . . well, we are business associates." Lilla had never had her very own business associate. Her father had many of them. "We simply work together."

Violet cut her gaze sideways at her. "I think you like him."

"I do like him," she admitted. "He's for the most part a very decent man."

"He likes you, too," Violet assured her. "I can tell by the way he looks at you. And he treats you nice, not like other men treat women."

Lilla turned to the girl. "The majority of the male population is not all bad, Violet. You mustn't judge every man by your father, or by the man he sold you to, or even by the men you've seen come and go at Sally's Saloon. There are kind, decent men in the world. I'd like to believe there are more good ones than bad."

Violet shoved her hair behind her ear. "I figure you haven't met as many bad ones as I have. Don't imagine I'll ever feel comfortable enough around a man to smile and laugh with him the way you did today."

Time was what Violet needed. And softer surroundings to forget her past. One of the reasons Lilla had fallen asleep after the noon meal was because Violet's nightmares had woken Lilla several times during the night.

A thought occurred to her. Maybe it was a far-fetched idea, but it was one that held possibilities. "Violet," she asked, "if you were given an opportunity to start your life over, to become someone else, would you?"

The young woman laughed. "What's the point of asking that when you and I both know no such thing could happen?"

"But if it could," Lilla persisted. "If you could go away from here and become someone else. Someone, say, like me—would you?"

Violet frowned. "If I could trade my life for yours I'd be plum stupid not to. You said I wasn't dense, remember?"

Lilla smiled and patted her hand. "I know you're not dense, Violet. I guess I'm wondering if you'd be brave enough to become someone different."

"Even a coward can see the obvious," Violet said quietly. "Even a coward would know better than to look a gift horse in the mouth. I'd trade my life for yours in a second, Miss Lilla, but I don't believe in dreams like that one. Those kind don't ever come true. I am who I am. My blood is tainted with my father's. I don't imagine no good can ever come of me. Not now."

"You mustn't think like that," Lilla said. "Dreams can come true, and someday you'll meet a fine young man who will make you realize how special you are."

Violet started to respond, but a dark shape materialized before them. Grady tipped his hat as he came into view.

"Ladies."

Heat crept into Lilla's cheeks. Would he comment about her sleeping the afternoon away? He paused, his gaze roaming over her like familiar territory.

"I hope you're rested up. I'm teaching you to ride in the morning."

"I'll be ready," she promised.

"Miss Violet." He nodded and strolled away.

Lilla stared after him. She felt Violet's gaze boring into her and turned back to the young woman. "What were we discussing?"

"Dreams," Violet said. "And love I think."

"Oh, yes." Lilla straightened. "I am no expert upon the subject of love, but I've often heard that it happens to the most unlikely of people."

"I think you know more about love than you're pretending to know." Violet actually smiled at her, although somewhat sadly. "You're in love with Mr. Finch."

A strong gust could have knocked Lilla over. She was shocked. "Don't be silly. I like Mr. Finch, as I admitted, but I also told you we're nothing more than business associates."

"Does he know that?" Violet's grin stretched. " 'Cause by the way he looks at you, I'm thinking he's in love with you, too."

Although Lilla was perfectly aware that Grady had feelings for her, she wouldn't call them love. He was attracted to her, as she was to him. Love was too strong a word for what they felt for one another . . . or perhaps too soft.

"A serious relationship between Mr. Finch and me would be pointless," she said primly. "And you are wrong about his feelings."

"I don't think I'm mistaken," Violet argued. "And what's wrong about you loving him, anyway?"

Uncomfortable with Violet's line of questioning, Lilla rose and stretched her legs. "Have you ever read poetry, Violet?"

"Not in a long time," the young woman mumbled.

"There's a poem I once read about a dove and a hawk who fell in love, but as you know, a hawk and a dove are two very different birds. The hawk is a bird of prey, and the dove a bird of peace."

"What happened to them?" Violet asked.

Lilla paused to watch the sun sink midway upon the horizon. The sight always took her breath away. "The hawk's life was a hard one. The dove, a gentle soul, could not live in the hawk's world. She needed the peaceful life she had known among other doves. But the hawk could not live among doves, and the dove could not live among hawks, and so she died."

"She died?" Violet blurted. "How come she died? Did the hawk kill her?"

Glancing away from the sunset, Lilla laughed. "No, Violet. She died of despair. You see, she could not live with the hawk, but she could not live without him, either."

Violet shrugged. "Sounds like a stupid bird, if you ask me."

Lilla rejoined her on the step. "I think you're missing the point. Two birds, or two people of such opposite natures, should not try to live together. One of them is bound to be unhappy."

"That's some silly poem," Violet scoffed. "You

may know a lot about manners, and fancy clothes and poetry, Miss Lilla, but you don't know much about real life. To me, if the dove had truly loved the hawk, she would have tried to be stronger for him. Or if the hawk had truly loved the dove, he would have tried to be gentler for her. With both of them trying, they could have been happy together. Any fool should be able to figure that out."

Violet's perception of the poem took Lilla by surprise. As did the wisdom of her words. "Maybe you should have written the poem," she teased. "Your ending is much better."

"My mother used to read me stories with happy endings," Violet whispered. "Guess that's where I get that nonsense." She rose and turned toward the front door. "The real truth is, the hawk would have never loved the dove. He'd have had her for a meal upon their first meeting, and that would have been the end of that story." Violet stepped into the house.

Chapter Nineteen

The hawk came calling later that night. At first, Lilla thought she must have been awakened by Violet's nightmares, but she listened, and realized the sound that woke her was the tapping of pebbles hitting her window. She wondered if it was already morning. A glance toward the window said darkness still painted the sky. Grady must have been trying to avoid any untoward suggestion by not just knocking at her door. But what could he want at this ungodly hour?

Slipping from bed, Lilla grabbed her robe. She went to the window, but couldn't make out anyone below. Maybe some crisis had arisen. Something pertaining to the ranch. When she pulled on her robe, she realized how sore her arms were from shoveling. Her back ached, too. He'd better have a good reason for getting her out of bed when her body needed rest. She made her way downstairs, wishing she'd thought to light a lamp and carry it with her. Even a candle would have been of use. She managed the darkened stairway without breaking her neck, opened the front door and walked out onto the porch.

She'd no more than started to call out when a hand clamped over her mouth. Lilla's immediate response was to struggle. She knew that whoever held her from behind was not Grady. He was smaller. The hand clamped over her mouth was smooth and soft, not the hand of a working man. She managed to pull back enough to bite him. He yelped. She elbowed him in the ribs, breaking free to run screaming toward the bunkhouse. He might have pursued her; Lilla wouldn't turn and look.

Sharp rocks cut into her bare feet. She hardly noticed the pain. The dark shape of the bunkhouse rose up before her. She was prepared to fling herself against the door, but she heard a loud creak and stumbled into a pair of familiar arms.

"What the hell is going on?"

"A man," Lilla gasped. "There's someone after me."

Grady pulled her inside. She heard him fumbling around in the dark. She had no doubt that he was looking for his gun. The sound of a horse's hooves racing away reached them in the darkness. Grady cussed.

"I can't catch him. I don't have a horse saddled and can't even find my damn clothes!"

Lilla's heart pounded against her chest. "What could he have wanted?"

More fumbling, and then a match flared in the darkness. She watched Grady light a lantern. A soft glow chased some of the darkness from the room. On trembling legs, Lilla walked to the nearest bunk and collapsed.

"What happened?" he repeated.

When she glanced up, she realized he wore only a blanket twisted around his waist. His feet were bare, and she saw no signs of longhandles sticking out from beneath the blanket.

"Are you naked?" she asked.

He blinked. "Yeah, but that's beside the point. What the hell happened?"

"The sound of pebbles being thrown against my window woke me. I went downstairs and out onto the porch to—"

"You did what?" He sat beside her on the bunk.

"I thought it was you," she explained.

"Why the hell would I be throwing pebbles at your window in the middle of the night?"

She sighed. "I don't know. That's what I came outside to find out."

He took a steadying breath. "Then what happened?"

"I started to call out for you, but a hand clamped over my mouth. I knew it wasn't you. I could feel him pressed up against my back, and he wasn't as large as you are, or as tall. His hands were smooth."

"Did he say anything? Did he tell you to be quiet, or identify himself?"

Lilla shook her head. "I bit him. Then I jabbed my elbows into his ribs and broke free. I started screaming and ran to the bunkhouse."

"Good thinking," he said. "Your screaming must have been what sent him running. He thought you'd roust the men."

Her hands were trembling. She twisted them together. "Do you think he was after me?"

He took her cold hands in his and rubbed them. "Sounds like it."

"But how did he know which room was mine?"

Grady lifted her fingers and blew his warm breath on them. "He must be watching the place. I suppose a man could stay some distance from the house and still see everything. He could have seen you at the window more than a time or two."

Just the thought made her shiver. "But why would he do that? If a person wanted to talk to me, why wouldn't they simply come to the house and knock on the door?"

"They would," he answered, "unless they were up to no good. Remember that day you drove the buggy from town? Could be the same man."

The thought of being stalked was terrifying. She tried to control her emotions. Lilla was no longer a prim-and-proper miss from St. Louis. She was a ranch hand, and she told herself she should act like one.

"I don't see what he would want with me."

Grady ran his gaze over her. "I do."

She waited for him to continue; when he didn't, she said, "What is it you see?"

He placed her hands back into her lap. "I see a beautiful, desirable woman. For some men, that's motivation enough."

His explanation wasn't one she could easily accept. "Are you suggesting that this ruffian intends to kidnap me, risk life and limb knowing the ranch is stocked with men willing and able to come to my rescue, just for the purpose of having his way with me?"

"It does sound a little far-fetched," Grady agreed. He turned to her. "But the men are gone now. He might have known that. If he's been watching the ranch, it could be the reason he grew so bold tonight."

Shivering again, she said, "That makes sense, but I still find it hard to believe that a man would go through so much trouble for . . . well, it isn't as if there were no other women in Texas."

"None as pretty as you." He rose, pacing back and forth in front of her. Lilla hoped he'd secured the blanket tight. They were alone, which wasn't proper in the first place at this time of night, and she was wearing just bedclothes and he next to nothing.

"Could this have anything to do with your father?"

She glanced up. "My father?"

"His money. Could someone be trying to kidnap you for ransom?"

If they were in St. Louis, she would have considered it a possibility. "No one here really knows who I am," she said. "They don't know that my father is that well-to-do. At least I don't think they know." She frowned. "You haven't said anything, have you?"

"No," he answered. "Most everyone only knows that your father is a business associate of the Langtrys. Unless Wade or Camile said something to someone, I don't think anyone would have reason to kidnap you. And I don't think Wade or Camile would be spouting off about your father. They're pretty tight-lipped about their business dealings."

She stood. A sudden suspicion arose in her. "The man might have been after Violet."

"But Violet wasn't driving the buggy that day he chased you," Grady pointed out.

Joining him in his pacing, she explained, "This could be a different man. Violet has a bit of a past. She ran away from someone. He might have just now found her."

"Would he harm her?"

Without a smidgen of doubt, she answered, "Yes he would. She sleeps in the same room with me. Perhaps it was her attention he tried to draw, and not mine."

"Yeah, about that." He took her hand and led her to the bunk. "Never answer the summons of a man who is throwing pebbles at your bedroom window in the middle of the night."

"But I thought it was you," she reminded. "I feared that some crisis regarding the ranch might have occurred."

He cupped her chin and turned her face toward his. "If there's a crisis, I'll come banging on the front door. If I pitch pebbles at your window in the middle of the night, don't get out of bed. I'm up to no good."

"Are you always so forthcoming regarding your improper intentions?"

"I figure that if I warn you, you have a fair chance of avoiding them."

Oddly enough under the circumstances, she felt safe with him—would have felt safer in his arms. Which was right where she was headed when Maria, holding a large cast iron skillet in one hand and Violet's hand in the other, stepped into the bunkhouse.

"I heard screaming," Maria said. "I thought it was Miss Violet having another nightmare, but then I realized the screams were coming from outside. I almost clobbered Miss Violet over the head when I found her sneaking around downstairs." Her dark brows lifted. "What are the two of you doing in here alone at this time of night?"

"It's not how it appears," Lilla assured her. "A man tried to accost me tonight."

"Someone came into the house?" Maria placed a hand against her chest. "While we were sleeping?"

"He threw pebbles at my window to draw me outside," Lilla said.

Maria frowned. "And you went? Are you loco?"

"She thought it was me," Grady said in Lilla's defense.

The housekeeper's frown deepened. "And you went? Are you loco?" She repeated.

All the excitement had caused Lilla's head to ache. And Violet looked terrified. "Maybe we could take this discussion into the house," Lilla said.

"And maybe Mr. Grady Finch could put some clothes on," Maria grumbled. "The rest of us will go inside and I will make coffee. I doubt any of us can sleep."

"Coffee sounds wonderful," Lilla said. "And you're right, I couldn't go back to sleep now."

Maria hurried Violet outside. A moment later, the woman reappeared. "You are coming with us while Mr. Grady gets dressed, are you not, Miss Lilla?"

"Oh." Lilla jumped up. "Of course. I—"

"On second thought," Grady interrupted, "you'd all better stay put and let me walk you to the house. We don't know for sure that the man is gone. We heard him ride out, but he could have circled around and come back."

At his words, Maria reached outside and pulled Violet back in. Lilla joined the women. They stood with their backs turned toward Grady. Violet's face looked pale in the lantern's glow. Lilla took Violet's cold hand in hers and squeezed.

"We're going to be fine," she assured her. "Grady will see to that."

Violet's expression of uncertainty reminded Lilla that the young woman's trust in men was shaky at best. She felt a little surprised at her own trust of a man she hadn't known for a long period of time. Grady wasn't a gentleman in the way she might have once defined the term, but he was honest, and she felt safe tonight because she knew he could protect them all.

A sudden thought occurred to Lilla, one she might never have considered had she not been given a taste of independence. Perhaps she and the other women should learn to protect themselves.

Guns and women weren't a good mix, in Grady's opinion. Lilla seemed too sure of herself, and Violet looked as if she thought about as highly of guns as she did of men. Maria had refused to join the shooting lesson, saying she'd do fine with her skillet. He'd gotten very little sleep that night, resting downstairs inside the house with an ear trained for trouble. It had been a short night.

He watched Lilla aim his gun at the target bottles. She fired, and missed. The gun's kick sent her back a couple of steps. She stomped her foot and took aim again.

"I wish I was as brave as Miss Lilla," Violet said

beside him. "The first day I saw her at Sally's, I wouldn't have given her credit for much spine, but she's proven me wrong."

"Yeah," he agreed. "She's surprised me, too."

It had taken a lot of courage for Lilla to fight off her attacker the previous evening. It took a lot of courage for her to make the decision to stay and earn her way home, when leaving would have been simpler, and smarter, for her. Now she stood before him wearing another pair of old buckskins, a long shirt and her silly boots, but holding a pistol instead of a parasol. If a man didn't know better, he might get the fool notion that she belonged to the rugged territory surrounding her.

"She says you're a good man," Violet continued, but she wouldn't look at him when she spoke.

He smiled. "She did?"

Violet nodded. "I think she's sweet on you."

His smile faded. "You do?"

Another short nod was Violet's response.

"I don't think so," he said, wondering how a man could feel pleased and uncomfortable at the same time. "She has better choices in men than me. She's—"

"A dove," Violet provided. "And you're a hawk."

He supposed that was a good example. Two birds but of different natures. "She'll forget all about me as soon as she's back where she belongs."

Part of him wanted Violet to argue the opposite, and part of him wanted her to agree with him. The girl said nothing.

Lilla fired again. She missed again. He waited for her to stomp her foot in frustration. She didn't disappoint him.

"I'm doing everything you said to do!" she called. "Why can't I hit the bottle?"

"It takes practice," he shouted back. "Keep trying."

Squaring her shoulders, Lilla faced the bottles again. Grady thought he should say something to Violet about her past, but he wasn't sure how to go about it. She was too young to have eyes so old. She was also very pretty, which he'd never noticed until Lilla cleaned her up.

"About men," he began. That was as far as he got before he felt stumped.

Violet turned to him. She lifted a brow. Grady plowed ahead.

"Not all men are mean-spirited. Not all men will lift a hand against a woman. In fact, I'd like to believe that most wouldn't."

"I'd like to believe that, too," Violet said. "I just haven't seen much proof of it."

"You will," he promised her. "As long as you don't go back to the kind of life you were living."

She turned those too-knowing eyes on him, and he saw the worry reflected there. "I don't want to, but I don't know what will happen to me. I don't have any money, anywhere to go, no family I'd want to return home to."

"Don't worry about that," he said. "We'll figure out something." Although Grady wasn't sure what.

He suspected that Wade and Camile would let her stay on and work at the ranch. But he wasn't sure she didn't need to get away from the past that was dogging her heels. Start fresh somewhere else.

"I appreciate you letting me come here," Violet said. "You and Miss Lilla are decent folks. My ma was a decent sort. Kind, gentle, educated. But my pa beat all of that out of her. I never could figure how those two got together."

Memories flooded Grady. Bitterness rose up inside him. "I knew a man like your father once, too. I know how a good beating on tender flesh feels. What it's like to see your mother struck down, treated worse than an animal. I also know there are ways to wound a person without ever throwing a punch, ever pulling a gun. I learned all that at a young age."

He was surprised to feel the light touch of Violet's hand on his. He glanced at her, and she quickly withdrew the offer of comfort, but she looked at him differently. As if she'd just realized that they were kindred spirits.

The blast of a gun and the shattering of a bottle drew their attention.

Lilla wheeled around, an excited blush staining her pretty face. "I did it! I hit one."

He smiled back at her.

"Your turn," he said to Violet.

"I-I'm not sure about this," she said. "I don't like guns."

"You don't have to like them, you just have to

respect them," he told her. "With the other men gone, I can't be around the house all day every day until they come to their senses and return to work. I'd feel better knowing you had protection if the need arose."

"I guess I would, too," she admitted. "I've seen what a gun can do. Seen men shot dead right in front of me. Not at Sally's, but at this other place I was before that."

Grady wanted to question her about the other place. About the man Lilla thought might be looking for Violet. His gut instinct told him the man wasn't after this young woman, but the one taking aim at another bottle. He'd make sure that Lilla stuck close to him in the days to follow. Real close.

The gun exploded—another bottle shattered. Lilla looked very pleased with herself and a little cocky as she approached him.

"What do you think of that, Mr. Finch?"

She pointed the gun at him while handing it to him. He ducked. "Damn, Lilla, don't point a loaded gun at someone like that. It might go off!"

"Oh." She jerked her hand down. The gun went off. A bullet dug into the dirt next to her foot. She screamed and dropped the gun. Grady dove to the side. Luckily, the gun did not discharge.

He sat, spitting dirt. "I think you're too dangerous to be trusted with a gun, is what I think. You'd do better with your parasol. At least I don't think you'll kill anyone with it."

The blush on her cheeks faded. Her face went

white. "My God, I could have shot you," she whispered.

Grady scrambled up and rushed to her side. She looked as if she might faint. He placed a steadying arm around her shoulders. "You could have, but you didn't. Take a few deep breaths."

She tried. He steered her toward the recently cleaned water trough. Dipping his bandanna in the trough with one hand, he used the other to snatch her parasol from where she'd hooked it on the corral fence. She never went anywhere without the thing, and today he was grateful for that. He popped it open and shoved it into her hand, then squeezed cold water from the bandanna and placed the rag against her face.

"Is that better?"

She nodded, but she still looked pale to him.

"Sit on this bottom board of the corral and lean forward."

As soon as she obeyed, he plucked the parasol from her fingers and balanced it on the top fence slat. He moved her hair aside and placed the bandanna against the back of her neck. It was a piece of skin on her he'd never seen up close. Soft, smooth, pale and kissable.

"Better?" he asked.

"Much," she answered.

"Are you all right, Miss Lilla?"

Grady glanced at Violet. She looked shaken as well.

"Are *you* all right?" he asked.

"It just scared me is all," the girl answered.

"Go to the house and get out of the heat," he said. "Your lesson will have to wait."

When Violet headed toward the house, he turned back to Lilla. "Do you think you can make it to the house? Maybe you'd better rest for a while."

Her head jerked up. "I am not going to rest. Not until we've done all we planned to do today. I can't keep sleeping my days away. And I'd appreciate it if you'd stop treating me like a tenderfoot. I'm not made of glass. I won't break."

His gaze widened. "Excuse the hell out of me for caring."

She buried her face in her hands. "I apologize. I'm angry with myself, not you. I can't believe I acted so irresponsibly with the gun. I could have shot you or Violet."

"Yeah, you could have," he agreed. "But you didn't, and you learned an important lesson about respecting a weapon. One you're not likely to forget."

She glanced up, her face no longer pale. "I believe I should stick to my parasol, the way Maria will stick to her frying pan."

"I think you'd better stick to me," he suggested.

A frown shaped her tempting mouth. "I wanted to be able to take care of myself."

"As far as I've seen, you've done a good job of it. Violet admires your courage."

Lifting a brow, she asked, "What were the two of you talking about while I practiced?"

"Private matters," he answered.

"What sort of private matters?"

He laughed. "The private kind."

She muttered something. He thought it might have been a curse word.

"You're nosy, you know that?"

"Nosy?" She straightened and removed the bandanna from her neck. "I prefer to think of it as inquisitive."

"Means the same thing in my book. Are you sure you don't need to rest before I start teaching you to ride?"

"Yes, I told you I'm fine," she insisted. "We're cooking daylight. Let's get started."

He rubbed his jaw. "The proper term is burning daylight."

Lilla waved a hand in the air. "Cooking, burning, it means the same thing in my book."

She made him laugh. And her digging into his business with Violet made him recall an aspect of their conversation he could tease her about.

"Violet thinks you're sweet on me," he said, grinning.

Her face turned red. "Is that what you were talking about? Because I can assure you—"

"Don't get your features all in a ruffle," he interrupted. "I know what you think of me."

"Y-You do?"

He nodded. "You think I'm a hawk." He started to help her rise, then figured she'd get huffy either way, if he offered, or if he didn't. Grady turned toward the horse he'd roped for her earlier. The old mare stood inside the corral waiting to be saddled.

"Come along, Dove. We're cooking daylight."

Chapter Twenty

Learning to ride a horse was not as simple as Lilla had thought it would be. Every time she more than walked the animal, she nearly slid off the saddle. Grady told her she needed to grip the saddle with her legs. Although her first instinct had been to inform him that a gentleman did not make mention of a woman's legs in her presence, she refrained. Manners, she realized, didn't count for much in the face of a challenge. And there were challenges aplenty waiting for her.

She knew that Grady was worried not only about the intruder, but about the cattle grazing on the range. He'd said that if word got out that his men were on strike, it might open the door for cattle rustlers to assume that the Langtrys' herd was theirs for the taking. Since she felt responsible for causing the trouble with the men, Lilla was determined to be a good hand for him.

She knew he planned to ride out on the range and round up the cattle, moving the large herd closer to the ranch for safety's sake. He couldn't do it alone. Or at least not as quickly as he could with the help of another rider. Violet had offered to throw in her lot with them, but Grady worried about leaving Maria alone at the house. Since Violet had proven skilled at learning how to fire not only Grady's pistol, but a rifle kept inside the house, both of them worried less about the women's safety.

"I think I'm getting the gist of it," Lilla said to Grady, easing the horse into a trot around the corral. She forgot to use her legs to grip the sides of the saddle and nearly found herself unseated. Upon recovery, she noted Grady's less than enthusiastic expression.

"I will improve," she assured him. "I think we should keep to our plan of riding out tomorrow to gather up the cattle. The longer we wait, the more likelihood there is that rustlers might beat us to the task."

He removed his hat and shoved a hand through his hair. "You're not ready. Not by a far stretch."

"I'm ready enough," she argued. "And I'll learn along the way. I won't have it said that I single-handedly split a town apart and sent Wade and Camile Langtry to the poorhouse. My presence here was supposed to improve conditions, not destroy them."

Replacing his hat, he sauntered toward her. "You haven't single-handedly destroyed anything, Lilla. I'm as much to blame as you are for the men leaving. I hear they're all camped on the outskirts of Langtry, waiting for the women to send up a white flag of surrender. Sounds like a standoff to me."

Lilla accidentally dropped the reins. The horse moved forward, and she nearly fell off while grabbing for the long leather strips. Grady stepped forward and grabbed the animal's bridle. He didn't say anything about her blunder, just gathered the reins and handed them to her.

"I-I could talk to the women, I guess," she said. "Maybe get them to call a truce until the men can come back and help you bring the cattle closer to the ranch."

"No, you can't," he said. "You can't give people pride in themselves and then ask them to give it up. This is something the men and women have to work out. We're not getting involved in it."

She felt relieved he'd said so, because she didn't for one moment believe she could go to the women and ask them to do any such thing. She only hoped the men would come to their senses quickly, or at least that Tanner Richards would and then ask Meg to marry him. It would be a small step in the right direction, and an important win for the women. It would show them all that they had choices—they didn't have to settle for the life they'd been dealt. No one did.

"You *have* single-handedly done one thing since you came to Texas," he said.

She lifted a brow.

"You've improved the scenery."

Glancing around, she drawled, "That isn't saying much."

He laughed. "Wait till I show you my future ranch. The river runs through it, and the grass is knee deep. Trees line the creek bed, and the stars hang down so close to the ground it looks like you could reach up and snatch one from the sky."

Excitement coursed through her. "Then we're going?"

Grady nodded. "We're going. Pack light. Only the bare necessities. What you can roll inside a blanket and strap on the back of a saddle."

A little of Lilla's enthusiasm faded. "Are you serious? I couldn't get much of anything rolled inside a blanket. Maybe a change of clothes and a hairbrush."

"That's why it's called packing light," he explained, then lifted his arms to help her dismount. "We can't weigh the horses down. I'll bring along a string for a fresh change of mounts, but we can only pack one of them with supplies. And those supplies will be food."

Lilla allowed him to help her down, though she would have to learn to mount and dismount on her own to save time. She had a problem with something else he'd said. "I suppose you'll make me do all the cooking. Although Maria has been educational to an extent in the kitchen, I'm not a very good cook."

"We'll take turns. That's the way ranch hands do things out on the range. Every man is equal and does his fair share."

"Or hers," she countered, smiling up at him. She liked the idea of being equal partners in their venture. She didn't know too many men who'd count a woman as their equal. As much as she hated to, Lilla supposed she had to give Camile Langtry credit for Grady's difference of attitude regarding gender roles. Camile hardly conformed to society's standards, and at the moment, Lilla began to find herself grateful to the woman for plowing new territory.

Grady still stood close to her, his hands resting upon her waist. She doubted that he realized he was touching her far more intimately than he would a bowlegged ranch hand. She liked that about him, too. He didn't mind touching, holding, giving. It seemed a natural part of his character. One she hoped would not get the both of them into trouble during their nights alone on the range.

"I think this is not a good decision," Maria fussed. "You are not like Camile. She has been raised around horses and cattle. I'm worried you could be hurt."

Lilla continued her attempt at rolling too many

clothes inside a blanket. "It's sweet of you to worry, Maria, but I'll be fine. Grady will watch out for me. It's not as if I were going alone."

"I worry about what he watches of yours," Maria muttered. "It is not proper. A young, virile man such as Mr. Grady and a young, passionate woman should not go off alone together. Trouble will usually follow."

Surprised, Lilla glanced up. "Who said I'm passionate? My nature runs to the opposite. I assure you I am very level-headed."

The housekeeper snorted. "I asked Miss Violet how you did with the dance. She said your dancing could make a whore blush."

"Oh, that." Lilla waved a hand in dismissal. "I was simply caught up in the moment."

"There are many moments to be found when two young people are left alone for days and nights together."

Lilla couldn't dispute that the possibility for trouble existed. Deep inside, she had to acknowledge that not only did the possibility exist, but the probability. When she felt tempted, she would recall the poem about the hawk and the dove. For good measure, she threw her study manual on etiquette into the blanket.

"I am touched by your concern for me, Maria," she said. "I truly am, but I am a grown woman. I made the decision to stay and help Grady, and I will stick to it."

"You are as stubborn as Camile," Maria complained. She suddenly smiled. "But I am proud of you. You have come a long way in your journey to Texas. I think your mother would be proud, too, if she could see you now."

Lilla felt her eyes sting with tears. "I would like to think so," she admitted, not bothering to add that she didn't believe her father would appreciate her new sense of independence. If he knew she planned to ride out on a horse and gather up cattle with a handsome single man, he'd puff up like a toad and bust the buttons off his best suit. But her father wasn't around to dictate proper behavior to Lilla, and her thoughts turned to more urgent matters.

"You're certain you and Violet will be all right here alone?"

Maria stepped forward and started thinning Lilla's clothing pile. "I was not an old woman when I first began working for Mr. Cordell. I have had to fight off many men's advances throughout the years. Violet and I will be fine. Besides, Wade and Camile could return any day."

Lilla hoped not. Not until she and Grady had straightened out the trouble. Wade and Camile might reconsider selling Grady his land, angry with him because of the strike, or feeling that he wasn't ready for the responsibility. She couldn't bear that. He had his heart set on the land. His eyes lit up when he spoke about the grass and the river and the stars. And some lucky woman would share it all with him.

Her last thought wasn't pleasing to her. Still, it stood to reason that he would marry. A man with a ranch needed a wife, and children to help him run it. Strong, sturdy boys like their father. And all of them handsome, too. The more pictures that formed inside her head, the less she liked the idea of Grady carrying on his life as if she had never existed.

Lilla closed her eyes and tried to see herself in the role of his wife. She couldn't picture herself here, among the cactus and the blowing dirt. She supposed she was still a dove. And not even the right kind of dove, as far as Grady was concerned. He seemed to prefer his soiled.

"Are you sleeping?"

She opened her eyes and tried to concentrate on packing. "No, just thinking. My boots are hardly appropriate for ranch work."

"I'll get you a pair of Camile's moccasins. Your feet look smaller, but you can wear extra socks. And I'll find you a hat and one of her jackets. The days are hot, but the nights and mornings are sometimes cool."

"Thank you, Maria," Lilla said. "Maybe I should let you pack for me and go downstairs to help Violet with the supplies."

"Yes," Maria agreed. "Mr. Grady will never let you take all of this in your blanket. I will decide for you what is necessary."

Lilla headed for the door. She paused. "Leave the book, Maria. I may have need of it."

The housekeeper picked up the book. "Is this telling you how to behave properly?"

She nodded.

"Yes, I will leave the book," Maria agreed. "And maybe put my Bible in for good measure."

Grady had the horses ready by sunup. He'd packed a sturdy bay gelding with cooking supplies, an extra blanket and slickers in case it rained. Not that he imagined it would. They didn't get nearly the rain they needed in the Texas Panhandle. Sometimes the river almost dried up and they had real problems. It was cold in the winter, hot in the summer, full of rattlesnakes and outlaws. No place for a lady.

When Maria had brought breakfast out to him earlier, she'd given him a good earful on behaving himself. He supposed he'd blushed like a boy when she'd told him to keep his snake in his pants. She'd never been so blunt with him, and he realized that the woman considered Lilla another chick she must look after. Anytime he got any fool notions about Lilla, he would try to remember that she was made for fancier things than barbecues and calf ropings.

He hoped she'd show up soon. He didn't want to spend his morning waiting for her to decide what silly hat she would wear, or what ribbon would look best in her dark hair. But when she arrived, he almost didn't recognize her. Lilla wore buckskins, moccasins instead of her fancy boots, a fringed jacket he knew belonged to Camile and a worn-looking wide-brimmed hat. He didn't see any bows in her hair.

"You could almost pass for a Texan," he said.

Handing him a bedroll that felt surprisingly light, she said, "I thought I could pass for one. At least from a distance, someone might mistake me for Camile Langtry."

"Camile has sunshine hair; yours is midnight. And longer. After Wade chopped hers off with a knife on the trail drive, she realized she didn't want it long again. Too much trouble, she said."

"A woman's hair should be her treasure. I'm, of course, quoting one Margaret Pendergraft Riley. At least that's what she used to tell us during lessons."

He smiled. "Well, she wears hers bobbed off now. Says it's not as hot or as much trouble to fix."

Lilla laughed, pulled her long ponytail over her shoulder and eyed it speculatively.

"Don't even think about cutting your hair," Grady said. "It reminds me of night on the water, the way it ripples and flows around you when you wear it loose. It feels like a fine silk dress my mother wore, and smells sweeter than the patch of wildflowers that grow up on the bluff overlooking my future land."

Her violet eyes darkened a shade. The flush of excitement she wore when she joined him deepened. "That was beautiful. You're a poet. Who would have thought?"

He felt like a fool for spouting poetry at her. Hell, he didn't even know it was poetry. He shrugged.

"Cut it if you want. It's your hair, and not for me to say what you should or shouldn't do with it."

It was a sad thing to see her pleasure fade. Like the sun moving behind a dark cloud, blotting out the warmth, the light. "Yes, well, I suppose that would be my decision. It is my hair. Are we ready to get started?"

He pulled her saddled horse forward. "As ready as we're going to get. Need a hand up?"

She shook her head. "I need to learn to mount and dismount by myself."

The horse was tall; she wasn't. It took her several tries to get enough height to hook her foot into the stirrup. She finally managed, pulling herself up into the saddle. He saw Violet and Maria coming from the house to see them off.

"Move out slow," he said to Lilla, then mounted and started forward, holding the lead rope to the four horses strung together. Maria waved at them, and he frowned when he saw what she held in her hand.

"You did not mean to forget this, did you, Miss Lilla?"

The object Maria held up was Lilla's dainty parasol. He glanced at Lilla. She chewed her lip, as he'd sometimes seen her do when weighing her answer.

"I was afraid it might spook one of the horses," she said. "But I would very much like to take it to keep the sun from my face and neck."

Her hat was meant to do that, but Grady knew

for a fact that didn't always do the trick. It depended on where the sun sat in the sky as to how much protection a hat could offer.

"Go ahead and take it," he said. "You can keep it in your rifle stock there on the saddle when you're not using it. Just be sure you warn me before you pop it open, and don't do it within eyesight of your horse if you're sitting on his back."

"I'll be careful," she promised, then leaned down and took the parasol from Maria.

The article fit perfectly inside the rifle stock. Grady supposed they could count it as a weapon. He'd seen her cower men with it before.

"You ladies remember to keep an eye out and stick together. Bolt the house up tight at night."

"Don't you be forgetting what I told you to remember," Maria warned him. Her gaze turned to Lilla. "Stay away from snakes."

At Lilla's confused expression, he nearly laughed. Maria meant the warning seriously, and he had promised her he'd behave himself, so he held his humor in.

"I most certainly will watch for snakes," Lilla assured her. "Violet, I trust you to take care of Maria during our absence, and likewise, Maria, for you to watch over Violet."

Both women nodded. Maria slipped her arm around Violet's slim waist, and Grady watched the young woman move a step away from her. Lilla had done the same thing the first time Maria hugged her. Fortunately, or maybe unfortunately for him,

Lilla didn't seem to mind being touched anymore.

"Time to go," he said. "If the men show up, send them out to find us."

"Those idiots," Maria fumed. "If they show up, they will get a good tongue-lashing from me first. And that Tanner Richards had better not show up back here without a wife."

Grady grinned. "I wouldn't hold my breath. He's pigheaded sometimes."

"It seems to be a normal condition around here," Lilla muttered, then moved her horse forward.

With a final wave, they left Violet and Maria behind. They hadn't gotten far when he asked, "Do you think I'm pigheaded?"

"About some things," she commented, and he could tell she tried to concentrate on her riding.

"Such as?"

"Once you get an idea stuck in your head, there's no jarring it loose."

"You mean like starting my own ranch?"

"Yes, about the ranch . . . and sometimes about people."

"I like to think I'd give any man a fair chance to prove himself."

"But would you do the same for a woman?"

He had no idea what she was getting at. "You know I would. I have. I gave you this one when you asked for it, didn't I?"

"Yes, but the stakes weren't very high. You had nothing really to lose by giving me a chance."

A curse came close to leaving his lips. "Nothing

to lose? Only my job. My dreams for my own place. Only Camile and Wade's ranch."

The color suddenly drained from her cheeks. "Well, now you've made me nervous. You didn't have to tell me so much was at stake. I mean, I knew, but when you just start rattling it all off like that—"

"Lilla," he said. "You're not making a lick of sense. Why don't you just get to the point?"

"I guess what I'm trying to say is that you still don't believe that a woman like me can survive in Texas. You still think I'm some silly, spoiled greenhorn without a thought in my pretty little head except what hat looks best with which gown and—"

"I never said that," he interrupted again. "What's eating at you?"

"Your wife," she blurted.

They moved so slowly that they were almost at a standstill. Grady drew his mount to a halt. "My wife? Last I knew, I didn't have one."

"But you plan to get yourself one someday, don't you?"

He was growing more confused by the minute. "I guess. What's that got to do with anything?"

Her back stiffened. "I would think it had something to do with the two of us."

A tiny sliver of light penetrated the fog clouding his mind. "Are you jealous of her?"

"You have been leading me on all the while, planning to marry her."

"I don't even know her!" he defended. "What do

you want? Do you want me to ask you to marry me?"

She glanced at him. "*Are* you asking me to marry you?"

"No," he quickly answered. "Why would I do a fool thing like that?"

Her lips went tight, and she urged her horse into a slow walk again. At the speed they were moving, they wouldn't make his land before nightfall. It was only a half day's ride if a person was moving faster than a lame turtle.

"I've made you angry," he guessed.

"Don't be ridiculous. I could never marry you anyway. I will marry a man of my father's choosing, just as he expects me to do. My husband will be wealthy and handsome, and of course he will build me the largest house in St. Louis. I will spend the rest of my life tending to his proper children and hosting his lavish parties so that all may come and envy me my perfect little life."

"Sounds horrible," Grady commented.

She lifted her chin. "I think it sounds wonderful."

"Not all men who have money are bound to be handsome," he pointed out.

"My husband will be," she assured him.

"I'll bet he has a short little . . ."

"A short little what?"

"Temper. And he'll spend his whole life yelling at you because you're so damned annoying."

"He will not yell at me," Lilla huffed. "I shall hit him with my parasol the first time he does."

"Good," Grady said. "It would serve him right."

"Who does he think he is?" Lilla demanded. "Does he think just because he has money, influence in the community, a fine house and a pretty wife, that he may abuse me and I'll stand idly by and allow it?"

"For his sake, I hope not," Grady answered.

Her stiff posture relaxed. "Your wife is a lucky woman. I know you would never abuse her. You'd never take her for granted. Treat her like a pretty possession and nothing more."

"And I don't have a short little . . . temper, either," he chimed in. "No. I'll treat my wife good. She'll be praying for sundown to hurry every night."

"Why would she do that?"

He suddenly realized they were discussing people who didn't exist. At least not yet. He hadn't even been one hour into the ride with Lilla Traften, and she'd driven him as loco as she was.

"When you meet the right man and settle down, you'll understand why," he explained, but he didn't like the thought of her understanding his statement with another man. He didn't like it one little bit.

"Bastard," he muttered.

Chapter Twenty-one

Lilla was still fuming about Grady's wife when the sun began to set. They'd been riding all day and she had yet to spot a cow. Her legs hurt, her back hurt, and she suspected her face was sunburned despite the hat. She'd tried to trot her horse a couple of times, thinking they'd never get anywhere at a slow walk. She had bounced, jostled and nearly fallen off.

Grady had been right. She wasn't ready to sit in a saddle all day long. She barely knew how to hold on when they walked the horses. If she didn't learn to go faster, they'd drag back to the ranch when they'd lost all their teeth and their hair had turned gray. But Grady hadn't complained, and it was more than she could say.

They'd stopped several times to let her walk the cramps from her legs. Attending to personal matters was a nightmare. She'd been hard-pressed to find a bush or a tree to squat behind. Even when she had, thoughts of snakes biting her in private parts kept her stops short and quick. What she wouldn't give for a long, hot soak in a tub, and a good night's rest on a feather bed.

"We're finally getting into some cattle," Grady said, nodding toward the distance where she saw tiny dots she supposed represented cattle.

"Thank goodness," Lilla breathed. "Now we just have to round them up and go back, right?"

He smiled sadly. "This is just a small portion of the herd. They're spread out for miles."

She groaned. "Can't we stop at least for the night?"

"I planned on it. Let's get to the top of that rise."

Lilla suspected she could walk up the rise faster than she could ride. And she worried she might fall off if an angle was involved.

"Why don't you ride with me?" Grady asked, as if he'd known her thoughts.

"Are you sure your horse can carry us both up?"

He nodded. "I wouldn't want to push him if we weren't ready to camp for the night, but he can make it."

Holding on to Grady sounded more appealing than trying to hold on to the saddle horn. "All right. What do I do?"

Grady moved his horse close to hers. "Just slide

over." He scooted back, allowing her room.

The exchange went smoother than she anticipated. He took the reins of her horse, wrapped them around the saddle horn, and they were off. Lilla leaned back against him and relaxed, totally trusting in his abilities. They reached the top of the rise, and she caught her breath. Below lay a stretch of land unlike any she had yet seen in Texas. The grass was tall. A creek ran through it, and large trees lined the banks. She imagined that at night the stars looked so close a person could reach up and snatch one from the sky, just as Grady had said.

"This is the land you want, isn't it?" she whispered.

"What do you think of it?"

"Grady, it's beautiful. Like a small paradise resting in a desert of rock and dirt."

"I told you it was a special place."

She turned to him in the saddle. "I don't understand why Wade and Camile didn't build here. It's a perfect place for a house."

"They considered it, but it was too far from Langtry. You see, Langtry was just a trading post. Wade bought the fellow out and renamed the post Langtry, and then the town started to spring up. I imagine someday they'll have a school and a church, everything a real town has."

And Grady and his new wife, who couldn't wait for sundown, would help populate that school, Lilla realized. He would be part of something that sprang up from nothing. She envied him in that moment. Building a town sounded more exiting than simply living in one that had been established for some time. A woman carving her notch out of this untamed land sounded more interesting than one who spent her days picking out china patterns or hosting parties. The life Lilla had planned—or which her father had planned for her—sounded lackluster and boring. A realization struck Lilla. She had become an adventurer.

"What are you thinking?"

Lilla was afraid to tell him. Afraid to give voice to her thoughts. Thinking and doing were two separate matters. She wasn't certain she had the courage to be anything but what was expected of her, or the strength to go against what her father wanted for her and claim her own destiny.

"I'm thinking that hot or cold, that creek represents a bath. Can we camp here tonight?"

He laughed. "I'll get supper started while you clean up."

The water was cool but not cold. Disregarding manners, Lilla stripped down to her chemise and drawers, thankful she didn't have to bother with corsets and petticoats. She waded into the creek, pleased to find that it deepened in the middle and if she sat, the water covered her up to her shoulders. Grady couldn't see her because of the trees. He'd set up camp farther down the creek bed, and the smell of coffee and fatback bacon drifted downstream to her.

It wasn't dark yet, but the sun had sunk below the horizon and the heat began to fade. She shivered, either from the sudden chill or from the delicious feeling of doing something slightly wicked. She'd never been out of doors unless completely dressed. Certainly not with a handsome man only a stone's throw away. Of course, that same man had already seen her in her underclothes, and she had seen him without his clothes altogether. Only a backside view, besides the incident when she'd been too terrified to look beyond his face. But she'd seen beyond his face since, and discovered a strong and caring person. Not only a man's man, but a woman's man, too.

She knew she had deep feelings for him. But were they deep enough to risk everything? To give up the life she'd known and embrace the unfamiliar? To risk ridicule from her social friends in St. Louis, and her father's disapproval? A moment's more thought and Lilla accepted that she had no real friends in St. Louis. Only acquaintances. She'd been closer to the women at Sally's than she'd ever been with the proper young ladies with whom she mingled.

There was still the biggest obstacle to overcome: Grady himself. His attitude toward her. His belief that she could never fit into his world or he into hers. The hawk and the dove. What had Violet said? If the dove truly loved the hawk, she would try harder to be strong, and if the hawk truly loved the dove, he would try harder to be gentle.

Trying to convince the hawk that the dove was really a lady hawk in dove's feathers would prove the true challenge. Lilla suspected she had a few days to do so. If only she didn't mess up the whole journey. And she had to stop complaining about the hardships. Prove to Grady that she had what it took to be the woman waiting for sundown.

Her spirits bolstered, Lilla tried to rise from the water. Her aching legs would not cooperate. She tried again, falling back and drenching her long hair in the process. If she couldn't walk out of the water, she decided to crawl.

That didn't work either. She got a horrible cramp in the top of her leg. Gasping with pain, she called out for Grady. She heard the crunch of his boots running down the creek bank. He was in the water the next instant, lifting her into his arms.

"I have a cramp in my leg," she said. "It hurts to move it."

He carried her to the campsite, placing her upon a blanket spread before the cook fire. His strong hands settled over her thigh, massaging the sore muscle. She moaned, unsure if she should label the sensation pleasure or pain.

"Give me a minute," he said. "I'll have it rubbed out."

She bit her lip while he continued. After he worked a while longer, the pain subsided. Lilla collapsed back on her elbows.

"The pain is gone."

He glanced up. "Are you sure? I can rub . . ."

His gaze had lowered to the front of her wet chemise. Lilla glanced down and realized her underclothes were transparent in the soft glow from the cook fire. Her nipples stood erect, due to the dampness of her chemise and the coolness of the evening.

"God," he whispered. "You're so beautiful."

Her first instinct was to cross her arms over her breasts, to shield her body from him. But the heated glow of his gaze mesmerized her. His hand still rested upon her thigh, the warmth of it burning into her flesh as hot as any brand. He stared deep into her eyes. She stared back, afraid to breathe, afraid to surrender to the feelings he stirred, but unwilling to show him her fear. Lilla meant to prove her courage to him. She couldn't think of a better way.

He glanced toward the fire. "You'd better cover up."

"What if I don't?" she asked.

Grady ran a hand through his hair, but didn't look at her. "You might catch a chill."

She wanted to recapture his attention. Wanted the heat of his eyes moving over her body again. "Is that all I'll catch?"

His gaze returned to her. It didn't stay focused upon her face for long. "It's only polite to warn you that the thoughts running through my mind are not honorable."

"You're feeling . . . manly urges?"

"Oh, yeah," he answered, his gaze fastened upon the front of her wet chemise.

"What if I'm feeling urges, too?"

He glanced up at her. "Whose week is it?"

"I don't recall."

"Yours, I think," he said, his eyes drifting downward again. "You'd better exercise some control here, because I'm running out of it fast."

"Show me what you want to do to me," she whispered.

A sound very much like a groan left his lips. "This isn't a good idea, Lilla."

"It isn't polite to refuse a lady's request." Her heart pounded wildly. She couldn't believe her own daring. Her time with Grady was limited, she knew that, knew she had to make the most of her decision to show him she was the woman for him. Rules and propriety must be forsaken. Tonight, she would prove to him she had the courage to take what she wanted in life. She wanted him.

He said nothing, but slowly his head bent. His tongue traced the outline of her nipples through the wet chemise. They hardened painfully beneath his tender onslaught. She sucked in her breath, allowed herself to feel as she'd never done before. To ache, to love and possibly to lose. He pulled her chemise down, his mouth closing gently upon one tight bud.

She arched upward against him, her sudden intake of breath spurring him to be less gentle. He gripped her firmly, a breast in each hand, before he trailed a path of kisses up to her lips.

"Do you know how bad I want you? How bad I've wanted you from the moment I saw you?" He didn't wait for an answer before capturing her mouth.

The kiss held all the fire of the last time. The moment when passion had ruled them both in the hallway of Sally's back rooms. She thrilled to the feel of his tongue moving inside her mouth, the weight of his body pressing her down into the blanket. The ground was not soft like a feather mattress, but she hardly noticed. She'd been waiting for this moment all her life. She just hadn't known it, not until it was upon her.

His shirt was wet from carrying her from the creek. Together, the heat of their bodies nearly steamed in the cool night air. She fumbled with his shirt buttons, desperate to feel his skin next to hers. He pushed her hands aside and unfastened his shirt, allowing her to peel it from his shoulders. He'd already worked her clinging chemise off her shoulders and down to her waist. His mouth seemed to be everywhere, against hers one minute, upon her breasts the next. His hands twisted in her hair. He rested his forehead against hers, breathing hard.

"You know where we're headed, don't you?"

She pulled his lips to hers in answer. A moment later, he wrestled them back. "Lilla, you'd better think long and hard about what you're doing. What you're letting me do."

Thinking was not an option for her. Feeling was. "I want you, Grady," she whispered. "Here, tonight."

He groaned and kissed her again, then pulled back to look down at her. "What will your husband think?"

Her hands strayed up his smooth chest. "What will your wife think?"

"I say to hell with them."

She giggled, never having believed she'd do so while engaging in an act of intimacy with a man. She'd always imagined the moment would be a somber, disgusting one. She did sober a moment later. He removed his clothing and sat before her naked, the firelight casting shadows across his tawny skin. Slowly he pulled the rest of her wet clothing down her hips and tossed them in the dirt. A fleeting thought drifted through her mind. She'd never get them clean again. Then he stretched out on top of her, and her mind focused upon a much bigger issue.

Sudden fear clouded her passion. She clamped her legs together tight.

"Easy," he said, and his tone was one she'd heard him use with nervous horses. "Don't be afraid of me. Trust me."

She'd trusted him many times in the past, but this was different. Feeling him pressed against her while confined by clothing was one thing, but unrestrained . . . well, the rumors about him were true.

"I'm . . ." She didn't want to say afraid. "Skeptical."

He brushed a stray lock from her face. "You know I'd never hurt you. Not on purpose. It's not too late to turn back. Just say the word and I'll leave you alone."

It was too late to turn back for her. She'd gone farther than she ever had with a man, and it was by her choice that she lay shivering and naked beneath him. If she couldn't commit to him with her heart, and her body, he'd never believe she could sacrifice all she'd known for him.

"I trust you," she said. "You may proceed."

He groaned. " 'You may proceed?' Hell, Lilla, if ever three words could wilt a man's flower, those are them."

"That's not true," she countered. "Your flower is not wilting. Not one little bit."

His kiss stopped further discussion. She tried to relax, to trust him like she'd said she would. The fact that he didn't immediately charge into places she knew he wouldn't fit helped considerably. His kisses grew deeper, wetter, wilder, forcing an even stronger response from her. Her arms crept around his neck. She found parts of her body pressing against parts of his.

"Not yet," he said, nibbling her ear. "I want to make sure you're ready for me."

She was there, lying beneath him naked. Kissing him. Pressing against him. How much more ready could she get? He slid down to her breasts, and she agreed she could stand more coaxing. He teased her nipples with his tongue. She twisted her fingers in his hair and pulled him harder against her breasts, urging him to suckle her like he'd done before. He did so with maddening slowness, licking and sucking until her nails bit into his scalp, until her hips arched against him.

Heat flooded her, centered at the pulsating core between her legs. His fingers were there a moment later, gently stroking, tenderly exploring. She fought embarrassment that he would touch her in so intimate a place, focusing instead on the pleasure he brought her. When he slid lower, his lips brushing her stomach, his tongue testing the depth of her navel, she began to tremble.

Lower still he slid, and she felt a moment of panic. Her knees clamped together, or tried to—the action was foiled by the presence of his body wedged between her legs. His mouth moved to an area where she felt it had no business being. Her fingers twisted in his hair, stopping him.

"Grady?"

"It's all right, Lilla," he said. "What I'm doing is only meant to give you pleasure."

A part of the proper Lilla still remained imbedded in her character. "That may be so, but what you're doing makes me uncomfortable."

To her relief, he slid back up, kissing her softly. "Does it make you uncomfortable for me to touch you here?" His fingers returned to her, causing a shiver to race up her spine.

"No," she whispered. "I like for you to touch me."

His mouth lowered to hers. He kissed her tenderly, his hand wedged between them, his fingers stroking her until she couldn't be tender in return. She moved against him, with him, a delicious tingle dancing beneath her skin. Her blood burned hot. Pressure began to build, a driving force that swept her up, trampling all in its wake except the rhythm of his fingers, the sound of his labored breathing, the warmth of his kisses.

She strained against him, wrapping her trembling legs around him with a need to grasp something solid. And then something oh-so-solid was suddenly poised at the entrance to her pulsing core. His overwhelming presence there caused her a moment of alarm, but only a moment.

The pressure increased, and all except the need centered beneath his fingertips fled her mind. A feeling unlike any she had known seeped into her—flooded her with sensation almost painful in its pleasure. She gasped, arched upward, then shattered, flying off into a million pieces. The pain came on swift wings, piercing her while she bucked and convulsed, still caught between ecstasy and torture. She cried out, but with which emotion she couldn't sanely identify.

Even the feel of him sliding deeper inside her, stretching her, coaxing her body to accept him, increased the ripples of pleasure still washing over her. The sensation waged a war within her to both push him away and draw him closer. She must have struggled, because he encircled her wrists and pulled them over her head.

He kissed her, and he kept kissing her until she surprised herself by trying to bite him. She had no idea what suppressed instinct made her lash out at him, except that the stinging reminder of the pain he had delivered made her almost believe he had somehow tricked her. He didn't apologize, nor did he stop what he was doing. As if he sensed that to hesitate would allow room for protest, he moved deeper inside her. He claimed her while she fumed about the pain no one had told her about.

"I thought you knew," he finally said, his voice ragged. "I thought someone had told you about the first time a woman is with a man, and what to expect."

She wasn't certain if she felt angry with him or with her maiden aunts for not making certain she understood all that was involved in intimacy. "I was told it was distasteful, that was all."

He moved deeper, causing her to gasp.

"If I had known, I would have explained, tried to prepare you."

She couldn't see where any type of explanation would prepare a woman for what he'd done to her, what he was still doing. Of course, no one had told her about the pleasure, either. She wondered if it had hurt him, too, because his body trembled.

"I won't hurt you again, Lilla. You'll have to trust me."

There was no going back now. She'd given herself to him. And there had been wonderful pleasure before the pain. She realized she felt no pain at the moment, only discomfort over the unfamiliar invasion of her body.

"Why do you tremble?" she asked.

He pressed his forehead to hers. "Because you feel so good. Like hot, wet silk. Because I'm fighting myself to be gentle with you, to remember you're a delicate flower. A sweet desert bloom."

"If I won't feel the pain again, does that mean I won't feel the pleasure, either?"

His tongue softly traced the shape of her lips. "No. I can give you pleasure again, and again, and again."

"And there will be no pain?" She wanted reassurance.

"Does this hurt?"

He moved. A slow, rocking motion. She couldn't say it hurt, but she couldn't say it felt good. Not until he continued. Then she began to understand the dance.

Loving her was torture. She was sweeter than anything he'd ever imagined, felt better than words could describe, and tonight she belonged to him, and only him. He wanted to make certain it was a night she would never forget. That he was a man she'd never forget.

The firelight reflected in her eyes and revealed the beauty of her flushed face. He could explode with the sheer pleasure of looking at her. He battled the need—continued to love her slowly. Inch by inch. A little at a time. Deeper and deeper he thrust, the moist, tight feel of her its own little heaven and hell. His body shook with his efforts not to crush her beneath his weight, and also with his determination to see her satisfied again.

Her hips arched, taking more of him inside her, his reward for being patient. She moved with him, against him. The sound of her breaths coming in short little gasps hammered away at what feeble control he still managed to grasp. Her nails dug into his back. She moaned his name, arched harder against him, and he lost the battle. He gave her all he had to give. Heart, body and soul. And she took it.

When her long, slender legs wrapped around him, gentleness went by the wayside. He grasped her hips and drove into her—buried his shaft. Again and again he thrust, angling his slick member to create friction against her most sensitive spot. Sweat ran down his back, but still he labored. Release was upon him when he felt her tighten, her convulsions squeezing him until he surrendered.

He moaned her name as she cried out, then pulled from her at the last second to spill his seed upon the blankets. He died the most exquisite death, one he had died before, but never so completely. One he wished he had the right to experience within her. Through the numbing pleasure, he understood the blaring truth. He didn't have the right to spill his seed within her; he had no right to lie between her legs, her blood staining his thighs. Grady Finch, a man who tried to live his life with honor, had done a most dishonorable act. He'd deflowered an innocent.

He lifted his head to look at her, his heart pounding wildly in his chest, his breathing ragged. She smiled at him like a sweet and trusting child. He'd never felt so good and so ashamed in his life.

"I'm sorry, Lilla," he said. Then he rolled off her. He rose and went to the creek, splashing his thighs to remove her blood, as if that would remove his sins.

Chapter Twenty-two

"Grady?"

Turning, he saw her standing on the creek bank, the blanket wrapped around her. The moon hung full above, bathing her in a soft glow. A long tangle of dark hair hung over her shoulders. His body responded again to the mere sight of her.

"Is this what's supposed to happen afterward? Does the man say he's sorry, then get up and leave?"

She deserved an explanation for his behavior. "I had no right, Lilla. No right to take what doesn't belong to me."

"I gave you the right."

"One day," he bit out. "It only took me one day of being alone with you to lose control. One day to ruin your reputation and prove how irresponsible I am. One day to shame the Langtrys, to shame you, to shame myself."

Her eyes glittered with tears. "I thought what we shared tonight was beautiful, but you've turned it into something dirty and disgraceful."

Grady felt lower than a snake's belly. "It was beautiful," he said. "You're beautiful, and deserving of a man better than me. Of a life better than the one I can offer you." He lifted his arms. "Look around, Lilla. Look at what I have. A piece of grassland and a little money saved to buy cattle. Land that's not even mine yet. All I have ahead of me is a long row to hoe. I love you too much to ask you to settle for that. Not when you can have the world at your feet."

Her eyes widened. "You love me?" she whispered.

He realized it was true. Denying it seemed stupid. He'd been guilty of doing the same thing Tanner Richards had done with Meg. "Of course I love you. I loved you from the moment I saw you. I didn't love everything about you yet, but that came with time."

She stepped toward him, but he lifted a hand to stop her. "Tonight I've proven my love is selfish. I wanted to put my brand on you. I wanted you to remember me. Even after you marry and have all those fine things you deserve as another man's wife, I didn't want you to forget me."

His admission didn't have the effect on her he

intended. She'd kept moving toward him as he spoke, and now she'd stepped into the water and stood before him. She should be as furious with him as he was with himself. But she didn't look angry. She looked soft and womanly.

"If ever three words could get a man who's in trouble out of it, those are them, Grady Finch." She lunged forward and threw herself into his arms. "I love you, too."

Her heart bursting with joy, Lilla stood on tiptoes and tried to kiss him. She didn't care that the blanket she held fell into the water. She did care that he took her arms and gently unwound them from around his neck, stepping away from her as if her skin burned his.

"I don't deserve your love, Lilla. At least save that part of you for someone else."

Anger quickly replaced the soft feelings uncurling deep within her. "How dare you say that to me? As if I would give any part of myself to a man I didn't love. You are crude and bad-mannered!"

"That's my point!" he ground out. "I'm no gentleman. You don't know anything about me."

He lied. She knew all about him. He was good, kind and caring. His dreams were admirable. He had courage, or at least she thought he did.

"What are you afraid of?" she whispered. "What is it you haven't told me?"

His gaze lowered. He ran a hand through his hair, calling her attention to the way the moonlight outlined the contours of his magnificent body. She could easily become distracted from the conversation.

"Do you want to know where I grew up?"

With difficulty, she focused on his face. "If you think it will matter to me."

"I think it will."

She lifted the soggy blanket floating around her knees. The night air and the water began to chill her, but she waited for him to continue.

"From the time I was six, until Tom Cordell brought me to Texas at the age of thirteen, I lived in a small storage room below a whorehouse. My mother worked upstairs."

"Y-Your mother was a . . ."

"Whore," he finished for her. "She put food in my belly and clothes on my back by lying on hers."

Although shocked, Lilla began to understand some of the comments he'd made in the past. The reason he treated the women at Sally's with respect, when other men sometimes didn't.

"And your father?"

"My father was a farmer. My mother was a farmer's wife up until a fever took him when I was five. She couldn't find work, so she married a man thinking he'd at least take care of us. He beat her. He beat me. After that, she did the only thing that seemed logical to her. She went to work in a place where her beauty was an asset rather than a drawback—a place where if a man took a notion to grab her or beat her, he at least had to pay for the privilege."

Lilla didn't know what to say—what he expected her to say. "Am I supposed to be repelled?" she asked. "I know women don't always have a choice, Grady. Texas has taught me that. I'm sure your mother did what she thought was best for you. I don't judge her for it, if that's how you thought I would react."

He seemed to have trouble looking at her. "Here's the thing." He cleared his throat and glanced back up at her. "I do. I hold it against her. I have for years."

The look of disgust upon his face, she suspected, was not for his mother but because of his own feelings.

"And you're ashamed of how you feel?"

"I'm ashamed because I took my resentment of her out on you in the beginning. I should have sent you back home that first day we both realized you'd been misled about Margaret's school. But I wanted you to suffer a little. At first I thought it was for her sake. Now I know it was for my own."

She moved to him, reached up and brushed a stray lock from his forehead. "Why?"

He pulled her into his arms. His body heat warmed her. "To me, you were the type of woman who pulled her skirts aside when my mother passed them on the streets. The type who stared right through us like we didn't exist. My mother told me not to pay them any mind, but she didn't know that down deep, I wanted her to be one of those decent women more than I wanted anything. I fought nearly every day on her behalf. Because of what some boy said to me outside the place she worked, or back behind the alley, or just about anywhere I went."

"It must have been hard for a little boy." Her hand slid up his back, trailing her fingertips across the smooth contours of his heated flesh.

"No harder than I imagine it was on her. She just didn't know, and I didn't want her to. I was ashamed to tell her what the boys said about her. I kept hoping some decent man would come along and take us both away from there. But none did. My mother died of disease when I was thirteen. Tom Cordell came into the place for a drink, heard about me and offered to bring me to Texas. He said I could work on his ranch."

Lilla placed her cheek against his chest, listening to the strong beat of his heart. "That was a nice thing for him to do. Give you a place."

"No telling what would have become of me if he hadn't," he agreed, absently playing with her hair. "Probably no good."

Her heart hurt for him. Hurt for Meg, for Violet, and for every child who had been abused, every woman who'd had her choices taken from her, and every boy who grew to manhood carrying a secret shame within him.

She reached up and cupped the back of his head, pulling his lips toward hers. "Your past doesn't matter to me, Grady. Only your future."

His mouth stopped a whisper from hers. "Yours

matters to me, too. That's why we can't be together. Not ever again."

He pulled away from her. More than the sudden chill made her shiver. He sounded dead serious. She dropped the soggy blanket. "Are you saying we can't be together because you don't think you're good enough for me?"

"No," he assured her. "I'm saying it because I don't think you know what you're doing. Now this life is exciting for you, but later you'll miss your fancy friends and your fancy life, and I won't have you resenting me for it. I won't risk seeing the light in your eyes fade into bitterness."

"You're wrong, Grady," Lilla argued. "You think you know me, but I didn't even know myself until I came here. You're not giving me a fair chance."

"I'm giving you a way out," he shot back. "I'll make you a deal. We'll go back to the ranch tomorrow. I'll take you to Tascosa and put you on a stage for St. Louis. You stay there for a while; then if you want to come back, I'll know you're serious."

She kicked water at him. "I just lost my virtue to a man on a rough blanket outside in the middle of nowhere! Don't talk to me about how serious I am!"

He took a step back, eyeing her legs with more than apprehension. "I admit that what happened between us is my fault. I'm the more experienced one. I took advantage of you, seduced you."

Lilla begged to disagree. "*I* seduced *you*, you conceited bastard." She grabbed up the blanket and stomped past him, then stomped back. "Leave. I need to wash."

"I've seen you naked," he said. "I'm seeing you right now."

"Go!" She pointed toward the bank. "I have private matters to attend to."

He left, and she kicked the ground in frustration. How could he be so ignorant? And bullheaded! Her feelings for him were not a fluke. She loved him, had loved him maybe from the moment he'd carried her piggyback across the desert because her feet hurt. His problem was exactly what she'd thought. He didn't think she was tough enough for Texas. He didn't think she had what it took to be his sundown woman. She would prove him wrong if it was the last thing she ever did.

Grady woke from dreams of a hot woman to the feel of a cold campfire. He pulled his blanket tighter around him, then remembered last night and sat bolt upright. He'd pretended to be asleep when Lilla finally returned to camp. He'd lain in his bedroll watching her eat the cold supper they had never gotten around to. It wasn't that he was afraid of her, but that his control seemed to go to hell when he was around her. She talked him into making foolish decisions. And he had no doubt that one sultry look across the fire would have sent him scrambling for her bedroll.

He needed time to think about his actions, her declarations, their future, if they had one together.

He'd spent most of the night mulling things over in his mind, watching her settle in, then listening until he finally heard the steady sound of her breathing, and the snoring. He'd grinned, knowing she'd be embarrassed if she could hear herself. He wasn't smiling now.

Her bedroll was gone. He glanced toward the creek and didn't see her. Scrambling up, he ran to where the horses had been tethered. One was missing. The one she'd ridden yesterday.

"Dammit," he swore, racing for his tack. He must have dozed off close to morning. What was she up to? Was she on her way back to the ranch? Or something even more foolish? Surely she hadn't thought she could round up a few head by herself.

Knowing her, he decided that was exactly what she'd try. She wouldn't run home. Not anymore. That would prove him right about her. Grady saddled his mount quickly. He left the campsite, worried she might get thrown, or her horse might get snake bit and leave her stranded. Countless dangers awaited a cowhand out on the range.

A blind man could follow the trail she left. She'd led her horse back up the bluff and down the other side. The footprints of her moccasins and the horse's hoofprints were clearly visible in the dusty soil around the bluff. He'd shown her the direction of the cattle the day before, could in fact still see a few grazing in the distance. He kicked his horse and headed toward them.

A few miles later he jerked his mount to a stop.

He should be able to see her by now, moving between the cattle, walking, lying on the ground. He squinted into the morning sun. Where was she?

Maybe he'd been wrong. She might have headed back to the ranch. Grady turned his horse and began looking for tracks again. He found some, but the horse hadn't been shod, and he knew Lilla's horse wore shoes. A few minutes more and he spotted her horse's prints in the dirt. She rode with someone, but whom? Fear suddenly clutched his gut. He had a bad feeling, and when he got one, he wasn't usually wrong.

It took him a while of backtracking to piece the story together. Lilla had ridden toward the herd once she reached the bottom of the bluff. Judging by the stride of the horse, she'd been walking the animal. The rider had come up behind her. She'd evidently noticed a rider pursuing her and had tried to run the horse. She'd fallen off and landed hard, from the looks of it. The other rider had dragged her to where her horse stood, then put her up on the saddle.

Someone had Lilla. The same man, he suspected, who'd tried to accost her on two separate occasions. What did he want with her? Grady's gut twisted. He would track them, and if the man had so much as lain a finger on his woman, he'd meet his maker in the blink of an eye.

Chapter Twenty-three

Was it night? Lilla couldn't see a thing. Her head pounded, and her body ached in every place imaginable. She brought a hand to her temples, then felt to make certain her eyes were open. They were. She couldn't imagine where she might be, or why. Slowly, memories came to her. She'd slipped away before dawn, after waiting all night for Grady to fall asleep. He hadn't fooled her for a moment with his pretense of dozing. But she had fooled him.

It had finally occurred to her to snore. She'd done so with great aplomb. After a few moments of making the most horrible racket, she had noticed his breathing steadied. As quietly as she could, she'd slipped from her bedroll and crept into the dawn. Saddling her horse took some doing, but she'd managed. She'd led the animal up the bluff, her legs screaming with soreness from riding the day before, and other parts of her aching as a reminder of what she'd done with Grady the previous evening. He'd been right that first day she met him. If anything had happened between them in Sally's back room, she would have known.

The pounding in her head made trying to remember difficult. She recalled turning to see a rider approaching her. It wasn't Grady. It was the same horse and rider she'd seen racing after her the day she drove the buggy from town. She'd kicked her horse's sides and taken off. Fear alone held her in the saddle for a few feet; then she'd lost her balance and gone tumbling to the ground. She couldn't remember anything else.

Where was she? And more importantly, was she alone? The soft whinny of a horse in the distance made her jump. She heard the shuffle of footsteps approaching. There was fumbling in the dark. A match struck against rock, then just as quickly went out.

"Damn matches," she heard a male voice mutter.

Oddly enough, the voice sounded familiar. Another match struck, and she saw a man trying to light a small fire. She felt her eyes widen.

"Gregory? Gregory Kline?"

His head whipped in her direction. The match went out. "Damn, Lilla. You scared me and made me blow out the match. I'll never get this piss-poor excuse for a fire lit!"

She thought she might be dreaming. That was it. She lay somewhere unconscious and her mind had conjured her old suitor Gregory Kline to entertain her.

"I wish I'd wake up," she muttered. "In the meantime, I'm in no mood for you. Go away, Gregory."

"You are not dreaming, Lilla. Why can't I get this fire started?" He struck another match. The light lasted for all of a second. He cursed again.

"Dream or not, you're beginning to annoy me with all that match-striking and cursing. The fire won't start because there is no air flow in this black hole. Even a greenhorn should know you need air to start a fire. And if you did manage to get it lit, you'd suffocate us because there is nowhere for the smoke to escape."

"Really?"

"Really," she repeated, irritated that she wouldn't wake up. Grady would probably find her passed out, sprawled upon the ground. She might have spiders or snakes crawling on her. She shivered at the thought.

Shuffling noises, like the scurry of mice, echoed around her. A moment later a hand touched her arm. She screamed. The hand hit her in the nose, she supposed in search of her mouth.

"Shut up, Lilla! Do you want him to find us?"

"Who?" she demanded.

Gregory sighed. "That tall cowboy who's been stuck to you since I finally managed to reach Texas."

"Grady?"

"How should I know who he is? All I know is, every time I get within shouting distance of you, either he shows up or you do something nasty like bite me and run screaming to him!"

She felt a prickle of unease. "At the house, that was you? And on the road from town?"

"If you would have slowed down long enough in that blasted buggy to let me catch up with you, or you would have refrained from beating me up at the house before I could get a word in, you would have known it was me."

Dreams were indeed strange at times. She found it humorous that her mind would create Gregory Kline as an evil pursuer. He was a blackmailer, and a coward, money-hungry to say the least, but he wasn't dangerous.

"Why are you laughing?"

She tried to control herself. "There is a flaw in the logic of this dream. Why didn't you just approach me at the house, or in town?"

His shoulder bumped hers when he settled beside her. "Because that brute of a cowboy has been holding you hostage. I'm rescuing you."

Another giggle escaped her. "What?"

"I couldn't believe the news when I heard your father had sent you to Texas. I know you, Lilla. Unless you were being held hostage, there is no reason in the world why you would stay in this awful country. And I saw you at the saloon, forced to enter that place, and do who knows what horrible acts."

The dream wasn't so funny anymore. It was ridiculous. "I went into the saloon to teach charm lessons to the women there. It was part of the agreement I made with Grady when I discovered Margaret had no school for me to teach in. No students."

The man beside her snorted. "I believe the fall you took addled your brain. The Lilla I know would never stoop to teaching charm lessons to whores. Oh, yes, I saw your students that day they rushed out to give you your forgotten articles. I couldn't mount that stupid beast I bought at Tascosa in time to catch you in town. Then the nasty brute threw me, and I had a devil of a time catching up with you. Whenever I try to hurry the horse, he bucks with me."

"Gregory, please pinch me."

"I beg your pardon."

"Pinch me so I can wake up, you twit! I want you out of this dream!"

He clamped a hand over her mouth again. "Be quiet or he might hear us. I'm sure the man is out looking for you by now."

If she had to dream, she could think of better ones to have, and a better man to keep her company. Lilla shoved his hand away and scrambled to her feet. She placed her hands along the rock wall.

"Which way leads out?"

She heard Gregory shuffle up. He touched her breast a moment later. She slapped out at him.

"Watch where you put your hands!"

"I'm sorry. I can't see a blasted thing!"

"Then keep your hands at your sides, or press them along the wall like I'm doing."

"Lilla, I think we should stay here until we're certain he has given up and stopped looking for you."

"I want him to find me, you idiot. Outside of dreams, you can't be nearly as silly as you are right now. If Grady Finch were holding me against my will, why on earth would I go running to him when you tried to approach me?"

"I meant to ask you that the moment I finally managed a word with you."

She stubbed her toe and cussed. "Which way, Gregory?"

"To the left, and you haven't told me why you'd want the very man holding you hostage to rescue you from me."

Feeling her way along the wall, she answered, "Because I'm in love with him. He's not holding me hostage, Gregory. I stayed in Langtry and taught lessons so I could earn my passage home. Now I'm helping him run the ranch because I caused a fight between the women and the cow-hands and everyone has gone on strike."

"Oh, my God, you're delirious," Gregory croaked. "A fine lady such as yourself would never consider falling in love with a cowboy. And your father could buy the state of Texas if he wished. There is no call whatsoever to make you earn your passage back to St. Louis. You're not making sense."

He tried to grab for her, but she avoided him and kept moving. "My father meant to teach me a lesson for bad-mouthing Wade Langtry to everyone who might listen. A lesson I believe he taught you, as well. You know what it's like to be banished."

"I have been trying to redeem myself ever since—as you know."

She snorted. "I suppose you had a difficult time dealing with the fact that you were never going to get your hands on either me or my father's money."

His breath brushed her neck. "I am offended, Lilla. You know you were always more important to me than your father's wealth."

"Save your breath, Gregory. I've wised up since my stay in Texas."

A light suddenly shone at the end of the black tunnel. Lilla hurried her step. She made out the shape of the horses standing inside the enclosure.

"Is this a cave?"

"Yes. I found it on the side of a cliff of sorts. I knew we'd need shelter, since neither of us are good enough riders to outrun the cowboy. I searched for a place to bring you after the man ordered you to break camp last eve."

"He didn't order me to do anything, Gregory. I

was tired. My legs hurt from all the riding we did yesterday."

"Did I just hear you mention private parts of the body?"

His censure made her smile. She had to be dreaming. The situation was too comical to be real. Since she felt certain that Gregory existed only because her imagination had conjured him, she said, "I did worse than that last night. I not only showed Grady my legs, I let him climb between them." She sighed at the memory. "We made hot, sweaty love on a rough blanket beneath the stars."

She glanced at Gregory, and in the dim light saw his mouth hanging open. His expression reminded her of what hers must have been the first time she met the women at Sally's and listened to their vulgar remarks. Since there could be no harm in baiting him, she added, "But afterward, we had a horrible fight. He doesn't think I belong in Texas."

"Cowboy or not, the man is right," he piped up.

"Nonsense," she argued. "I love Texas. Especially the place where he plans to build our future home. It has grass and a creek, and at night—"

"You're not thinking of marrying this man?"

He had grown pale in the fading darkness. "But I am," she assured the specter disguised as Gregory Kline. "I only have to convince him that he wants to marry me, as well."

"Why the devil wouldn't he? Is he insane? With your father's money—"

"He doesn't care about money," she interrupted.

"Or having perfect manners. Or mixing with dull society. He cares about honesty, and he's concerned I'll grow tired of his way of life and miss my former one."

"A very smart man, if you ask me," Gregory said.

"Also a thick-headed one. He's as stubborn as a mule," she fumed. A moment later she smiled. "But he's also hung like one, which makes up for a good portion of his faults."

Kline's mouth fell open again. "You must be an impostor. The Lilla Traften I know would never say anything so vulgar."

She turned and kept moving, hoping the light at the end of the tunnel would be the end of her dream. That she would wake in Grady's arms and he would hold her—whisper words of love to her, ask her to stay and be his sundown woman. She wondered why she still had to be so sore in her dreams. Or why Gregory had to be breathing down her neck. She'd thought him a gentleman at one time. Considered him a good catch. God, had she ever been that naïve?

The horses felt real enough when she bumped up against them, crowded inside the mouth of the cave. She laughed. Her parasol still rested in the rifle stock of her saddle. Dreams weren't usually so detailed.

"Lilla, I must forbid you to leave the shelter of the cave," Gregory huffed. "This Grady person has obviously brainwashed you into believing you are in love with him. I will return you to the safety of your father's keeping as soon as possible. Once home, I feel certain you will regain your senses and return to the Lilla Traften I know and love."

A thought occurred to her. "And you believe my father will be so beholden to you for your daring rescue that he will let you back into his good graces?"

"Well, I had rather hoped to talk you into marrying me before I returned you to your father. I thought being forced into the vile company of these Texans, you would appreciate the comfort and companionship of a gentleman with whom you are well acquainted. Then I realized you were being held against your will, and knew I must rescue you from your dire circumstances."

Although she felt more than ready for the strange dream to end, Lilla also found herself curious. "Why on earth would you think I'm being held against my will?"

"I have seen what's been going on. I have seen you doing laundry and work around the ranch. The people there have obviously made a slave of you. Then those disgusting trips to the saloon in town. And I saw for myself that you had a black eye. I didn't dare approach the house when I first arrived, fearing a run-in with the gunfighter Wade Langtry and his equally dangerous wife, but then I realized they weren't present. I could only assume you would not stay without at least Margaret in residence to act as a proper chaperone. Not of your own free will."

"I wouldn't have stayed at first," she admitted. "But Father insisted I earn my passage home by helping Margaret with her school. He said I didn't know the value of money, since I had thoughtlessly jeopardized his dealings with Wade and Camile Langtry. He said I should learn some manners."

"Rather boorish of him," Gregory muttered.

"I thought so, too," Lilla agreed. "At least in the beginning. But then I decided I liked being independent. For the first time in my life, I was neither under my father's thumb, nor society's. I began to see the world in a different light. Learn about people. Even discover things about myself I didn't know. The person you're seeing is not the impostor, Gregory. The impostor was who I was when I first arrived in Texas. A woman trying to live up to her father's grand expectations, and her mother's saintly image. A spoiled brat who had managed to stumble through twenty years of living and learn nothing of real value. I have no desire to be a man's ornament. To spend my days decorating his home and having tea with women who totally bore me. Texas is where I belong. I can grow here. I can love here. I can be anyone I want to be. Even myself."

Gregory straightened, his expression stern. "You're starting to unsettle me, Lilla. Your father would be most distressed to hear you speaking in this manner. You leave me no choice but to drag you back to St. Louis if I must. I'm certain that, once away from the bad influences surrounding you, you'll be grateful to me."

"I'll never marry you, Gregory," she bit out. "And I wish you would try to drag me away. This dream would be much more enjoyable if I could bite you again. In fact, it would give me an opportunity to test a move I saw Grady make in a barroom brawl. He kicked a man right between the legs and—"

"Don't take another step."

She wheeled around. Grady stood behind her, his gun drawn and ready and pointed at Gregory, who, without her realizing it, had made an advance in her direction. The dream had taken a turn for the better. She hurried to Grady's side. She reached up and touched his face—ran her fingers down the front of his shirt.

"You feel real," she said, beginning to think she might not be dreaming.

"Are you all right, Lilla?" he asked. "This bastard hasn't hurt you, has he?"

"Gregory?" She laughed. "Don't be absurd. He couldn't hurt anyone, except maybe himself."

"You know him?"

"Allow me to make introductions. Gregory Kline, Mr. Grady Finch, foreman of the WC Ranch. Grady, Mr. Kline is the man I believe I mentioned to you who only wanted to marry me for my father's money. Oh, but you may recall him more easily as the man who tried to blackmail Wade

Langtry into getting the deed for the Circle C from Camile."

"E-Excuse me," Gregory said weakly. "Uh, do you mind lowering the gun? I fear it may go off."

Grady didn't oblige him. "Yeah, I remember hearing about him. What's he doing here?"

"I thought he was here because I was having a dream. He says he's trying to rescue me from you. I am dreaming, am I not?"

He flashed her an odd look. "No. Are you sure you're not hurt?"

"I took a fall from my horse," she hated to admit. "I thought I might be lying unconscious somewhere, and that I'm having this odd dream while spiders and snakes crawl over me."

Again, the glance he cast her was one of worry. "You're not dreaming." To Gregory he said, "Maybe you'd better explain what you're doing here."

"I find it hard to converse while a gun is pointed at me."

Grady lowered the weapon, but he didn't put it back in his holster. Lilla had a sickening realization: If she wasn't dreaming, she'd really made those shocking remarks to Gregory.

"Gregory is the man who chased me that day in the buggy," she explained. "And the man who tried to accost me at the ranch."

"Why didn't he just come to the house and speak to you?"

"I—"

"He thought you were holding me there against my will, forcing me to do labor around the ranch. He also thought you forced me to visit the saloon and perform disgusting acts He's nothing but a coward. A coward with a big mouth, I might add."

With the last thought uppermost in her mind, Lilla snatched her parasol from the rifle stock of her saddle. She advanced upon Gregory.

"Lilla, stay away from him!" Grady ordered.

She wasn't the least bit afraid of Gregory Kline. He backed away from her, coming up flush against the damp rock walls of the cave. She pointed the tip of her parasol at his heart.

"If one word of what I said to you earlier ever leaves your lips, I will hunt you down. I will . . ." Threatening people was not her strong suit. She glanced at Grady. "What is a good threat?"

He stepped up and pulled her back, lifting his gun again. "I thought I would have to rescue you from him. I didn't know it would be the other way around."

"Believe me, threats need to be made before we leave here," Lilla said.

Grady sighed before fastening a steely gaze on Kline. "She'll peel your hide off in strips. Stake you to an ant hill without your clothes on and smear honey over your privates. She'll cut your tongue off and make you choke on it—"

"I get the idea," Gregory said. "May I please leave now?"

"No," Grady answered. "You're coming with us

until I get this story straight. And until *I* decide you're not dangerous."

Lilla had a nasty bump on the side of her head. Maybe that was the reason she'd acted so strangely in the cave. He'd taken her and Gregory Kline back to the campsite, since he'd left the horses and their supplies there that morning. Now he stood barefoot and calf deep in the creek, with Lilla perched on a big rock, while he looked her over.

"I can't believe you tied him up," she said. "You've probably scared ten years off his life."

"Me?" he scoffed. "You're the one who wanted to run him through with your parasol. What was it you said to him that you don't want repeated, anyway?"

Her gaze lowered to the vicinity of his belt, then rose abruptly. "Nothing."

"You didn't act like it was nothing." He took the bandanna he'd dipped in the creek and wiped a smudge of dirt from her cheek. When the dirt didn't come off, he realized it was a bruise.

"Do you hurt anywhere besides your head?"

She lifted a brow. He didn't need an explanation.

"You shouldn't have crept off this morning," he said. "You could have killed yourself falling off that horse. And this Gregory fellow could have just as easily been someone more dangerous."

"I wanted to herd some cattle in on my own," she explained. "To prove to you I could. To show you I can be tough."

He laughed. "Hell, I already knew you were tough. It's not spine you lack. It's skill."

"Which will come in time," she ventured.

"You won't need to ride and rope in St. Louis. You already know everything you need to know to survive there."

By the sudden frown shaping her mouth, he knew she hadn't said words she wanted to hear. Grady tried to be rational. Since he'd failed miserably at it last night, he planned to make up for it today. He loved her too much to have her for a time, only to have to let her go. She acted brave without the restraints she'd grown up with, but he wondered how brave she'd be about telling her father she wasn't coming home. He believed she loved him, but he wouldn't give himself false hope, or picture her in the role of his wife, until he knew she could stand up to her father about what she wanted and didn't want.

"I think my knees are cut," she said. "Would you have a look?"

The knees of her buckskins didn't show signs of blood, and they weren't torn. "Probably just scraped them a little."

"They sting," she insisted. "I need your help. I still feel a little dizzy. I wouldn't want to topple over into the creek and drown because I passed out trying to tend them myself."

He tugged at his collar. "You'll have to shuck those pants."

"You did tie Gregory up good, didn't you? I

wouldn't want him to see me undressed."

"He's not going anywhere," he assured her, then turned his back. He'd seen her naked before, but didn't think it was a good idea to watch her peel those tight buckskins down her hips. Just thinking of her doing so aroused him. Grady tried to will the problem away.

"All right. You may turn around."

Legs. Long, slender, bare legs. "Where are your, ah—"

"I didn't have time to bother with them this morning," she explained. "I did well to find a clean shift."

It was clean, and he could see through it. "Why'd you take your shirt off?"

She lifted her arms. "My elbows are scratched up, too."

Grady ran the wet bandanna across his forehead. He realized what he'd done and dunked it again, wringing out the water. God, he wanted her. Right then, right there. He'd told her last night that what happened between them couldn't happen again. He'd meant it.

He washed the red scratches marring the soft skin on her elbows. She held them at a level where his gaze couldn't help but stray to the front of her chemise. He saw the darker shade of her nipples through the thin fabric. She lifted one leg, perched it on top of the rock, and gave him all kinds of ideas.

Her thighs were a work of art. Smooth, pale, perfectly sculpted. She'd raised her chemise only above her scratched knees, but with her leg propped up on the rock . . .

"Delores says I have the prettiest legs she's ever seen. Of course, considering what hers look like, I'm not sure to take it as a compliment. What do you think?"

His gaze met hers. A half smile rested upon her full lips.

"They're fine," he said, then had to clear the huskiness from his throat.

"Fine?" She frowned. "I think they're better than fine. Maybe you didn't get a good look last night, with it growing dark and all. Feel free to study them at your leisure now that it's broad daylight."

"I've seen them before in broad daylight," he reminded. "That first day when you had your petticoats shoved up past your knees inside the coach."

"Oh, yes. What were you thinking when you saw me half undressed inside the coach?"

Running the cloth over her scratched knee, he glanced up. "You know what I was thinking."

"And what are you thinking now?"

His gaze narrowed. "You know what I'm thinking. Lilla," he warned. "I told you that what happened last night can't happen again."

She shifted, lifting the other knee for his inspection. "I don't see why not. If you insist on sending me back home, I might as well leave with a proper education."

He knew she could be tough; he didn't know she

could be merciless. "I gave you a good enough education already," he muttered. "There, your knees are cleaned up. Get dressed."

Her legs were suddenly wrapped around him, drawing him closer. "What were you going to do last night when I stopped you? When you said you only meant to give me pleasure?"

The sun suddenly felt ten degrees hotter, and it was already sweltering. He grasped her legs, thinking to unwind them from around his waist, but instead, he pressed up against her. "You're killing me. You know that, don't you?"

Her cheeks were flushed, her lips parted. "I never got to touch you," she whispered. "I wanted to wrap my fingers around your—"

That was all he needed to hear. Grady leaned forward and kissed her, unfastening his gun belt. He broke from her long enough to toss it toward the bank. Her hands were at the fastenings of his pants a moment later. He should stop her, he should stop himself, but he couldn't resist. Having tasted her sweetness the night before, experienced the heat and wetness of her, the tight, silky madness of her, he couldn't say no. Not for all the good intentions in the world.

Chapter Twenty-four

Lilla fully knew that her behavior was less than ladylike. And her motives for being brazen were somewhat on the shady side. She had every intention of working her way beneath Grady's skin, the way he'd worked his way into her heart. She meant to prove to him that no other woman but her would do for a wife, and she didn't care if she had to take on the mannerisms of a whore who fully enjoyed her profession to get his attention, and to keep it.

It wasn't that Lilla didn't feel passion for him. She burned with desire to have him make love to her again. But being so bold as to unfasten his pants and grasp his straining member was perhaps too wanton an act to perform in the name of love.

His shaft felt hard, but smooth as velvet. Certainly impressive in thickness, for her small hand couldn't encompass the full width of him. As for length, she slid her hand up his entire organ, but lost her estimation of its size when he groaned, pressing his forehead against hers.

"Am I hurting you?" she whispered, concerned by his reaction. His body trembled and he gasped slightly.

"Your hands feel so good on me."

With that bit of encouragement, she slid her hand down him, then back up. When he responded in the same manner as before, she repeated the process. She intended to continue, but his hand stopped hers.

"Keep that up and I'll be no good to you later."

She didn't understand. He removed her hand; then his hands were sliding up her thighs.

"I believe you asked me earlier to improve your education."

He grasped her hips and gently moved her where her legs dangled off the rock. The height of the boulder allowed them to meet where their bodies were of a mind to join, she sitting and he standing, but he didn't complete the union. He knelt before her, the water covering his pants up to the knees. He kissed the insides of her thighs, running his tongue the length of one and back down again.

Embarrassment threatened to engulf her as it had the previous night, but she fought it down. Her skin began to tingle beneath his tongue, her nipples to tighten. She closed her eyes, allowing the sun to warm her, while he made her hot in places the bright rays couldn't reach. Her body jerked when his mouth found the place he sought. It took all of her will not to clamp her legs closed, or twist her fingers in his hair and stop him. In the seconds she battled modesty, he conquered her fears.

He used his tongue like others might wield a weapon. He knew exactly how to turn her knees to butter, where her sensation centered, when to apply pressure and when to ease up. Instead of clamping shut, her legs opened further in trusting surrender. Sweat ran between the valley of her breasts, and lower, she grew moist with more than the wetness of his mouth.

His hands strayed to her breasts, his thumbs brushing her nipples through the fabric of her shift. She wanted to tear the material from her skin—wanted him on top of her, inside her, but she wanted him to continue the slow torture with his mouth as well. Her body trembled. She leaned back, allowing the smooth surface of the boulder to steady her. The torturous sensation grew, fueled by the steady pressure of his tongue. Her thighs shook.

She moved against his mouth, helpless to stop herself. His hand slid down from her breast and he penetrated her with one long finger. She shattered, writhing and moaning, caught within a force that sent pleasure pounding through her. Until he pulled her up, she hadn't realized she'd collapsed and lay upon the bolder, her legs still dangling.

His eyes scorched her as he grasped her hips and

positioned her so that she slid onto him. He filled her completely, causing her to gasp, then to moan when the fading waves of pleasure intensified once more. He thrust deeper, harder, faster, his hands placed firmly upon her hips to keep her in place. She wasn't sure if it was the urgent demand of his body pumping into hers, or watching him stare into her eyes that sent her off again, but she took him with her. His handsome face contorted into a beautiful mask of pleasure. He groaned, thrust to the very core of her, then gasped as his body trembled and bucked.

He held her until the storm calmed, his heart pounding wildly against hers, both of them struggling for air. Then gently he scooted her back, slowly withdrawing. He readjusted his clothing, then leaned against the boulder, his head resting on his arms.

She started to reach down and smooth his dark hair back, but he uttered a word that stilled the motion. At first she thought she'd misunderstood him, and even though he didn't repeat it, she knew he'd said, "Shit."

Grady had never seen a woman run hot and cold as quickly as Lilla. She sat across from the campfire, eating a meal she had prepared with a great amount of banging and muttering.

Granted, "shit" was not a good word to say after making love to a woman, but he'd tried to explain his reaction. He'd not only gone against his own decision and given in to his desire for her; he'd been too caught up in his pleasure to consider the possible outcome of his actions. He hadn't withdrawn at the last minute to spill his seed somewhere other than in her tempting flesh. Instead, he'd given her all he had to give—pumped her full of possible trouble. He couldn't send her home with a baby in her belly, and he couldn't force her to stay because of his carelessness, either.

"Might I have some more, please?"

The hand that held the tin plate toward Lilla shook. Grady eyed Gregory Kline, thinking the coward had just shown the first sign of bravery he'd seen in him.

"If you have two hands to dish it up, be my guest," she snapped.

Grady had to smile at that one. His smile faded when Lilla's heated glance landed upon him. The light of desire didn't shine there, but the glow of anger sure as hell did. She had every right to be mad, he admitted. He said one thing and did another. He'd been taking one step forward and two back since the day he met her.

The sound of Kline spooning up a second portion distracted her. Anytime her gaze encountered the man's; Grady noticed how she quickly looked away from him. He hoped the fancy dude didn't have as big a mouth as Lilla insinuated, because he'd sure as hell have plenty to talk about to her social friends in St. Louis. When they'd returned to the camp, Lilla in a snit and Grady trying to dig his way out of the mess he'd started with that one little word, Kline's face had been beet red. Grady figured that if Kline hadn't seen them down at the creek, he'd sure as hell heard them.

Snoring wasn't the only thing Lilla did loudly.

"Are you going to tie me up again?" Kline asked. "Because I cannot sleep trussed up like a—"

"If you stop talking, I might consider it," Grady interrupted. "In the meantime, eat and be quiet."

"Why don't you just let him go?" Lilla muttered. "He's not dangerous. If he makes it back to civilization without the rattlesnakes or the coyotes getting him, I doubt we'll ever set eyes on him again."

"I had hoped to escort you back to St. Louis," Kline reminded her. At her frosty glare, he continued, "Of course, that seems unlikely now."

"Unlikely is too hopeful a word. Try impossible." She rose, grabbed her bedroll and shook it out. "Here's what I'm looking for." She shoved a book into Grady's hands and stormed off.

He glanced down. It was her manners book. "Whatever impression you might have had of Lilla in St. Louis, Kline, forget it. She's gone wild, and you'd best respect that side of her."

Kline wisely chose not to comment. By the way he stuffed food into his mouth, Grady figured the man hadn't had a decent meal in a while. Not that Lilla's was all that decent, but at least it stuck to a man's ribs. He flipped open her book and began reading.

"Should one of us check on Lilla?"

He glanced up. The food was gone and the fire had died down. He must have lost track of time while reading. He rose, stretching his legs. "I'll check on her. You stay put."

A big moon lit the sky above. The sounds of crickets chirping soothed his restless spirit as he waded through the tall grass. He found her on the rock where they'd made love. She sat staring up at the sky. Her arms were wrapped around her knees. Her long hair hung down her back. He wondered if she might be praying, but then she reached up as if trying to touch the stars. He smiled.

His heart made a funny lurching motion. He'd never seen a person look more at home than she did sitting on that rock. He had a feeling it would be her thinking place in days to come. Where she'd go to ponder things, or when she was angry with him.

There was no use fighting the inevitable. It only took this one picture, one that would be planted in his mind forever, to know that she belonged here, on his place, by his side. She was his sundown woman.

His footsteps were silent in the grass, but she must have sensed his approach. She turned, and her face bathed by moonlight was the most beautiful sight in the world to him. He walked up to her and said the first thing that came to mind.

"Marry me."

Her eyes widened. "What?"

"I'm asking you to marry me."

She scrambled up, and he wasn't too sure she didn't look poised for flight. "Do you think you can just traipse up to me, ask me to marry you, and I won't be furious with you anymore?"

He gave it a moment of thought. "Yeah."

She drew a shaky breath. "I hate it when you're right."

A moment later, she was in his arms. She kissed him, tears suddenly streaming down her cheeks. "What changed your mind? I thought you wanted me to go home, to think about things, and then if I wanted to come back—"

"You and that rock changed my mind," he said, interrupting her, then kissed her again. "I can never bring another woman here to live without looking at that rock and wanting you. I'd beg you to stay if I had to. I'd—"

She placed a finger against his lips. "You don't have to beg me to stay. I want to stay, but I need to know something."

"You know I love you."

"Yes, I know you love me. But if the only way you could have me was to give up this land, to give up this life, would you?"

The thought of having to leave his dreams to pursue her had never crossed his mind. He'd never wanted any other life but the one he lived. It was a fair question, though. By staying, she'd be giving up the only life she'd ever known. Her friends, life in her father's fancy house, servants. He glanced around. The grass was still knee deep, and the stars were still so close he thought he could touch them, but without her, he realized it was just a piece of land. Without her, his dreams were not so grand anymore. He thought about her leaving, and he knew without a doubt that if she didn't return, he would go after her. If she couldn't fit into his world, he'd read her silly manners book, get himself a fancy suit and try like hell to fit into hers.

"Yes. If I had to give it all up for you, I would."

He guessed it was the right answer. She pulled him down into the grass. Things might have gotten out of hand again had not the sound of a horse speeding away echoed off the rocky bluffs.

"Damn! I should have known he couldn't be trusted."

"Let him go." Lilla's fingers curled around his neck and pulled him back down. "He's only in the way."

A woman's lips, especially this one's, could be very convincing. Grady didn't see where Kline was any real threat to them. He didn't plan on letting Lilla out of his arms for the rest of the night—for the rest of his life.

Later, he held her while the campfire danced with orange and red colors. She had fallen asleep hours ago, exhausted from an eventful day.

He'd kissed her, touched her, held her, but he hadn't given in to his passion for her. All things in moderation, he thought, and he knew her body needed rest. He drifted off, visions of them sleeping together with a roof over their heads, and a nice soft mattress beneath their backsides for a change, lulling him into peaceful slumber.

What seemed like only moments later, a loud cough woke him. He glanced up to see Sparks Montgomery staring down at him. The big-eared man's face was redder than Oklahoma dirt, and his mustache twitched like he might be trying not to laugh. That wasn't the worst of it. Sparks wasn't alone. Grady's whole damn outfit was there.

"Hate to you wake you, boss, but, ah, there's been a development back at the ranch."

Lilla mumbled something in her sleep and snuggled closer to Grady. He knew she'd die of embarrassment if she woke up with Sparks's ugly mug staring down at her.

"What is it? And keep your voice low," he whispered.

Sparks scratched the back of his neck and grinned. "Seems that woman snuggled up to you has company. Her daddy's come to fetch her home."

Grady was glad Lilla was not awake, because he muttered that word she didn't like.

"My father?" Lilla's stomach made a gurgling noise. "My father is here?"

"At the ranch," Grady specified.

She wrung her hands. "What's he doing here?"

Grady stuck a cup of coffee between her palms. "I imagine he's answering the letter you sent him. You know, the one spelling out all your horrible circumstances in Texas, telling him what heathens we all are and begging him to come take you home?"

"Oh, that letter," she whispered. Lifting the coffee tin, she noted that her hands shook. Grady watched her closely. She tried to act calmer. "What a nice surprise," she said with enough sarcasm to indicate the opposite.

"Yep." He took a sip from his cup. "Well, we knew we'd have to tell him eventually, right?"

"Right," she agreed, wishing the butterflies in her stomach would settle down. "I would have liked a little more time to prepare." Ten years or so would have been sufficient, she decided. "Tell me again what else has happened."

Grady stared at her for a moment over the rim of his cup, his eyes smoky gray. "The boys decided to return to work. Tanner Richards ran off with Meg. Word is they got married in Tascosa and just kept going."

She felt pleased for Meg, and hoped Tanner would make a good husband. "And what about the other women?"

"Rosita slipped away with her Mexican lover. Sparks says Delores doesn't look so bad with the hair off her legs. He's thinking about making an honest woman of her. Smitty White admitted that when Kate keeps her mouth closed, she's downright pretty. Besides, he's the most likely candidate as a husband for her. His brother's a dentist in Dodge."

Lilla giggled, although it sounded a little hysterical even to herself. "I bet Sally is fit to be tied."

"Sparks said when they were in there one night drinking, and the girls were keeping themselves to the back, Sally offered her own services. When she failed to get a response, she declared she was just serving drinks from then on out. She was through with women, and men."

"Langtry doesn't need a whorehouse," Lilla said. "It does need a church and a school."

"I'll be sure we put those at the top of the list," Grady said.

She felt so happy. She loved him so much, but knowing that her father waited for her at the ranch cast a dark cloud over her happiness. "And the Langtrys, along with Mr. Cordell and Hank and Margaret Riley, have returned as well?"

He nodded. "Wonder what they thought about arriving upon the heels of a distraught father with a missing daughter, cowhands returning from a strike they knew nothing about, and a young lady of questionable background residing in their home."

"Violet," Lilla gasped. "She must be terrified."

"I'm sure Maria has made up some story to pacify them all. Once she takes a chick under her wing, that chick stays there for life."

"She's a wonderful woman," Lilla said. She'd developed a soft spot in her heart for Maria. If she could just get rid of the lump in her throat. She didn't want Grady to know how terrified she felt about facing her father. He'd sent her to Texas to learn a lesson. Well, she had learned a few, and some of them he wouldn't approve of at all.

"No use putting it off." Grady rose. "If we don't ride in soon, he'll just get angrier. I told the men to wait for us on the other side of the bluff. Figured it'd look better with all of us riding in together than just the two of us."

"Good idea," she said, then poured the rest of her coffee into the fire.

"I'll tell him about us," Grady said. "As your future husband, I should be the one to approach him. I'll ask him for your hand in marriage, like it says I should do in your book. If he says no, I'll just shoot him."

She glanced up. He looked dead serious. His slow smile eased some of her tension. "I think I should talk to him first. You should probably hide until he calms down."

He lifted a brow. "Can he shoot?"

"He's an expert marksman."

A frown shaped his mouth. "Maybe I should stay out here and find some sand to bury my head beneath."

Lilla took a deep breath and rose. "I know you're not a coward, Grady. I'm only asking you to give me a chance to tell him. And to give me time to tell him in my own way."

"That way wouldn't happen to be miles from here, would it?"

She walked over and touched his face. "I'm not going anywhere. You're going to have to trust me."

* * *

Grady's gut churned with fear—with his own damn insecurities. Not fear of her father, but fear that her father still held a greater influence over her than he did. Fear that her father would just snap his fingers and tell her to come along, and she would follow. Then things would have to get nasty. Real nasty.

He wasn't above telling the stuffy man he'd taken his sweet daughter's virginity, or telling him that he had more than likely planted his child inside her. To keep Lilla, he'd fight dirty—he'd fight any way he had to.

As she gathered up their bedroll, he admitted that what he needed most was for Lilla to fight for herself. To stand up to her father the way he'd seen her stand up to anyone foolish enough to go toe to toe with her. There came a time in every woman's life when she had to let go of her father's hand, and take the hand of her husband. He hoped Lilla was ready to do that. He'd counted on it last night when he'd asked her to marry him.

"I guess we're ready," she said, handing him a perfectly rolled blanket. "We might as well go and get it over with."

She started to turn toward the horses he'd saddled, but he took her hand and pulled her into his arms. He kissed her with all the desperation he suddenly felt. She responded, her arms creeping around his neck. He suddenly wanted to take her to somewhere unknown, and right away. Steal her away. But only a coward or a man who didn't love a woman would do that, he decided. She loved her father; her father no doubt doted upon her. He wouldn't come between them—not unless the old man left him no choice.

The man didn't look that old as they drew closer to the ranch. He assumed the man standing next to Wade and Camile must be Lilla's father. He wore a fancy suit and a fancy hat. An Easterner if Grady ever saw one. A very upset Easterner, from the way he stood stiff as a dried pile of manure. He glanced at Lilla. She was chewing her lip to beat the band. A sure sign of her nervousness. They'd ridden all morning, not saying much to one another the whole time.

He thought he caught a glimpse of money being exchanged between the men. At first, he'd been conceited enough to think they'd bet on whether or not they'd find Lilla in his bedroll. Now, he wondered if they'd bet on whether he or Lilla's father would be the man left standing after the smoke cleared.

"Are you all right?" he asked Lilla, not looking at her.

"I'm fine."

She didn't sound fine. Her voice sounded soft and anxious. He wanted to reach across and take her hand—would have if he hadn't promised to let her tell her father in her own way.

"He's just a man, Lilla," he said dryly. "He's not God."

"Tell him that," she muttered.

For the first time, a realization occurred to him. "He didn't mind the idea of you marrying Wade, and he's an ex-gunfighter, not a fancy gentleman."

"Wade is a man of many talents, and putting on manners when the need arises is one of them. My father didn't know Wade Langtry was an ex-gunfighter when we were seeing one another, and by the time he found out, it was of no consequence. Wade had married Camile, making the issue of marriage to me moot."

He sighed. Grady had never been one to worry whether his boots were clean enough, or his jeans too worn or his shirts too frayed. Damn, he wished he'd shaved before they'd left. He probably looked like a saddle tramp.

A moment later, he didn't know why he'd worried about it. The group had drawn close enough for him to see that Miles Traften only had eyes for one person—his daughter. The man's eyes grew rounder with each step that brought her closer to him.

Although she looked beautiful to Grady, he admitted that Lilla looked a little the worse for wear. Her hair hung down her back beneath the mule-eared hat she wore. Her buckskins, shirt and jacket were all dusty from her fall from the horse. She had a bruise on her cheek, swollen lips from his kisses, and a place on her neck where he guessed he'd bitten her too hard during love play. Funny, he hadn't noticed it this morning, but now it stood out like an eight-day-old tick on a three-day-old puppy. He fought the urge to reach over and pull her collar up closer around her neck. Instead, he stared a hole through Miles Traften, trying to get him to look at him even once.

"Why are you looking at my father like that?" Lilla said through her teeth.

"Like what?" he ground back.

"Like you're about to bare your fangs and start growling over territorial rights."

He blinked and looked away from the man. Seeing Camile, a baby boy perched on one hip, and Wade, a baby girl in his arms who tugged at his earlobe, made him smile. Of course, they weren't smiling back. If Miles Traften hadn't given him a passing glance, the two of them were eyeing him plenty. He figured they remembered his wilder days and wondered what the hell he was doing, or had done, with Lilla Traften out on the range.

Lilla sat stiff in the saddle until they'd nearly reached the house. Then she went loco on him. She jumped from her horse and ran toward the man. "Father!" she shouted.

Fascinated, Grady watched her throw herself into her father's arms. If it were some type of tactic that she hoped would soften the man's displeased expression, it failed. Her father set her firmly away from him.

Grady pulled his horse to a halt before the group, holding the reins of her discarded horse and hoping he didn't hold the remains of his discarded heart.

"Lilla Traften, what are you doing in that get-up?" her father blustered. "And where on earth have you been? I hope what I've been told is a lie. Surely you're not foolish enough to go off somewhere with a young, unattached man without a proper chaperone?"

She shrank before Grady's eyes. He didn't care if the man might be his future father-in-law, he had no right to start chastising her in front of everyone. And why in the hell couldn't the man at least hug her and tell her he was happy to see her before he lit into her? Angry, he nudged his horse closer.

"I-I—" Lilla stuttered.

"She was perfectly chaperoned." From out of nowhere, as seemed to be the man's habit, Gregory Kline appeared. Grady misjudged the man's courage. One glance at Wade and Camile indicated that both were planning to put down the babies and fetch their guns.

"What the hell is he doing here?" Wade growled.

Kline held up his hands. "I assure you my motives for being here only involve Miss Traften. I heard she would be coming to Texas and only meant to offer my services as a proper escort for her. In fact, when I saw her riding out to the range, I joined her and the foreman to offer my help, and to serve as a chaperon."

What was the fancy dude up to? Grady wondered. Lilla's father eyed the man warily.

"You were with them the whole two days . . . and nights?" Miles Traften asked meaningfully.

"I certainly was," Kline lied. "And I can assure you, nothing untoward went on during the journey." He held out his hand to Lilla. "Except that it gave your daughter and me a chance to reinstate our friendship. We have become the best of friends. Isn't that right, Lilla?"

She stared at the man's offered hand, then slowly took it. "Yes, we have. I fear that Gregory is somewhat misunderstood. If in the past he felt tempted into acts of blackmail and underhandedness, it has always been with our family's best interest at heart. He simply adores us."

Grady understood the ploy now. Kline was determined to weasel his way back into Lilla's father's good graces, and he had found an opportunity. He had to give the man credit for having brains.

"I even saved poor Lilla's life," Gregory bragged.

"Her life?" Miles blustered. "When was her life endangered?"

"Gregory." Grady heard a warning note in Lilla's voice.

Kline's brow lifted. "Remember that day at the creek?"

Her face paled. Grady tensed, ready to stuff a fist down the man's big mouth.

"I told you to be careful on those rocks, and had I not warned you about them, you might have stumbled, hit your head and drowned. Remember now?"

Her stiff posture relaxed. "Yes, I do recall that

now," she said, then turned to her father. "It appears as if Mr. Kline has become invaluable to me. I do hope you'll forgive and forget his past indiscretions. I believe he has learned his lesson and will forsake his wicked ways."

Miles frowned at the man. "I suppose I owe you a debt of gratitude for watching over Lilla in my absence. You may return with us to St. Louis. Come," he snapped, turning toward the house. "Lilla, I want you to pack immediately. Business does not allow me to chase all over the countryside in search of my wayward daughter. You'll no doubt be anxious to return to your friends and your social obligations."

For an awful moment, Grady thought she'd fall behind him as ordered. She did take a step, then she dug in her heels. "I cannot leave, Father."

Grady's heart swelled with pride. Miles Traften was about to get a glimpse of the real Lilla.

The man turned. "What?"

At his stern tone, she shrank again. "For one thing, I haven't earned my passage home as yet. I planned to help Gra—Mr. Finch—"

"Oh, nonsense." Her father waved away her concerns. "I think the important lessons have been learned. You did learn the value of a dollar, did you not?"

"Yes," she admitted.

"And you did learn that even though some people are different from those with whom you usually associate, they deserve respect, did you not?"

"Yes, I did," she answered. "But—"

"Then my work, and yours, has been done. Come along."

The man set off again for the house. Lilla glanced at Grady. She looked at a loss. He started to climb down from his horse. If she couldn't tell her father, by damn, he would. She cast him a pleading look, then straightened.

"Father," she clipped. "Where are your manners?" When she regained the man's attention, she continued, "I have just returned and haven't even been allowed to thank the Langtrys for the hospitality of their home while they were away. I have not been able to greet Margaret, whom I have not seen in some time, and yet you expect me—"

"Oh, dear," her father breathed. "I have been lax in my manners." He walked back, took her arm and guided her to the others. "Forgive my breach of etiquette," he said to the small party gathered in front of the house. "I had been long from my business obligations, only to arrive home to find a letter from my distraught daughter. I had forgotten she has not been afforded an opportunity to thank you, and to have a short reunion with Mrs. Riley."

Lilla felt a moment of relief that she'd at least been granted a short reprieve to gather her courage. Her father was overbearing and intimidating. He'd always been so with her, but she loved him deeply, and wanted to find a gentle way to tell him she wouldn't be going home with him. Besides his business dealings, she had been his life for the past twenty years. She didn't expect he'd take the news well.

And Grady. He was breaking her heart. The other men had moved away, but he sat mounted on his horse, waiting for her to find her backbone. Her father was bound to notice him at some point and wonder why the man wouldn't get on with his own business and leave them to theirs.

Kline, she noted, had wisely hung back from any interaction with the Langtrys. She was surprised that he had the courage to face them again, but then money had always been a strong substitute for courage as far as Gregory was concerned.

"Lilla, it's good to see you again," Wade Langtry said.

The daughter he held was his mirror image. Dark hair, green eyes, and dimples when she displayed one shiny tooth. Lilla melted on the spot. Wade appeared to be happy, and as handsome as ever. Even the scar on his cheek looked less conspicuous than the last time she'd seen him.

"I thank you for the hospitality of your home in your absence," she said. "Maria has been like a mother to me." She glanced around the group, spotted the woman and reached to take her hand, squeezing it for a moment before releasing her.

Violet looked relieved to see her, and Lilla stepped up close to the girl. She whispered, "Dreams can come true, Violet. Both yours and mine. Are you brave enough to reach for them?"

The girl looked confused, but nodded. Her gaze strayed toward Grady. "I reckon if you're brave enough, I'm brave enough, too. But I don't have any idea what you're talking about."

"I'll have to explain later," Lilla said. Remembering her manners, she moved away from Violet and turned toward Camile. The hellion looked tamer bouncing on her hip a baby boy with blond curls and sky blue eyes. She was a beautiful woman, and from all indications, a very happy one. And her wardrobe was a sight nicer than Lilla's. Camile didn't wear a dress, but she wore a pretty starched shirt and a split skirt.

"I must get one of those skirts," Lilla marveled, then remembered she currently wore an outfit from the woman's wardrobe. "Mrs. Langtry . . . Camile," she amended. "I do hope you will forgive me for borrowing your clothes. I couldn't very well help around the ranch wearing a dress."

"No, dresses aren't for ranch work," Camile agreed. She smiled at her. "You look better in those buckskins than I do. If I didn't know better, I'd say you've turned Texan on us."

Camile's comment received a shiver of pleasure from Lilla, and a frown, she noted, from her father. He took out his pocket watch and glanced at it, then impatiently shoved it back into his pocket.

"I'm sorry we weren't here to act as host and hostess during your stay," Camile said, recapturing her attention.

"I managed quite nicely on my own," Lilla assured her.

The woman's gaze strayed past her, and Lilla knew she'd glanced at Grady. "So it would seem. You haven't met my father." Camile turned to a handsome older gentleman in a wheelchair. "Father, this is Miss Lilla Traften. Miss Traften, Thomas Cordell."

Lilla was impressed by Camile's polite ways. She supposed that when her own father had told her Camile Langtry could fit into any setting if she felt the inclination, her misgivings had been wrong. Of course, she had wanted badly to dislike Camile, embarrassed that she'd been made to look the fool. She took the older man's hand, and immediately noticed where Camile had come by that hard blue stare of hers.

"It's nice to meet you, Mr. Cordell. You have beautiful grandchildren."

She'd hit upon the correct subject to melt his stern features. He smiled. "That I do. Those two keep me plenty busy these days. Hell," he chuckled, "they keep us all busy." He glanced at the babies. "Now Clint there, he's quiet, but sharp as a tack. Little Cammy, she's her mother all over again. Always into one mess after another. Can wrap her daddy around her little finger with those sweet dimples of hers, too."

Miles Traften cleared his throat impatiently. Lilla didn't know why her father didn't just get a cattle prod to move her along. She still felt Grady's gaze boring into the back of her head. It took every ounce of her willpower not to turn and look at him.

Margaret and Hank were next in line. Lilla smiled fondly at the older woman and hugged her. "Margaret, you look wonderful. I love your hair bobbed."

The older woman patted her short hair proudly. Then she looked miserable. "I'm so sorry, Lilla. My letters about the school. I didn't realize there was such a shortage of women farther south of Tascosa. I—"

"It's all right, Margaret," Lilla soothed her. "I'm glad about the misunderstanding. Otherwise, I would never have come to Texas. I would have missed out on so much. I've made so many remarkable discoveries here."

The older woman's gaze strayed past her shoulder. "I'm sure you have," she muttered. "Guess the rumors about him are true."

Lilla blinked, thinking she'd misunderstood Margaret's remark. When the woman winked at her, she felt her face flood with color. She quickly directed her attention to the man standing beside Margaret. "This must be Hank."

The leathery-faced man grinned at her. His mouth was packed with tobacco. "Pleasure to meet you, ma'am. I mean, I remember seeing you in St. Louis, but don't recollect if we were ever introduced."

"Well, we have been now," she said, offering her hand. He glanced around, spit a stream of tobacco juice, then pumped her hand enthusiastically.

"Hank," Margaret said dryly. "You'll pry the young woman's arm from the socket. And I told you to get rid of that disgusting tobacco before Lilla joined us." She shrugged. "He's still a work in progress."

They made a handsome couple, and since Hank Riley didn't appear to be the type easily reformed, Lilla suspected Margaret had her work cut out for her.

"It was a pleasure to meet you, Mr. Riley," Lilla said, then realized she had reached the end of the line. Her father had come to the same conclusion.

"All right, then. Sorry if I seem rude, but as I've said, I must get back to St. Louis. I'm working on the merger in Wyoming," he said to Wade, including Camile and the Rileys. "I think it will increase our holdings admirably."

"I assume you'll call a meeting when all the details are set," Wade asked.

"Certainly," Miles answered. "Can't make decisions without the approval of the stockholders."

All nodded agreement, and it seemed there was nothing left to talk about. Except one thing. Lilla's father took her arm and turned. He ran into a brick wall.

"I haven't been introduced." Grady stuck out his hand. "I'm Grady Finch."

Lilla glanced up. Grady wasn't looking at her father; he stared at her.

"Grady . . . Mr. Finch is the foreman of the WC Ranch," Lilla provided.

Her father finally took Grady's hand. "Nice to meet you." He tried to brush past him, Lilla in tow.

Grady blocked his exit. Wade Langtry appeared beside his foreman. He slapped Grady on the back, a little hard, in Lilla's opinion.

"Grady is the best foreman in the country," Wade bragged. "I'll hate to lose him."

Her father's brow furrowed. "Is he going somewhere?"

"I'm selling him a prime piece of land to start his own spread. Soon he'll be an asset to the community. In fact, we might be wise to consider taking him in with us as a partner."

Only the mention of business made her father give Grady a second glance. "Is that so?"

"No, it isn't." Grady shrugged Wade's hand off his shoulder. "I want to stay independent if I can. And currently, I'm concerned about a different partnership. One which I'm seriously worried is in jeopardy of collapsing."

If he kept staring at her that way, her father was bound to realize that something was amiss. Lilla wanted to tell her father in private, not while surrounded by a group of people.

"Well, good luck, then." Her father stepped around Grady and proceeded toward the house. Lilla was left to face off with him.

"Grady," she whispered frantically, not caring if Wade stood next to him. "What are you doing?"

"What the hell are *you* doing?" he shot back. "When are you planning to tell him, Lilla? When you get back to St. Louis?"

"It isn't as simple as you think. You don't know him the way I know him. He's—"

"Dammit," Wade suddenly interrupted. His eyes narrowed upon Grady. "Have you been messing with her?"

Grady stared back at him, his gaze also narrowed. "Yeah, I've been messing with her. A lot."

Wade glanced at her and back at Grady. "Are you crazy? You and Lilla Traften? She's . . ."

Lilla placed her hands on her hips. "I'm what?"

He looked momentarily embarrassed. "Well, I wouldn't have paired the two of you up. You don't seem right for each other."

"I thought so too, once," Grady said. "But she proved me wrong. At least I thought she did."

"Don't talk about me as if I'm not standing here," she snapped at him.

"You're not standing here," he snapped back. "Not the Lilla I know. Not the woman I love. It makes me sick to see your father snap orders at you like you're some kind of pet dog. Stick up for yourself."

"Lilla!" Miles called impatiently. "Are you coming? I'm in a hurry!"

She glanced at her father. He stared at her as if confused by her behavior. Even while appearing puzzled, he managed to look stern. Grady didn't understand the bond between a daughter and father. He couldn't even understand the bond between a son and father.

"Grady," she pleaded. "Give me time to tell him the way I want to tell him. You were willing to give me time before."

The hurt reflected in his eyes stunned her. For the first time since she'd met him, she saw doubt there. He wasn't sure of her. He wasn't sure of himself.

"I didn't mind giving you time, Lilla. But you said you wanted to stay. You said you wanted to be my wife. Say it to him. Say it out loud so I know you meant it."

"Is there a problem?"

Her father's impatient voice sliced between them. He'd walked to where she stood, his expression still puzzled, and annoyed. His gaze darted between her and Grady. She wanted to blurt it out, wanted to announce to the whole world that she loved Grady Finch and intended to marry him. And it seemed as if the whole world was suddenly listening.

Camile had joined Wade. Hank and Margaret had moved in closer. And Maria and Violet as well. The words she wanted to say suddenly stuck in her throat.

"Lilla? I've asked you more than once to come along," her father fussed. "You know I'm in a hurry to depart. What's gotten into you?"

She glanced at Grady and swallowed hard. "He's gotten into me," she said, then straightened. "Father, I'm not going home with you. My place is here with Grady."

Grady sighed as if relieved. Her father's mouth dropped open.

"Grady? This . . . this cowboy?"

She took Grady's hand, because he looked as if he meant to set her father straight. "Yes," she answered proudly. "I love him."

Her father's shocked gaze moved from her to Grady, then back to her. "I think the sun has fried your brain," he bit out. "This man is—"

"In love with your daughter," Grady said, his voice low, dangerous. "I plan to marry her."

"You what?" her father roared. "You, sir, are not a suitable match. Lilla is accustomed to the finer things in life. She's delicate, well bred, educated. She does not belong in Texas. And she certainly doesn't belong with a man—"

"Father," Lilla interrupted. "Sending me to Texas was the best thing you ever did for me. I have grown, become who I am instead of who you expect me to be. This is where I belong, where I can be myself, please myself instead of trying to please you and everyone else."

"I will hear no more of this," her father clipped. He grabbed her arm. "You're coming home with me this instant."

"No." Lilla dug in her heels. "Can't you see? I'm not my mother. I will never be her. I'm strong. I'm stubborn, and I'm going to help Grady build his ranch from the ground up. Together, we'll help

Wade and Camile make Langtry into a town, with schools and churches and shops. I am not a socialite, a pretty glass doll that has to be kept upon a shelf. I am an adventurer. I am a Texan."

"You are coming home!" her father thundered, then yanked her toward the house. Grady had maintained a firm grip on her hand and he didn't let go.

"She's not going anywhere," he warned her father.

She felt pulled apart by the two men she loved the most. And she was furious with both of them. She'd told Grady she would handle the confrontation with her father, but he had stepped in and thrown his weight around. Her father wasn't behaving much better.

Lilla yanked free from both men's grasp. "Stop it this instant! Can't we all behave in a civilized manner?"

"Excuse me, Lilla," Camile called from the porch. "This is Texas, remember? This is about as civilized as things get."

Lilla realized that the crowd had moved to the porch, where they had all seated themselves as if preparing for a play. Violet and Maria served tall glasses of lemonade. The scene reminded her of the dance in Langtry, and Grady fighting four men to the tune of a badly played waltz.

The rattle of a buggy drew her attention. She glanced to the left. A buggy loaded with brightly clothed, shouting, waving women lumbered toward the house.

"Good God," her father croaked. "Who are those women?"

Lilla sighed. She hoped her father had a strong heart. "Those are my students," she answered. "Actually, those are my friends."

The women jumped from the buggy and hurried toward her. Lilla was swept up in a whirlwind of giggles and embraces.

"Did you hear about Meg and Tanner?" Kate asked.

She smiled. "Yes. I'm so happy for them."

"We've all gone respectable now," Delores said, then noticed her father. "Who is this?"

Delores might have claimed respectability, but she eyed Miles Traften up and down to the point she made him blush.

"This is my father, Delores. I hope you will excuse me if I can't make proper introductions at the moment." She glanced nervously between her father and Grady, who were back to a stare-down. "I'm in the middle of something."

"Oh." Delores lifted a brow. "You two finally got together, huh? I knew you would when I saw you dance that flamenco. And I figure it would have been a lot sooner if that fight in the saloon hadn't rousted the two of you from the back rooms." She laughed and jabbed at Lilla. "I told the girls, just you wait and see. Miss Lilla and them waxed legs of hers are going to get that Grady Finch."

Lilla suspected her eyes were as wide as her father's were. Miles glanced at Grady, and his eyes narrowed again. Her father did something she thought she would never see in her lifetime. He bellowed like a bull and charged the man she loved.

"Fight!" Kate shouted, and the women hurried off to join the other spectators on the porch.

It seemed that Camile Langtry could be shocked, after all, Lilla noted. Camile didn't look at all poised when a flock of soiled doves, turned respectable, perched upon her porch. Wade, she noted, was grinning. At least until his pretty young wife poked him in the ribs. Kate grabbed the baby from Camile's hip and grinned at him. The child let out a bloodcurdling wail. His mother quickly snatched him back.

The sounds of a scuffle drew Lilla's attention back to Grady and her father. They'd obviously rolled around in the dirt, but each stood now. Both had their hands lifted, fists clenched.

"Don't you dare hit my father, Grady Finch!" she yelled.

He glanced at her, and received a solid jab to the jaw for doing so.

"Father!" she shouted. "You *are* going to be reasonable about this, aren't you?"

Grady, it seemed, was of a mind to listen to her. Her father, on the other hand, was not. He hit Grady again, causing him to stumble back a step.

"What am I supposed to do, Lilla?" Grady

shouted. "Just stand here and take it off the old buzzard?"

Lilla groaned. A man with marriage on his mind should not refer to the woman's father as an old buzzard. At least not in front of the father. She supposed that such matters were not addressed in her manners book.

"Just run away from him," Lilla suggested.

"Like hell I will," Grady shouted, and received another punch in the bargain. "You can beat me senseless," he said to her father. "But that's not going to change how I feel about Lilla. You can try to take her away, but I'll come after her. I'm not going to disappear from her life. Not ever! Understand?"

Her father did not understand. He walloped him.

She'd stood still long enough for this ridiculous introduction between her father and the man she loved. Lilla glanced around, spotted her horse and raced to the animal. She retrieved her parasol from the rifle stock. Armed, she marched toward the men, placing herself between them.

"Father," she warned, the tip of her parasol aimed at his middle. "You will stop this nonsense at once. You have embarrassed me in front of the people who have been polite enough to grant me a stay at their home."

"That's all right," Hank called from the porch. "We're enjoying ourselves."

Lilla fully expected Margaret to give her husband some form of indication that his interruption had been rude. The former charm school teacher simply smiled at Lilla and nodded in agreement. Lilla sighed and turned back to her father.

"You will not hit Grady again. And you will apologize to him at once! This is the man I love. The man I will marry, with or without your blessing. The man whose child I may be carrying even as we speak."

"Lilla," Grady warned. "I thought you were trying to calm him down."

She wheeled around, her parasol pointed at Grady. "And you! I told you to stay out of it, but you couldn't. You had to rush to my rescue and prove how big and strong you are." She jabbed him once for good measure. "If I need your help in the future, I will ask for it. If I don't ask for it, that means to leave me the hell alone! You will show my father the proper respect and never refer to him as an old buzzard. I'll love you for the rest of my life, Grady, but I've loved him all of my life. I'm asking you to love him, too."

Grady glanced toward her father, his jaw tight. Slowly he relaxed. "For you, I will," he promised.

She smiled at him, then sobered and turned toward her father. "Grady is a good man, Father. He has ambitions—he has dreams. I want to be a part of them. A part of his life. He holds me when I need to be held. He's never too busy for me. He loves me for who I am, not who he expects me to be. Feelings are more important to him than business. Honesty is more important to him than manners. If you truly love me, then you must love him as well. We come as a matched pair."

Her father lowered his gaze. When he glanced up again, his eyes shown with tears. "When your mother died, I knew I had to raise you, be a good father to you. But I think I fumbled my way through life, lost myself in the business of making money rather than the business of life. But always, Lilla, I have loved you with all my heart. Your happiness means more to me than all the wealth I have acquired. If this man makes you happy, then I can ask for no greater riches in life."

Tears streaming down her cheeks, Lilla walked into her father's arms. He hugged her, held her so tight she couldn't breathe, as if he could make up for all the missed opportunities over the past twenty years.

"I want something from you," she said softly. "A wedding present."

He drew back. "Of course. I will bring this young man into the business. I will see that you have the biggest house and—"

She placed her fingers against his lips. "No. Grady will take care of me. I don't mind doing without while we build our lives together. What I want from you has nothing to do with cattle, or mergers, or fine things."

His brow knit. "What do you want?"

Drawing a deep breath, she answered, "I want

you to take a young lady back to St. Louis with you. Her name is Violet. I want you to let her live in our—your home. I want you to protect her, to give her a new life."

"What?" Her father looked even more confused. "Who is this girl?"

"Violet is a dove," she answered. "A beautiful bird with a broken wing. She needs to mend, to be treated kindly, gently. You are the only person I can trust with her future."

"That is a rather odd request, Lilla," her father said. "I don't even know this young woman. What is her name?"

"Violet," she said. "Violet Mallory."

His brows lifted. "The same last name as my sister? Your cousins in Boston?"

"Exactly the same," she said meaningfully.

"Oh." He nodded. "I see. And you would give up all that I can provide for you and your young man, for this girl's sake?"

She stepped away from her father and took Grady's hand. "I have all that I need. She has nothing. Has never had anything. I want her to see a different side of life, the way I have seen a different side now."

Miles Traften shook his head. "I don't know who this outspoken young lady is standing before me now, but I like her. I'm proud of who you have become."

Lilla smiled at him. "I like her, too." She took

her father's hand, joining his with that of the man she loved. They shook respectfully. Lilla supposed it was a little too early to expect more than that from them.

"I trust you will take care of my daughter," her father said to Grady.

"You have my word on it, sir."

"Grady never goes back on his word," she assured her father. "Well, hardly ever." She cast Grady a smug look from beneath her lashes.

His face flushed. "Only under extreme pressure."

Her father frowned. "I believe you two need a word in private. I'll wait with the others."

Lilla hugged her father once more, then let him go. Filled with love and joy, she walked into the arms of the man she would marry. The cowboy who had won her heart.

"Do you know how proud I am to be the man you love?"

She reached up and touched the handsome face staring down at her. "No prouder than I am to be your woman."

"Things might be rough going at first," he warned her.

"I'll be there to help you," she teased.

His face lowered to hers, and not caring that they had an audience, she stood on her tiptoes to meet him halfway.

"Hold it."

They both turned their heads to see Wade Langtry, a rifle in his hand. "You may recall an incident not long ago, Finch, where you had a mind to hang me because I'd broken the cowboy code of conduct with a certain spitfire. I believe I got the choice of a wedding or a hanging. I'm giving you the same choice."

"Hell, Wade, you can plainly see I have every intention of marrying Lilla," Grady said.

Wade glanced at Miles Traften. "I don't know about you, Miles, but after hearing your daughter say a child might possibly be on the way, I say it's time to fetch the preacher and make certain the knot gets tied."

Her father nodded agreement.

"Now, hold on," Lilla said. "I wanted a fancy wedding. One with all my friends present."

"I thought these were your friends," her father reminded.

Staring at the happy faces of her students and all her friends, new and old, Lilla surrendered. "You're right. All my friends and everyone I love are present and accounted for."

"Smitty, Sparks, I see you hiding back there watching the show," Wade called. "You two ride hell for leather to Tascosa and have a preacher back here before dusk."

"Be our pleasure, boss," Sparks called out. "Hey, Delores! What say we make it a double wedding?"

All heads swung toward the saucy brunette standing on the porch. She turned thoughtful, then shrugged.

"All right, but I hope our kids don't have your ears."

"And I hope they don't have your legs!" he called back.

"Kate!" Smitty called. "We might as well join in!"

The Irish woman grinned. "First stop on our honeymoon, your brother's place!" she called.

If anyone had told Lilla her wedding day would be decided by a shotgun, and shared with two former soiled doves turned respectable, she'd never have believed them. She'd have thought it was one of those tall Texas tales meant to frighten a woman.

"You're not going to run out on me, are you?" Grady asked.

She shook her head. "I'll be dogging your heels until you're old and cantankerous, Grady Finch."

"After the wedding, what do you say we slip away and spend our wedding night on a rock?"

"I say a rock sounds cozy to me."

"I-I've been thinking." He suddenly looked serious. "How would you feel about naming our ranch The Flying F?"

The name was horrible. "No," she said firmly. "I've heard the men swearing at night in the bunkhouse with the door wide open. They're always saying they don't give a flying f about this, or a flying f about that. We are not naming our ranch The Flying F."

He smiled, and she knew he'd been teasing her. "No," he agreed. "I'm naming it the Sweet Desert Bloom Ranch, after you."

"The DB for short," she decided.

He kissed her, and she didn't care who saw, she kissed him back with all the joy that bubbled up inside her. A cheer went up from the crowd gathered on the porch, and the men hiding behind the barn.

"I hope that preacher hurries," he said against her lips.

"I'm waiting for sundown," she whispered back.

"Oh, my gosh, I'm getting married," she heard Delores squeal. "I'm suddenly so nervous I could—"

"Oh, no," Lilla groaned.

ABOUT THOSE TWO BIRDS

I'm not much of a poet, but I'll do in a pinch.
Miss Lilla did in fact marry that hawk Grady Finch.
The wedding was short, for three couples who wed,
The preacher was drunk, and half out of his head.

Lilla's father was angry, which he couldn't hide,
But anger was sweet, compared to the wind from one nervous bride.

Desert Bloom

The air filled with more than well wishes and
cheers,
The "I doing" was said amidst snickers and jeers.

But the hawk and the dove made their own sol-
emn vows,
Words that had nothing to do with ranches or
cows.
The hawk said for her, his heart would be tender,
The hawk said for her, he gave all in surrender.

The dove said for him, she'd be strong and unerr-
ing,
But for their children, she swore, she'd be gentle
and caring.
She vowed to stand by him, through thick and
through thin,
She promised devotion, to no man but him.

Their words touched me deeply, brought tears to
my eyes,
Though I said I'd trust no man, I think that I
lied.
I wanted what they found, much more than I
knew,
I wanted to someday be part of a two.

If a dove and a hawk can find love everlasting,
There is hope in my heart, my fears will be passing.
The dove gave me wings when mine had been
broken,

The hawk gave me strength, with one soft phrase
spoken . . .

he told me to fly.

Written by Violet Dalton Mallory, upon her journey to St. Louis

Ronda Thompson

Scandalous

Christine is shocked that she's agreed to marry. Her intended, Gavin Norfork, is a notorious lover, gambler, and duelist. It is rumored he can seduce a woman at twenty paces. The dissolute aristocrat is clearly an unsuitable match for a virtuous orphan who has devoted her life to charity work. But Christine's first attempt to scare him off ends only with mud on her face. And, suddenly finding herself wed to a man she hasn't even met, Christine finds herself questioning her goals. Perhaps it is time to make her entrée into London society, to meet Gavin on his own ground—and challenge him with his own tricks. The unrepentant rake thinks she's gotten dirty before, but he hasn't seen anything yet. Not only her husband can be scandalous—and not only Christine can fall in love.

___4805-1 $5.50 US/$6.50 CAN

Dorchester Publishing Co., Inc.
P.O. Box 6640
Wayne, PA 19087-8640

Please add $2.50 for shipping and handling for the first book and $.75 for each book thereafter. NY and PA residents, please add appropriate sales tax. No cash, stamps, or C.O.D.s. All orders shipped within 6 weeks via postal service book rate.
Canadian orders require $2.00 extra postage and must be paid in U.S. dollars through a U.S. banking facility.

Name____
Address______________________________________
City____________________ State______ Zip__________
I have enclosed $______ in payment for the checked book(s).
Payment <u>must</u> accompany all orders. ❑ Please send a free catalog.

CHECK OUT OUR WEBSITE! www.dorchesterpub.com